The Evolution of Song and Dance in Hindi Cinema

Exploring the evolution of song and dance in the popular Hindi film, this book examines how these quintessential elements have been and continue to be theorized.

As song 'picturizations', as they are frequently called, have evolved, shifting from little more than impromptu moves around tree trunks to highly choreographed affairs featuring scores of professional dancers and exotic backgrounds, their theorization has also developed beyond the initial, peremptory dismissals of earlier critics. Featuring a landmark collection of essays from leading theorists, as well as newer contributions from up-and-coming scholars, this book develops new and exciting ways of thinking about song and dance in Hindi cinema and, in turn, explores how these elements work to (re)define popular Hindi cinema in the twenty-first century.

This collection will be of interest to students and scholars of Hindi cinema, musicals, and global popular cultures. It was originally published as a special issue of *South Asian Popular Culture*.

Ajay Gehlawat is the author of several studies of popular Hindi cinema, including *Twenty-First Century Bollywood* (Routledge, 2015). He is Professor of Interdisciplinary Studies, Theatre and Film at Sonoma State University, Rohnert Park, USA.

Rajinder Dudrah has authored numerous studies of Indian cinema and is the editor of the *South Asian Popular Culture* journal. He is Professor of Cultural Studies and Creative Industries at Birmingham City University, UK.

The Evolution of Song and Dance in Hindi Cinema

Edited by
Ajay Gehlawat and Rajinder Dudrah

First published 2020
by Routledge
2 Park Square, Milton Park, Abingdon, Oxon, OX14 4RN

and by Routledge
605 Third Avenue, New York, NY 10017

First issued in paperback 2021

Routledge is an imprint of the Taylor & Francis Group, an informa business

© 2020 Taylor & Francis

All rights reserved. No part of this book may be reprinted or reproduced or utilised in any form or by any electronic, mechanical, or other means, now known or hereafter invented, including photocopying and recording, or in any information storage or retrieval system, without permission in writing from the publishers.

Trademark notice: Product or corporate names may be trademarks or registered trademarks, and are used only for identification and explanation without intent to infringe.

British Library Cataloguing-in-Publication Data
A catalogue record for this book is available from the British Library

Typeset in Minion Pro
by codeMantra

Publisher's Note
The publisher accepts responsibility for any inconsistencies that may have arisen during the conversion of this book from journal articles to book chapters, namely the inclusion of journal terminology.

Disclaimer
Every effort has been made to contact copyright holders for their permission to reprint material in this book. The publishers would be grateful to hear from any copyright holder who is not here acknowledged and will undertake to rectify any errors or omissions in future editions of this book.

ISBN 13: 978-0-367-78567-3 (pbk)
ISBN 13: 978-0-367-33560-1 (hbk)

Contents

Citation Information

The chapters in this book were originally published in *South Asian Popular Culture*, volume 15, issue 2–3 (July 2017). When citing this material, please use the original page numbering for each article, as follows:

Introduction
The evolution of song and dance in Hindi cinema
Ajay Gehlawat and Rajinder Dudrah
South Asian Popular Culture, volume 15, issue 2–3 (July 2017) pp. 103–108

Chapter 1
Synchronicity and continuity of sound and image in early Indian cinema
Gregory D. Booth
South Asian Popular Culture, volume 15, issue 2–3 (July 2017) pp. 109–122

Chapter 2
Two dances and a conference
Philip Lutgendorf
South Asian Popular Culture, volume 15, issue 2–3 (July 2017) pp. 217–223

Chapter 3
Dance Musicalization: Proposing a choreomusicological approach to Hindi film song-and-dance sequences
Usha Iyer
South Asian Popular Culture, volume 15, issue 2–3 (July 2017) pp. 123–138

Chapter 4
Romance, piety, and fun: The transformation of qawwali and Islamicate culture in Hindi cinema
Pavitra Sundar
South Asian Popular Culture, volume 15, issue 2–3 (July 2017) pp. 139–153

Chapter 5
A.R. Rahman and the aesthetic transformation of Indian film scores
Jayson Beaster-Jones
South Asian Popular Culture, volume 15, issue 2–3 (July 2017) pp. 155–171

Chapter 6

Bollywood's variation on the firanginess *theme: Song-and-dance sequences as heterotopic offbeats*
Monia Acciari
South Asian Popular Culture, volume 15, issue 2–3 (July 2017) pp. 173–187

Chapter 7

Kehte Hain Humko Pyar Se Indiawaale: *Shaping a contemporary diasporic Indianness in and through the Bollywood Song*
Sangeeta Marwah
South Asian Popular Culture, volume 15, issue 2–3 (July 2017) pp. 189–202

Chapter 8

The picture is not yet over!: The end credits song sequence in Bollywood
Ajay Gehlawat
South Asian Popular Culture, volume 15, issue 2–3 (July 2017) pp. 203–216

For any permission-related enquiries please visit:
http://www.tandfonline.com/page/help/permissions

Notes on Contributors

Monia Acciari is a VC2020 Senior Lecturer in Cinema and Television History at the Leicester Media School at De Montfort University, UK.

Jayson Beaster-Jones is an Associate Professor of Music in the Global Arts Studies Program at the University of California, Merced, USA.

Gregory D. Booth is a Professor of Ethnomusicology at the University of Auckland, New Zealand, and has been engaged in the study of Indian music and culture for more than thirty years.

Rajinder Dudrah is the editor of the *South Asian Popular Culture* journal. He is a Professor of Cultural Studies and Creative Industries at Birmingham City University, UK.

Ajay Gehlawat is a Professor of Interdisciplinary Studies, Theatre and Film at Sonoma State University, Rohnert Park, USA.

Usha Iyer is an Assistant Professor of Film and Media Studies in the Department of Art and Art History at Stanford University, USA.

Philip Lutgendorf is Professor Emeritus of Hindi and Modern Indian Studies at the University of Iowa, Iowa City, USA.

Sangeeta Marwah received a PhD in Cinema and Media Studies from the University of Southern California, Los Angeles, USA.

Pavitra Sundar is an Assistant Professor of Literature at Hamilton College, USA, where she teaches courses on global film and literature.

Notes on Contributors

INTRODUCTION

The evolution of song and dance in Hindi cinema

Ajay Gehlawat and Rajinder Dudrah

The history of Hindi cinema is in many ways the history of song and dance. Put another way, the evolution of Hindi cinema can perhaps most accurately be seen through its song and dance. Since the advent of sound, popular Hindi cinema, now known as Bollywood, has made song and dance key—some would even argue, *the* key—features of its on-screen ecumene. Beginning in the 1930s with features such as *Alam Ara* (1931), India's first sound film, the use of music, song, and dance, as Ashish Rajadhyaksha and Paul Willemen note, was established as 'the mainstay' of Indian cinema (253). Yet the ways in which these elements have shifted over the ensuing decades—since the use of a single-system camera and the simultaneous recording of image and sound—are myriad in their manifestations, reflecting at times the serendipitous method not only of incorporating these elements into the film story but also, more broadly, of the development of the cinema itself as a storytelling device. Alternately hailed and bemoaned, fetishized and stigmatized, song and dance have continued to play an outsized role not only in the world of the Hindi film (and those of all the other, regional cinemas it has influenced) but also in the burgeoning world of Hindi film scholarship.

Indeed, until recently, song and dance became the essentialized elements paradoxically used by critics to peremptorily dismiss this cinema. Yet even as critics like Satyajit Ray lambasted Hindi films for the inane ways in which they incorporated song and dance (note our avoidance of the term 'integrated,' which would have made Ray wince), they did, even if begrudgingly, acknowledge the 'striking' nature of the tunes and their orchestration, and admire the 'brashness' and 'verve' of their instrumental combinations (Ray 75). Similarly (to continue using Ray as a particularly eloquent representative of such views), even as critics deplored these elements' disruption of the film's continuity and verisimilitude, they (or at least Ray) found, for instance, the practice of 'hav[ing] each lyric sung against a different scenic background … a daring innovation' and one 'wholly cinematic' (Ray 74).

Even as such song 'picturizations,' as they are frequently called, have evolved, shifting from little more than impromptu moves around tree trunks to highly choreographed affairs featuring scores of professional dancers and exotic backgrounds, their theorization has also developed beyond the initial, peremptory dismissals of critics like Ray, Kobita Sarkar, and Chidananda Dasgupta, to name but a few, to what has arguably become a highly specialized (sub)field of an increasingly theorized cinema, a development even more startling for the 'overnight' nature of its arrival. Yet behind the apparent suddenness of this (sub)field's gestation—and belying it—lie the aforementioned and ongoing shifts in these elements themselves—their inner workings and recordings, choreographies and productions—as well as how they interact with the rest of the film in which they appear. It is precisely this evolution—not only of song and dance but also how they are deployed; not only how they are deployed but also how they have been and continue to be theorized—that constitutes the basis of this special issue in which we collectively explore the history and ongoing development of what Sujata Moorti and Sangita Gopal have called 'the single most enduring feature of popular Hindi cinema' (1).

Not the same old song and dance

Even as we embark upon such a project, however, we must ask, as a way of both inflecting our endeavor with the previous scholarship informing these themes and distinguishing our own path, how have song and dance previously been approached and constituted as a field of scholarship? Which discourses have crucially informed and, at times, underinformed this area of study? It may seem obvious to state that different disciplines approach song and dance from different perspectives, foregrounding certain elements and (perhaps unintentionally) downplaying others. Part of the evolution of this field as an area of study is precisely the growing diversity of such disciplinary perspectives. Whereas previously 'song and dance' was articulated as one category, now, with the advent of ethnomusicologists and dance scholars, among others, song and dance can be separated, disjoined, and deconstructed in their differing (disciplinary) details. While Gopal and Moorti's edited collection, *Global Bollywood* (2008), marks one of the first book-length studies dedicated to song and dance in Hindi film, it also routinely conflates these terms, beginning literally on the first page by making reference to 'song-dance' (1) and employing the singular verb. As an initial endeavor, then, and as a way of simultaneously disarticulating both these (conflated) terms and our intervention from those which have come before it, we shall refer to these as separate terms—song and dance—and approach them as such, that is, as separate entities that have frequently been conjoined, not only in their cinematic representations but also, just as importantly, in their theorizations. Doing so—disarticulating 'song' from 'dance'—will paradoxically not only allow us to more precisely understand how and why they have been conflated but also more clearly grasp the underlying technological issues—those concerning images, sounds, bodies, and voices—informing these categories.

Such a move will, in turn, allow this collection as a whole to chart new ways of writing and thinking about song and dance in Hindi cinema and, in turn, how these elements work to (re)define this cinema, contemporaneously and retrospectively, in the twenty-first century. If Gopal and Moorti begin by arguing that 'song-dance' determines—perhaps unfairly—the form of Hindi cinema itself (1), we begin this special issue by asking how, through not only considering song and dance as separate (though frequently conjoined) elements but also focusing on the elided and omitted issues related to these elements, can the form of Hindi cinema, and the broader field of Hindi film studies, be reconceptualized?

It should come as no surprise that such a question—and intervention—comes precisely at a time when many scholars are noting the passing of song and dance, their subsumption by Western-oriented film logic bent on eliminating these latent 'irrationalities' of the Hindi film form. Several scholars, including Ian Garwood (2006), Gopal (2011), and Tejaswini Ganti

(2012), have recently argued that song and dance are already things of the past, pointing to new iterations of the cinema once (and only just recently) called Bollywood, which define themselves by eschewing this latter form's very defining features. Yet declaring such a shift may itself be premature, given both the ongoing roles song and dance play in this cinema and, equally importantly, the multiple technical innovations on display with regard to the numerous elided elements lumped under the general rubric of 'song-dance.' It is precisely such details that concern us here and that this collection wishes to highlight and use, in the process, to reconceptualize Bollywood, its use of song and dance, and their theorizations today.

Chapters and verse

The individual essays collected here, each in their own ways, contribute to this special issue's larger aim of simultaneously highlighting and rethinking the historical and theoretical paradigms, as well as the related technologies, associated with song and dance in Hindi cinema. Our collection commences, appropriately enough, with Gregory Booth's exploration of the changing dynamics of music, timbre, and cinematography during Hindi cinema's shift to playback technology in the 1930s. Focusing on the textual, aesthetic, and historical engagement of song and dance, as well as the embodiments involved in all of these, Booth examines song and dance as storytelling devices and how, in turn, the various changes related to these elements during the first decade of sound were both unforeseen and unexpected. Booth is particularly concerned with the shifts in vocal timbre, song structure, and cinematographic techniques that took place in the films of two studios during and around 1935: those of Prabhat and New Theatres. Through his analysis of this key early historical period, he argues that the challenges which arose for these studios led, in turn, to innovations in shooting and vocal production which were themselves intertwined with new technological practices in film song production. These early shifts in many ways serve as harbingers of subsequent technological innovations in Hindi cinema and as instances of the type of improvised solutions developed to accommodate new forms of sound and movement.

Meanwhile, Philip Lutgendorf steps back to look at the Bollywood song and dance form's historical lineage, examining Uday Shankar's recently restored dance drama *Kalpana* (1948) as well as, more broadly, the influence of classical Indian dance forms such as Kathak on the choreographies and trajectories of dance in Hindi cinema. In the process, Lutgendorf also considers the importance of focusing on dance, rather than merely collapsing it with the song, as well as how such paradigm shifts are, in turn, complemented and contradicted by the different methodological approaches taken toward song and dance in Hindi cinema. In her subsequent essay, Usha Iyer is concerned with issues relating to dance in Hindi cinema. Applying choreomusicological theory, Iyer examines the long shared history of cinema and dance in an attempt to excavate what she argues has frequently been overlooked, namely dance, in the study of popular Hindi cinema. As she persuasively argues, much of the discussion of song and dance numbers in this cinema has focused on music rather than on dance or, following our earlier remarks, has treated song and dance as a combined entity. Iyer instead posits that a focus on film dance can provide new models for theorizing the Hindi film song-and-dance sequence. Employing a broad range of historical examples, she outlines a body-space movement framework that explores the spaces of dance, the movement vocabularies employed and the resulting construction of star bodies in these film texts. In the process, Iyer's essay reconsiders terms like the aforementioned 'song picturization,' which suggest the primacy of the song, instead proposing a reverse paradigm of 'dance musicalization' as a way of foregrounding previously elided elements and reengaging with attendant issues of stardom, gender, and genre.

In the following section, Pavitra Sundar examines the Hindi film qawwali, not only as a musical sign of Islamicate culture but also as a vehicle for romance. Examining the use of qawwalis in a diverse array of films, including *Mughal-e-Azam* (1960), *Amar Akbar Anthony* (1977), and *Jodhaa Akbar* (2008), Sundar argues that these films reflect a shift from the use of qawwalis to stage a playful seduction or competition, to an emphasis on spirituality popularized by A.R. Rahman. Sundar also examines the more recent phenomenon of what she calls 'techno-qawwalis,' such as 'Kajra re' in *Bunty aur Babli* (2006), claiming that, in many ways, the historical functions of this song form have become fused with the sexual energy of item numbers which, in turn, can be seen as a reflection of the broader transformations concerning religion and identity currently taking place in popular Hindi cinema.

Extending Sundar's discussion of A.R. Rahman, Jayson Beaster-Jones examines a relatively un(der)explored issue, namely the use of orchestral scores in Hindi cinema. Such scores, he argues, have largely been ignored by both fans and scholars due in part to the spectacular nature of Hindi film songs. As he notes, the award for 'Best Background Score' was not even introduced in the Filmfare Awards until 1998 and then, too, only as a technical rather than an artistic category. In his essay, Beaster-Jones examines how mainstream composers such as Rahman began to change their approach to film scoring in the first decade of the twenty-first century, including new compositional techniques such as the development of musical themes unrelated to the other film song melodies. Through a comparative analysis of *Taal* (1999) and *Swades* (2004), Beaster-Jones argues that it is A.R. Rahman's film scores from this period that marked a significant turning point for the use of background music in Hindi films. This shift, he goes on to note, in many ways anticipated the decline of the lip-synched song sequence in the ensuing years, even as such background scores blurred the boundaries between film song and score.

The evolution of Bollywood song and dance is not just limited to on-screen representations but also manifests itself in broader cultural contexts, as Monia Acciari and Sangeeta Marwah demonstrate in their essays. Acciari focuses on representations of foreign bodies in Hindi cinema which, in her view, highlight the beginning of gradual changes for interracial romance on-screen. Using Michel Foucault's notion of heterotopic spaces, Acciari uncovers the existence of parallel spaces of 'foreignness' in Bollywood and uses these varying contexts to examine how white bodies have transcoded Bollywood narratives, creating new sites of cultural meaning and production. In a complimentary turn, Sangeeta Marwah looks at how Hindi film songs travel amidst the Indian diaspora, creating spaces in which notions of Indianness are formulated, challenged, and reconstructed. Looking closely at the Hindi film song's ability to transcend barriers of space and language, Marwah examines how such songs create a unique cultural currency which, in turn, allows diasporic audiences to articulate spaces for collective identification. In doing so, Marwah utilizes a combination of fieldwork and content analysis to understand how a diasporic Indianness shapes the Bollywood song and, in turn, gets shaped by it.

Rounding out our special issue is a contribution from Ajay Gehlawat. In his essay, Gehlawat examines the recent phenomenon of the end credits song sequence, which simultaneously distinguishes this film form from others in a global mediascape and reflects its continuing evolution in the twenty-first century. Looking closely at a series of end credits, starting with those of the *Dhoom* series (2004–2013), Gehlawat argues that these sequences, featuring increasingly choreographed and semi-autonomous song and dance, function in multiple innovative ways, including as remixed reprises, epilogues and, at times, as compensatory devices for the parallel diminution of song sequences within the Bollywood film. By focusing on this particular iteration of the song, Gehlawat also develops a more nuanced understanding of the contemporary Bollywood film and the particular role that song and dance now play both within and outside of it.

Conclusion

The essays collected here comprise a significant intervention into the study of Bollywood today, taking up, as they do, two of the most well-known elements of this film form—song and dance—at precisely the moment when many voices are questioning the tenability of such elements. Rather than merely retreading familiar ground, however, this special issue takes a more nuanced approach, addressing this subject from new and differing perspectives, which aptly reflect the interdisciplinary backgrounds of the contributors and their cross-disciplinary engagements. As noted at the outset, the history of Bollywood can, in many ways, be encapsulated in the evolution of its song and dance. Yet these elements have never been stable and continue evolving in fascinating ways, belying recent claims of their demise. One of the most significant indicators that song and dance continue to evolve and continue to play outsized roles in defining and redefining Hindi cinema is the increasing attention given to these moments by people all around the world. One need not be a film theorist or an ethnomusicologist to understand the allure of Bollywood song and dance—their energy is indeed infectious and hard to resist. What becomes more difficult is distinguishing between the hype surrounding song and dance—whether that comes from adoring fans or skeptical critics—and looking at these elements both on their own terms and vis-à-vis the numerous new perspectives being brought in to the study of popular Hindi cinema.

In assembling this special issue, we have tried to create new itineraries for the study of song and dance in this cinema, that challenge previous trajectories even as they provide new histories of how song and dance have been created, deployed, and appropriated over the decades and around the world. Individually, each of the contributions here provides new perspectives on a familiar theme, whether that theme be the use of dance to create narratives or the use of song to interrupt them. Taken as a whole, this collection creates a new tune from several discordant elements, one that we feel desperately needs to be heard today, when song and dance in this cinema paradoxically seem in danger of being eclipsed by their very familiarity. While song and dance are pleasurable elements and while several of these essays were no doubt written while humming a favorite Hindi tune, there are also elements of the unfamiliar we have tried to imbue this collection with, which challenge previous paradigms that insist upon relegating song and dance either to collapsed/ unified identities or to bygone eras. Such scholarship, even as it problematizes our familiar understandings of song and dance, can itself be pleasurable, and it is our hope that these essays make for both challenging and entertaining reading, much like a Bollywood song and dance, which looks easy to perform, until one starts to perform it.

Disclosure statement

No potential conflict of interest was reported by the authors.

ORCID

Rajinder Dudrah http://orcid.org/0000-0002-0295-724X

References

Ganti, Tejaswini. "No Longer a Frivolous Singing and Dancing Nation of Movie-makers: The Hindi Film Industry and Its Quest for Global Distinction." *Visual Anthropology* 25 (2012): 340–65.
Garwood, Ian. "The Songless Bollywood Film." *South Asian Popular Culture* 4.2 (2006): 169–83.
Gopal, Sangita. *Conjugations*. Chicago, IL: U of Chicago P, 2011.
Gopal, Sangita, and Sujata Moorti. "Introduction: Travels of Hindi Song and Dance." *Global Bollywood: Travels of Hindi Song and Dance*. Ed. Sangita Gopal and Sujata Moorti. Minneapolis: U of Minnesota P, 2008. 1–60.
Rajadhyaksha, Ashish, and Paul Willemen. *Encyclopaedia of Indian Cinema*. London: BFI, 1999.
Ray, Satyajit. *Our Films, Their Films*. New Delhi: Orient Longman, 1976.

Synchronicity and continuity of sound and image in early Indian cinema

Gregory D. Booth

ABSTRACT
This study examines a small sample of song scenes from Indian films produced between 1931 and 1935. It considers the impact of the technological constraints imposed by the absence of post-production technology for sound editing and for sound-image synchronization. That impact included the common practice of simultaneous sound and image recording (to ensure synchronization of sound and image) and of filming song scenes in single takes (to ensure musical continuity). The study traces the evidence available in cinematic texts suggesting that film-makers recognized the cinematic limitations of scenes filmed in these ways and sought technological solutions based on the use of the continuous sound track as the 'master' track for a song scene and other musically and technologically inventive ways to produce cinematically (as well as musically) interesting song scenes. The implications of early film production practices for the relationship of song scenes to the diegesis are also considered.

In most accounts of sound in the Indian cinema history, two dates and two films stand out in matters of first-ness: 1931's *Alam Ara* and 1935's *Dhoop Chaon*. As the first Indian film to have a sound track, the former's first-ness is reasonably concrete, more so, in some ways, than the first-ness of Warner's *The Jazz Singer* (1927) as Hollywood's first sound film. *Dhoop Chaon*'s first-ness, however, is more complex. While it is also based on technological change, the film's importance has been shaped by industrial practices and cultural developments that were unique to India. The mute or silent synchronizer – newly introduced in India in 1935 and first used in the production of *Dhoop Chaon* – allowed film-makers to merge two strips of celluloid, one carrying a sound track, the other an image track, on a new single strip on which the movements of the image track would appear (if proper care was taken) to be synchronous with the sounds of the sound track.

Synchronism and continuity

Synchronism – of limbs, bodies and lips with sound (and especially with words) – is an essential characteristic of all cinemas. From *Alam Ara* to *Dhoop Chaon*, in the absence of the technological means to ensure synchronicity of independently recorded sound and image, early Indian film-makers most commonly recorded sound and image simultaneously, with camera and microphone both sending signals to the same strip of film. To some extent, early Indian films were recordings of fully staged performances of scenes or parts of scenes and, of course, of song scenes. In the case of many song scenes of this period, actors were simultaneously acting and singing for the camera, in costume, on set and moving into and out of musical modes of expression sometimes with no break in the filming.

Naturally, the simultaneous recording process created challenges for both the actors (who were performing, in effect, as they might have done on stage: in costume, with appropriate actions and emotional expression) and for production staff who had to stage and film scenes that offered suitable perspectives of the actors and their settings, but that kept the microphone out of the scene and that located any accompanying musicians close enough to the microphone to be recorded, but also out of the camera's view.

This dynamic is apparently responsible for one of the most widely reported characterizations of song scene production between 1931 and 1935, that of musicians lurking in the bushes or behind the sets to provide musical accompaniment while actors stood in fixed positions and sang into hidden microphones. Composer Naushad Ali invoked this image frequently in his accounts of early film making practice.

> Song picturization … created problems. … Not only microphones, but musicians were also hidden from the camera view. On location … at Powai Lake, some musicians were perched on the trees with their instruments and some sat at the very edge of the lake. (Kinikar 56)

Beyond the demands for appropriate cinematography and staging, and for sound-image synchronism in general, filming staged performances carried an additional set of problems that emerged most clearly in the recording of song scenes. This second set of problems stemmed from the fundamental importance of both stable pitch or tuning and temporal regularity (or at least predictability) in the construction of musical meaning. When unplanned, even relatively small changes in these two, key music elements are perceptible to most listeners and have a negative impact on the musical-aesthetic experience. In a technological environment that permitted little or no post-recording sound editing and given the challenges of editing sound on optical film in any case, musical continuity was as much of a challenge as was synchronism.

Naturally, image sequences in the cinema also require a form of continuity; but the semiosis of a meaningful sequence of images depends on a series of iconic signs that are clearly referential (they are signs of something) in ways that the contingent, indexical signs of music are not. Image-track continuity can be maintained through more abstract or conceptual semiotic processes than can the continuity of a musical sound track.

Synchronism was most readily achieved through simultaneous sound/image recording, as I have noted, which acted as one kind of constraint on early Indian film making. That constraint lasted until 1935 and the appearance of the silent synchronizer in Indian studios, as I have noted. Musical continuity, however, imposed yet another constraint on recording, one that persisted much longer. The easiest way to produce a musically continuous sound track was to record each song scene or musical scene in a single, continuous take. In practice, it was almost impossible to stop filming at any point during a musical scene without leaving an audible (if not visual) trace, in either the pitch or melodic content or in the tempo or rhythm, or both. Musical continuity continued to be a challenge long after the problem of synchronism had been solved. Beginning-to-end song recording remained Indian filmmakers' solution of choice through the 1980s (Booth 75).

The combined needs for synchronism and continuity in the technologically limited Indian cinema of 1931–1935 had aesthetic, cinematic, and musical outcomes that are visible and audible in the films, songs, and song scenes produced between 1931–1935; these scenes occupy an odd, liminal sort of space between India's pre-1931 silent films and the films that came after *Dhoop Chaon*, in which Indian film-makers gradually institutionalized the production practice based on playing back songs that had been pre-recorded in order to film while actors mimed rather than sang. We know relatively little, and have relatively little familiarity, with the musical and cinematographic outcomes of this short, technologically defined and uniquely Indian interregnum. Given the brief period of time, the relatively few films (fewer still accessible), the increasingly remote history, and the enormous, prolonged impact of what came after, both Indian and Western writers have tended to ignore the 1931–1935 period or to treat these early songs as a primitive aberration. Morcom's study of Hindi film song, largely contemporary, ignores the majority of the Hindi cinema's past. Beaster-Jones' explicitly chronological study begins the 'at the end of the colonial era' tracing the 'emergence of *filmi* style' with a study of the 1943 film, *Kismet* (25). Pandit Ashok Ranade, does refer to pre-1935 songs; but argues that 'most, if not all of the early "songs" were in reality examples of verses, couplets or partial recitations' and that they 'stopped short of becoming "songs"!' (110).

Method and sample

It is difficult and probably inappropriate to assess song scenes from 1931–1935 on the same basis as song scenes that were produced after the silent synchronizer's arrival. It is important, however, to understand how the song scenes from these early years do and do not relate to the conventional song scenes that developed after 1936 and to ask what such scenes tell us about the aesthetic and cinematic goals of their producers. As I will show, some early song scenes represent distinct musical-cinematic forms that disappeared once synchronizers appeared in Indian studios. In other cases, the creators of these early scenes seem to have been pushing as hard as their technology allowed them towards post-1936 practice. In these examples, we can see how the dual needs for sound–image synchronism and sound continuity interactively constrained the development of film song and the filming of song scenes. This study is my quite basic attempt to contribute to that understanding. Simultaneous and continuous recording aside, how did early directors construct emotionally and cinematically successful song scenes? What strategies or techniques did they use in their attempts to stretch the limitations of technology? How do we, as scholars, connect the songs and aesthetics of the pre-synchronizer period with what came afterwards?

We have very few reliable resources that can help us answer such questions. No one living was on the sets when these scenes were filmed, and to the best of my knowledge, no one has taken the trouble to talk to those who were. Few of those working on those early films have left accounts for us to examine. To a large extent, we are reliant on what can be deduced from the texts themselves and an understanding of the available technology and film-making practice.

This study is not an attempt at a comprehensive survey of pre-synchronizer sound films. Instead, I explore the key technological, musical and cinematographic features of song-scene production in the first years of Indian cinema through the analysis of visible and audible evidence in the song scenes of a small selection of pre-1935 films. My conclusions are conclusions about practices that were possible and that were actually used in the production of these films. Although I use a small sample of the sound films made before 1935, the issues were the same for everyone. Given the limited number of variables, the technological 'work-arounds' that I discuss would have inevitably spread from film-maker to film-maker, either through explicit sharing or through imitation.

As this study will show, relatively static songs scenes, in which actors and cameras seemed to be literally tied to hidden microphones (as the cameras literally were in some cases), neither moving from their opening position, are readily found in Indian films. Such scenes are clearly the result of Indian film-makers' acceptance of the easily discerned limits of pre-synchronizer technology. As will also be apparent, however, even in the earliest years of the Indian cinema, directors and cinematographers were manipulating sound and movement in creative ways, pushing the technological boundaries to produce scenes that were cinematographically quite complex. The song scenes of 1931–1935 show a group of film-makers moving as fast as (and sometimes faster than) technology would allow them toward the more sophisticated song scenes of the 1940s onward.

Finally, I have reported (Booth) that at least from the 1950s onwards, film musicians have generally spoken of film songs as having a *mukhda*, or refrain, in which the lyrics remain the same throughout the song and two or more *antara*(s), verses, in which the lyrics are different for each repetition. Although these terms are taken from traditional or classical musical terminology, the meanings of *mukhda* and *antara* as used in the film music industry are closer to the English refrain and verse than to their traditional meanings. North Indian classical songs, in contrast, are more commonly described in terms of an *asthai* (an initial melody, set in the lower half of the raga/scale) and an *antara* (a consequent melody set in the upper half of the raga/scale). Both have a single set of lyrics. Variety is most commonly produced through musical variation (composed or improvised) rather than through multiple sets of lyrics or verses. The songs in this study are more closely aligned to the *asthai-antara* model of traditional or classical music than they are to the *mukhda-antara*(s) model of post-1950 film song.

Immobilities: Microphones, cameras, actors

Pre-1935 film-making technology could only produce a truly synchronous recording by simultaneously recording sound and image. No system of editing existed that would allow a film-maker to match sound and image in post-production so that the recorded images of an actor's bodily gestures, breathing and lip movements would appear to be synchronous with the recorded sounds. This was an especially crucial factor in the recording of song scenes as I have argued.

In most cases, movement by the actor during simultaneous sound and image recording was recorded not only on the image track but also on the sound track. Actors and directors had to manage, and in most cases limit, their movements; turning away from a microphone might result in changes in recorded sound and volume. The opening spectacle of *Ayodyecha Raja* (1932) features a chorus of courtiers whose voices move audibly closer to the microphone as their persons move visibly closer to the camera, as they proceed ritually onto the set. This early Prabhat film reflects the company's well known connections to stage drama, in this use of sound in an 'off-stage' mode. That mode appears in the film again, more explicitly, when Narada – Hinduism's messenger of the Gods – enters the court of the Gods (approximately 11 min into the film) singing 'Aati sundar Narayana', accompanied by *paun pethi*, or pedal harmonium, violin and tabla. Narada is waiting in the wings, so to speak, to make his entrance. He is not physically present in this part of the scene and is some distance from the microphone, which (we must assume) is located somewhere above the actors who are visible in the scene at this point. Narada's voice on the sound track, therefore, carries all the perceptible, iconic signs of distance: increased reverberation, low volume and so on. Distance is clearly perceptible because the voices of the other actors – who are on the set and thus closer to the microphone – embody a near-ness that highlights Narada's distance. Indeed, the King of the Gods and his courtier stare off into the distance (presumably in the direction from which the sound is coming) and the King asks, 'What's that?' in response to the distant sounds. As Narada's song continues, he enters the scene (in a very long shot); the volume of his voice continues to increase as he moves closer to the microphone. At this point, the 'non-prose-item', to use Ranade's (110) term, develops into a full-blown song-scene (shot in largely static medium close-up).

Sounds of movement in a sound track are realistic in that such a sound track replicates the effect of distance in human hearing. Nevertheless, sounds of movement were not expected in recorded song; for the most part, such realism disappears from Hindi song scenes once the practice of pre-recording songs became established. The easiest way to avoid signs of movement on sound tracks was to ensure that the song scene was set up so as to demand little or no movement from the actor. The 1933 release by J.B. Wadia's Wadia Movietone, *Lal-e-Yaman*, featured the child singing star, Feroze Dastur. In each of his three featured song scenes ('Tasvir-e-gham bana hua', 'Torde hardam parwar aas', and 'Mashoor the jahaa mein jo ijjo shaan') Dastur sits almost completely motionless.[1] His gaze is consistently directed upwards either in the philosophic contemplation of the fateful events about which he sings or with an eye on the microphone into which he is singing. The camera is equally motionless, so that the scenes are effectively devoid of nearly all interest other than that generated by Dastur's voice.

Although these scenes offer excellent recordings of Dastur as a singer, the almost complete lack of movement makes them less visually engaging than they might be. In a medium that was fundamentally visual and that could record movement, directors did not consistently accept the technological limitations of simultaneous recording, even within the context of a single film.

Among other things, the cinematographic limitations of simultaneous recording only came into effect when a scene required visible synchronism. If there were no images of moving mouths, or if the images were not intended to be moving rhythmically to the music, film-makers could sometimes successfully record sound and image in completely separate takes or sources. The short song, 'Gaafil bande kuch soch zara' features *Lal-e-Yaman*'s other important singing actor and music director, Master Ghulam Mohammad, who plays a Sufi dervish with magical powers that save the day more than once in the story. The scene suggests that director J. B. Wadia realized the cinematic limitations of the kinds of scenes that featured Dastur and sometimes chose to privilege movement in the production of song scenes.

'Gaafil bande kuch soch zara' is slightly longer than 30 s and features a single asthai-antara-asthai repetition. In a very long shot, and using some very creative image editing meant to illustrate the dervish's magical powers, a figure who appears to be Master Mohammad enters, and descends the stairs to his cave. Although the voice is unmistakably Master Mohammad's, the distance is such that not only is it impossible to judge the sound–image synchronism, it is impossible to determine whether or not the figure is indeed Master Mohammad. For the rest of the scene, although the camera moves closer, we see this figure only from behind for the few remaining seconds of the song. At that point, he is completely motionless and displays none of the physical signs of vocal performance (such as breathing).

Master Mohammad is shown singing in other scenes in which his sound and image were clearly recorded simultaneously. In 'Gaafil bande kuch soch zara', however, synchronism was unnecessary. It is easy to imagine that the scene was shot continuously, but with Mohammad at the microphone and a suitably dressed double in front of the camera.

A more technologically sophisticated method of producing this scene is also possible, one that was used in Hollywood, by Warner Brothers' Studio during the Vitaphone, sound-on-disc, era (1926–1931). This involved making a simultaneous and continuous recording of the song scene but using two or more cameras to film images from multiple perspectives. This produced one sound track but multiple synchronous image-tracks (Altman, R., email communication, 2017). The strip carrying the continuous sound track became what was, in effect, the 'master' recording. Image frames from the master could be replaced by the same number of frames from any of the other cameras that had been running (or indeed any other frames) without affecting the continuity of the sound track and without damaging the sound–image synchronicity in the frames that followed the insert.

This limited form of editing was 'a matter of selecting the required parts of several simultaneous takes from each of the cameras that had been running, and then relocating them in sequence to make up the edited picture track. This final edited picture track had to be exactly the same length as the individual camera takes' (Salt 188). In other words, as Rick Altman has noted, in this process 'the soundtrack provided the base line, with the images fitted to the sound' (email communication, 2017). The scenes in this study show that Indian film-makers must have been using similar techniques. Many of these scenes could not have been produced without two cameras running simultaneously or without the insertion of new sections of silent image track into the base line sound track. As I will describe, sudden changes in lighting, actor position, and other factors make clear that these scenes were not shot continuously on a single camera.

Prabhat's Marathi-language *Ayodhyecha Raja* (1932) starred Durga Khote as Queen Taramati. Unlike her co-star, the famous stage actor and singer Govindrao Tembe, Khote was not a trained singer and says of her singing in the film that it was 'nothing to write home about' (Gokhale 60). She was nevertheless featured in a number of song scenes. 'Anand de' is a fully developed song (2′20″ in total), with the then common structure based on complementary *asthai-antara* melodies. In this composition, both *asthai* and *antara* have their own complementary melody. The majority of Khote's performance in this scene is devoted to repetitions of the *asthai* melody and its complement. Many repetitions include relatively straightforward melodic variations that, given Khote's lack of musical training, may well have been pre-composed and memorized. Like most songs of the Marathi theatre (from which early Prabhat films borrowed content of all kinds), and other classical and light classical, raga-based song forms, variety is produced by musical not lyrical means.

'Anand de' opens with a very long shot. Khote is seated on what is presumably her bed, and presents her left profile to the camera while a maid stands behind her, braiding her hair.

The hidden *paun pethi* plays a fragment of the *asthai* or main melody and Khote begins singing. She faces what appears to be a devotional icon of some sort; but is presumably the disguised microphone on a stand. Except for her breathing, slight head movements and the movements of her mouth, Khote is motionless during the scene. The maid's small movements as she pretends to braid, and the wind-blown hanging plants high on the wall are the only other movements in the beginning of the scene. As the scene progresses, however, the camera (apparently on a trolley) moves closer in an unbroken shot until the distance is medium or medium long. At this point the image track is interrupted; but the sound track continues.

That this is a cut in the image track is clear from the abrupt repositioning of the camera (back to a very long shot). That this is actually a separate shot – as opposed to a second camera's perspective of the same shot – is clear from a change in the maid's position relative to Khote (she stands much further from Khote in this shot, and holds the end of Khote's braid, which is now almost horizontal). The sound track is just as clearly uncut; but Khote – who is now admittedly at some distance – does not appear to be singing; she seems to sit completely still, while Harishchandra, the King, enters the scene. This cut appears to have been achieved by the replacement of select frames from the original image track with frames from a separate image recording of the same scene, while leaving the sound track portion of the film intact. A second, later cut in this scene seems to have involved a cut in both image and sound recording, although the music continuity is managed so as to be almost undetectable.

Khote's positioning and her motionless-ness were, like the scenes featuring Feroze Daastur, responses to the technological challenges of recording sound in this era, but being able to sit without any actions or required movement and, one might say, without any emoting or acting, no doubt made it easier for this inexperienced singer to focus her singing. When actors had to sing as well as move, scenes and sound tracks become more complex for both actors and film-makers.

Managing movement

In what may well be the Indian cinema's first item number, an unknown performer sings and dances for the entertainment of the gods in *Ayodyecha Raja*. Although heroines and heroes have consistently been depicted singing and dancing simultaneously in post-1935 films, in actual practice, the physical exertion of dancing produces unavoidable breathing and positioning issues that are difficult to mask when one is singing. In the simultaneous recording era, singing and dancing (at the same time) were much more challenging, not only because of the physical and breathing issues, but because of the inevitable changes in volume and clarity that would result if an actor's dancing changed the direction or the distance of the actor's singing voice relative to the microphone. In this 1932 scene, therefore, the dancer either sings or dances; she never does both. Because the singing portions of her performance were constrained by microphone placement issues, she moves her arms and her head, but remains rooted in her designated position near the microphone. Once she shifts from song to dance, she becomes more completely mobile, moving from place to place and engaging in the circular *chakar* cadential movements that are so much a part of many Indian classical dance forms.

Like 'Anand de', it appears that this song scene was filmed in two different shots. The entire song performance was recorded in a medium length shot that includes two complete repetitions of the song; this shot concludes with a dance performance that ends the scene. It appears that once the song and concluding dance were filmed, the camera was then repositioned for a very long shot that only includes dance but also contextualizes the dance by including the audience. Both shots recorded sound and image, however, and after shooting, frames from the second shot were inserted into the middle, so to speak, of the first scene. The changes in shot length make for a cinematically more satisfactory scene; but changes in lighting make the changes visually abrupt and although the musicians and the editor seem to have attempted to minimize the impact of the cuts, the sound track is perceptibly discontinous. The discontinuity is exacerbated by the repositioning of either the microphone or the musicians so that the recorded volume of some instruments (a function of the distance between the microphone and the musicians) is noticeably different at both cuts.

As in 'Anand de', the creators of this scene clearly tried to manage the demands of musical continuity of the sound track by editing as carefully as possible in musically appropriate places; but as noted, given the technology available, cuts in a musical sound track are inevitably perceptible and always at least slightly disruptive. Other pre-1935 song scenes, such as those discussed below from *Amrit Manthan* (1934), show that Shantaram and other directors did learn how to avoid this problem.

New Theatres films of the early 1930s also demonstrate the challenges of simultaneous recording and the importance of the sound-track-as-master process. In the studio's Bengali language version of *Chandidas* (1932), Debaki Bose used the sound track as the master to produce scenes that were sometimes extremely long. Some of these musical scenes are so unlike post-1935 song scenes that they must be understood as a distinct approach to the cinematic music drama. A more complete examination of early New Theatres films would reveal the extent to which the practice I describe here was common to this studio's productions in the pre-playback era.

This first cinematic version of the Chandidas story opens with a long (11 min in total) scene on the riverbank, where Rami, the film's heroine (played by Sunila) is washing clothes; the film's protagonist, Chandidas (Durgadas Banerjee), sits fishing on the opposite bank. The first sub-section takes up the first 5 min and 30 s of the film (not including the title sequence). Thereafter, Chandidas's wife enters and engages in an emotional exchange with Rami. She exits at about 10 min into the scene, which continues for a further minute focusing again only on Rami and Chandidas.

For the first 6 min of this scene, there is no spoken dialogue, only silence, song or background music. Thereafter, the two women are the focus of a scene that features dialogue, song and background music. The final minute of the scene, after Chandidas' wife has exited, returns to the entirely musical focus of the opening. In total, a full 5 of the film's first 11 min feature song, with background music (or melodic interludes between sung melodies) for most of the rest of the scene. What is more, with the exception of one short response by Banerjee (I assume) at the end, all the singing is done by Sunila. In the first Rami–Chandidas scene, Sunila sings for 3 min and 28 s.

Almost all of Sunila's singing is unmetered. Broadly speaking, she sings five repetitions of a single extended melody, composed of four phrases, accompanied by *bansuri* or bamboo flute, cello, *paun pethi*, and what sounds like a North Indian vina. Each phrase is separated by a short pause, often partially filled in by her instrumental accompanists. Each melodic repetition is set to new lyrics. In fact, unlike most song scenes, in which the *mukhda* lyrics usually become the title of the song, there is no obvious way to put a lyric-based title to this scene; nothing is repeated. The melodic repetitions themselves are separated by other action in the overall scene. There are small melodic variations in each repetition; but more importantly, the explicit two-part form that is so common in Indian film song is largely absent. At the end of this extended performance the song ends very distinctively with an orchestral cadence that is clearly harmonic.

Unlike Feroze Dastur or Durga Khote, Sunila moves constantly throughout this extended scene. Her character is a washerwoman and she is shown scrubbing clothes, wringing them, rinsing them and so on. Although she stands or kneels in place for the most part, when she is singing, she is continuously working with the garment she is meant to be cleaning. When she turns her back to the camera (roughly 2′10″ into the scene) the sound of her turning – that is to say, the reduced volume and clarity or her voice – is audible. In addition to Sunila's movements, all of which are accompanied by background music that continues the modal and melodic content of her song, the camera 'moves' as well, panning as it follows Rami moving to and from the riverbank, and cutting to show Chandidas' silent irresponsiveness across the river.

In making his cuts, director Bose was using the same practice described above, either shooting simultaneously with two cameras, or most probably inserting shots of Chandidas responding (or not) to Rami's singing. These additional image recordings were then spliced into the image tracks on the strip containing the continuous sound track. In the initial 5′30″ sub-section, there are nine cuts in the image track; but only two in the sound track.

Prabhat Studio's 1934 hit, *Amrit Manthan* (1934), reveals an improvement in the quality of the microphones being used to record sound and a more sophisticated and consistent approach to recording. Director Shantaram was clearly aware of the advantages of shooting so as to obviate the need for simultaneous recording and seems to have mastered the technique of using the sound track as the master into which images tracks could be inserted. The breaks in musical continuity described above in *Ayodhyecha Raja* are largely absent in this 1934 film.

Amrit Manthan (1934) features actress (and singer) Shanta Apte in her first major role, as Princess Sumitra. In her famous song 'Raagi mammad', Shantaram inserted shots that shift the scene from Apte sitting (and singing) desolately in the night, to the reactions to her singing, first those of two watchmen who hear her voice and then that of her brother Prince Madhavgupta, played by G. R. Mane. The song continues uninterrupted, throughout these image-track cuts. The song was clearly recorded in a single take, with Apte sitting still on her rock, emoting and singing while the camera rolled. The inserted frames were probably shot without sound. In any event, the only sounds heard during the inserted frames are those of the original master sound track with Apte's voice. The resulting sonic and musical continuity are unimpeachable. But while the sound track is retained intact; the added images advance the narrative by showing others' responses to the song (an aesthetic convention that is familiar to modern viewers of Hindi cinema). When the reactions are established, the final portion of the scene cuts back to Apte, still singing, whose image is still in synch with the sound track.

Apte is also featured in a longer and more complex scene early in the film that eventually also includes her brother. Before he appears, however, Apte performs the song, 'Sukhi, sukhi taaren' as the Princess moves playfully around her room, singing, lighting lamps and

Seconds	Image track	Sound track
0	(VLS) Apte entrance	BG (pno, vln)
10		
20		
	Night sky/stars	Song
30	(LS) Apte - action	asthai
40		
		antara
50		
		Silence
60	(MLS) Apte - action	Song - antara
		Silence
70		Song - antara
		Silence
80		
		Song
90	(MS) bed	Silence
	(MLS) Apte - action	Song - antara
100		
	Night sky/stars	
110	(LS) Apte - action	2nd line
120		
		asthai
130		
	(CU) Apte - reaction	Silence
140		

Figure 1. Image track and Sound track cuts in song scene, 'Sukhi, sukhi taren.'

preparing a surprise to scare her brother. Including the introductory 20 s of background music and the final 5 s of silence, the song scene lasts roughly two-and-one-half minutes, shown as seconds in Figure 1. As can be seen, Shantaram constructed this scene using nine separate shots within which the camera is moving almost constantly, using pans and trolleys to track the Princess' movements, making for a fluid and cinematically interesting song scene.

If the image track is relatively easy to assess, however, the sound track is, in some ways, less so. The song itself is oddly structured in that there are no melodic interludes (no 'music' as the Mumbai industry would call it). Instead, sections of total silence are interspersed between sung portions of the song. The shifts from song to silence and *vice versa*, account for four of the cuts in the scene's sound track. As noted, Apte is very mobile throughout the scene, leaping across beds and twirling around the room. Because these sections were filmed without sound, the demands of musical continuity are mitigated. In effect, the song and (most importantly) the sound track 'restart' after each silent section. As shown in Figure 1, at 60 s and at 95 s the sound track restart aligns with a change of shot, so that the entire recording process could stop without affecting continuity. The camera could be repositioned; but Apte could also catch her breath (so to speak) and ready herself for the next part of the song.

It is also worth noting that the sections between these two restart points comprise the most complex portions of the scene. Among other things, some of the singing does reflect the realistic outcomes of Apte's mobility, through changes in vocal volume, clarity and, at one point, increased reverberation when she turns her back to the camera, singing, in effect, towards the wall, at which point the microphone begins to pick up the echo of her voice from the walls. This portion of the scene also includes some of the most involved action, as Apte arranges one of the beds with pillows and bed-covers to deceive her brother. She is bent over, arranging, unfolding, smoothing and so on. Given that Apte was 17 or 18 years old when *Amrit Manthan* was filmed and that this was her first singing role, the silent shooting may have been a practical as well as aesthetic choice. In the final song section of this middle portion of the scene, it is not clear that Apte is actually singing. The singing begins as she is bent over, arranging cushions and covers on the bed. As she comes upright, it is difficult to see her mouth; but at points she does not appear to be singing. Her motions are largely not responses to the musical rhythm. Because this shot, from roughly 85 to 90 s, is preceded and followed by silent shots, it is entirely possible that Apte recorded the sound track first, and then performed the scene or even the other way around. Whether or not Apte pre-recorded the shot, and whether or not the recording was developed and played-back (it hardly seems worth it for approximately 5 s of film), scenes such as this have the potential to change our understandings of the impact of playback. What is more, this scene from 1934 is not the first time that a Prabhat scene had pointed the way toward playback.

Shantaram's efforts to produce cinematographically appealing song scenes were responsible for the remarkable final song scene of *Ayodecha Raja* (1932). In 'Jiva Shankara', the royal family, consisting of King Harischandra (Tembe), Queen Taramati (Khote) and Prince Rohitdas (Master Vinayak), is transported back to Ayodhya on a magical flying vehicle (it is simply not clear what this was intended to be). The trio sing 'Jiva Shankara' in praise of the deity as they fly through the air. In the first portion of the scene, the actors are seated facing the camera as their vehicle flies vertically into the scene, against a painted backdrop of clouds and sky. In this portion of the scene, the actors' facial expressions and movements are readily visible. The images are unmistakably those of people singing.

The clarity of their singing voices on the sound track and the volume of the voices relative to the orchestra suggest that the actors were singing directly into the microphone and that they are closer to the microphone than was the orchestra. The sound track in this song scene is continuous; but, given the visual and aural clarity of the actors in this scene, the most important clue to understanding this scene is that the singers' lips and bodies are clearly not in synch with the sound track.

In this scene, the illusion of flight was achieved by the superimposition of two different image tracks and a single sound track. A background image track carried the painted sky, and later, buildings in silhouette under a full moon. The second image track carried the images of the vehicle and its passengers, which, when manipulated against the sky background, give the illusion of ascent and flight through the clouds.

Given the absence of synchronization in this portion of the scene (the only portion of the song scene in which such an assessment is possible), it is not possible to know whether Tembe, Khote, and Vinayak recorded the sound track along with the image of them sitting on their flying vehicle. This would have been normal practice; but if that is the case, the sound track somehow became separated from that image track. The other alternative is that the song was recorded separately (probably along with the background image track) and that the image of the singing trio was recorded as a silent scene in the hope that the two strips could be successfully synchronized. Whatever the process of its production, the continuous sound track somehow seems to have ended up on the background image track, so that when the image track carrying the flying vehicle and its occupants was superimposed onto the background film strip, the images of singing were un-synchronizable with the sounds of that singing. Although it is only evident for the few seconds of the scene, those seconds demonstrate the aesthetic results that forced simultaneous sound–image recording in India prior to 1935. What is also clear, and more important from the historical perspective, is that as early as 1932, Indian directors were sometimes trying to produce the more sophisticated cinematic results that would only be possible after 1935.

Conclusions: Songs, song scenes and the transition to playback

As noted above, the late Pandit Ashok Ranade has argued that many pre-1935 song scenes were actually 'non-prose … recited or partially sung items' (110). He has attributed the development of the conventional film song of the 1940s–1990s (at least) to Naushad Ali who 'succeeded in meaningfully tightening the musical concept of a film song as distinct from singing in a film. Through a careful structural crystallization, he made film-song a unified though somewhat predictable entity. Musical introduction, refrain, musical interlude, about three stanzas, perhaps an end-flourish form the structure' (Ranade 195).

As one might expect, Pandit Ranade's distinction is primarily musical, especially his analysis of what he calls the 'musical concept' that Naushad-saheb may have standardized. The idea of the 'non-prose item', however, which he seems to equate with the notion of 'singing in a film', is both more tenuous and more dependent on cinematic and/or lyrical criteria. In part, it distinguishes between the often rather generic romantic lyrics of the latter Mumbai cinema, with their potentially interruptive 'relationship to the diegesis' (Gopalan 19) on the one hand and on the other, the more discursive song lyrics and the perhaps more consistently contextualized performances of the 1931–1935 era (at least). In part, it is these attributes of the early song scenes (or non-prose items) that enabled their potentially closer, more unobtrusive relationship to the diegesis.

At the extreme non-prose item end of the musical spectrum are films such as the 1932 *Chandidas*, in which the only character to sing explicitly performed, strophic songs, is the village priest, whose songs are all devotional and who sings them in the context of his socio-religious role. The rest of the film's singing is of the kind I describe above: largely unmetered, loosely structured, and – however emotionally expressive – discursive. In this film at least, it might be more precise to describe this singing as sung prose, rather than non-prose. It would be amusing for some European music scholars at least to reflect on the concept, recitative, in this context.

At the broadest level, the closeness of the relationship that a song scene may have to the diegesis of its film is the result of the aesthetic, conventional tendencies in Indian music drama both staged and filmed, and is to some extent subjective. At another level, that relationship is also an outcome of the baseline technological processes of song scene production in the pre- and post-synchronizer eras. The process of song scene production after 1935 – in which sound was recorded separately and first, and later merged with the image track to form a synchronous scene that was still physically separate from the rest of the film – formed a foundation for an understanding of the song scene (of all song scenes) as a physically as well as aesthetically distinct unit that was then inserted into the flow of the narrative.

Before the synchronizer's arrival in India, however, and in purely technical terms, the fewer cuts there were or were needed in the sound track, the easier the production was to manage. Even if simultaneous sound/image recording sometimes lead to relatively static (and visually boring) shots, that process was nevertheless technically easier and provided fundamentally better results than any alternative. This is not to suggest an inevitably holistic production process that merged prose and non-prose portions of a film into an unavoidably organic whole. It is to suggest that a more integrated, if not holistic result was more likely, especially when combined with that other fundamental of pre-1935 song scenes: the combination of singer and actor in a single individual. I offer a final example to clarify this point.

Roughly half-way through *Ayodhyecha Raja*, the young prince, Rohitdas, asks Harishchandra, his father, why the King is performing manual labour in Kashi when his kingdom is Ayodhya. As Harishchandra explains his religious logic to his son, there is an image–sound cut in which the camera shifts from the medium shot of both Rohitdas and Harishchandra to a close-up shot of Harishchandra. This proves to have been preparation for a song and, after another few seconds of prose, the orchestra quietly provides the necessary musical cues. Actor Govindrao Tembe pauses as if in thought, while he orients himself musically, and then begins the song 'Parama dharama', the lyrics of which continue – with almost no interruption in the subject or the flow of the discourse – the homily that he had begun in prose.

The song is over three minutes in length; both sound and image were continuously (as well as simultaneously) recorded. The camera remains fixed on Tembe for the first minute, then pans down to his son listening for about 40 s, and then returns to Tembe for the remainder of the shot. Tembe's song has the usual two complementary melodies; but there is both lyrical and musical variation. As he comes to the end of major musical sections, he demonstrates his purely musical skills through a series of elaborate musical improvisations. The end of the song, is also the end of the shot.

The relationship of 'Parama dharama' to the diegesis could be said to be relatively strong in that the physical surroundings do not change and that the lyrics, which emerge out the preceding spoken dialogue, are similarly discursive despite their musical format. At the same time, the song is a fully musical composition, with an established melodic identity and structure delivered so as to explicitly display Tembe's musical virtuosity. What is more, the song does not dissolve back into the prose context from which it emerged. The cut at the end of the song is followed by a completely different scene with different characters. Its strong diegetic relationship is only evident at the beginning of the song scene.

In comparison to the songs of the 1940s onwards, which is the framework within which Ranade-saheb constructed his argument, 'Parama dharama' and the other song scenes I have analysed here do demonstrate a consistently stronger connection to their narrative than do the songs that began to emerge, gradually, after 1935. Many are considerably more than non-prose, however; as a sample of pre-1935 film songs they present the viewer with a much wider range of musical styles, and often more musical practices, than later film songs. What they, and the cinematography, make most clear is that although the technological limits of pre-1935 production encouraged films whose song scenes were closely connected to the diegesis, there was already a well-formed understanding in the minds of Indian film-makers that song scenes *were* different and should be treated (and filmed) in ways that were distinct from the cinema's narrative scenes. When synchronizers arrived in Indian studios, they offered film-makers the practical, technological means of producing the kinds of song scenes they were already imagining.

Note

1. The entire film is viewable at https://www.youtube.com/watch?v=Cj3kGMtmJBs. Dastur's three song scenes occur at approximately 21, 52, and 89 min, respectively.

References

Altman, Rick. "Re: Indian Cinema Query." Message to Greg Booth. 6 Jan. 2017. E-mail.

Beaster-Jones, Jayson. *Bollywood Sounds: The Cosmopolitan Mediations of Hindi Film Song*. New York: Oxford University Press, 2015. Print.

Booth, Gregory D. *Behind the Curtain: Making Music in Mumbai's Film Studios*. New York: Oxford University Press, 2008. Print.

Gokhale, Shanta, trans. *I, Durge Khote: An Autobiography*. By Durga Khote. Delhi: Oxford University Press, 2006. Print.

Gopalan, Lalitha. *Cinema of Interruptions: Action Genres in Contemporary Indian Cinema*. London: British Film Institute Publishing, 2002. Print.

Kinikar, Shashikant, ed. *Notes of Naushad*. By Naushad Ali. Mumbai: English Edition, 2004. Print.

Morcom, Anna. *Hindi Film Songs and the Cinema*. Aldershot: Ashgate, 2007. Print.

Ranade, Ashok. *Hindi Film Song: Music Beyond Boundaries*. Delhi: Promila, 2006. Print.

Salt, Barry. *Film Style and Technology: History and Analysis*. London: Starword. 1992. Print.

Filmography

Alam Ara. Dir. Ardeshir Irani. Imperial Movietone, 1931.
Amrit Manthan. Dir. V. Shantaram. Prabhat, 1934.
Ayodhyecha Raja. Dir. V. Shantaram. Prabhat, 1932.
Chandidas. Dir. Debaki Bose. New Theatres, 1932.
Dhoop Chaon. Dir. Nitin Bose. New Theatres, 1935.
Lal-e-Yaman. Dir. J. B. Wadia. Wadia Movietone, 1933.
The Jazz Singer. Dir. Alan Crosland. Warner Bros., 1927.

Two dances and a conference

Philip Lutgendorf

Philip Lutgendorf participated in an international symposium on the evolution of song and dance in Hindi cinema hosted at Sonoma State University in April 2017, where he also attended two-related events – a screening of Uday Shankar's recently restored dance-drama *Kalpana* (1948) and the world premiere of Leela Dance's *Son of the Wind* – both of which he discusses below.

The event

A symposium on 'The Evolution of Song and Dance in Hindi Cinema' was held at California's Sonoma State University in April 2017. Organized by Rajinder Dudrah and Ajay Gehlawat, its presentations, which generated the articles featured in this special issue of *SAPC*, offered an array of new perspectives on this cinema's musical and choreographic dimensions, with notable and especially welcome attention given to the latter. For despite general agreement among scholars of popular Hindi cinema that the presence of music and dance is one of its trademark features, scholarship on this formidable entertainment industry has often focused on its narratives as texts, and to a lesser extent on acting, camerawork, and *mise-en-scène* – largely ignoring the music and dance sequences that may constitute as much as a third of a film's running time, or even dismissing them as insignificant add-ons or 'spectacles' of emotional excess (see, e.g. Prasad; Dissanayake and Sahai). And if song itself has been (to venture a pun) downplayed in most Indian cinema scholarship, the films' choreographic component has usually been still more overlooked. This is perhaps natural given that most film and cultural studies scholars lack specialized training in musicology (or the emerging discipline of 'choreomusicology' highlighted in Usha Iyer's contribution), and though two ethnomusicologists who presented at the symposium have produced important books on Hindi cinema (Beaster-Jones; Booth), scholars (like me) who lack such training are often painfully aware of their inability to effectively analyze in musical terms what is going on in song/dance sequences. In bringing together eminent ethnomusicologists with other scholars who write on Bombay cinema and with two whose work focuses on dance and its practitioners, the symposium demonstrated the potential richness of a more wholistic approach to (what one participant called) the 'layered assemblage' of Hindi films.

It was thus, especially, appropriate that the academic presentations were bracketed by two dance performance events happily arranged to coincide with the symposium – a screening of the newly restored print of dancer and choreographer Uday Shankar's much-discussed but rarely seen 1948 film *Kalpana*, and a live performance: the world premiere of a full-length ballet in Kathak style, 'Son of the Wind', by the San Francisco Bay area-based dance company Leela. That neither piece exemplified the mainstream, cinematic productions that were the focus of the academic symposium made the cumulative package even richer and more provocative – especially in compelling participants to think more about the centrality of dance in cinema, and indeed about the tenuous boundary-line dividing 'dance', as conventionally understood, from the more encompassing choreography of any physical movement accompanied by diegetic or extra diegetic music.

As a fortunate spectator and discussant at the symposium, I was given the task, for this journal, of commenting on the Shankar film – an assignment about which I felt some trepidation, as I am neither a film specialist nor a scholar of music and dance. In what follows, I have drawn not only on my own response to seeing the restored print (and several viewings of a poorer quality one that is helpfully archived, with extensive scene-by-scene commentary, on the extraordinary internet site Indiancine.ma), but have also benefited from several insightful analyses that place the film in the wider context of Shankar's career and legacy (Erdman; Munsi; Purkayastha). Although he was largely scorned, for decades, by a classical dance establishment that branded his work 'inauthentic' even as it quietly adopted some of his innovations in pedagogy, ensemble work, and story ballets (for example, in the Shriram Bharatiya Kala Kendra of Delhi's mounting, since 1957, of an annual 'Ramlila' as a spectacular dance-drama), Shankar has received more appreciative assessment in recent years as a visionary innovator who singlehandedly developed a style of modern dance in India that was neither purely 'classical' nor 'folk' but, notwithstanding its foreign influences, unquestionably 'Indian'. The restoration of *Kalpana* offers a welcome opportunity to reassess his impact on both cinema and dance (Figure 1).

Figure 1. Uday Shankar as Krishna in a dance sequence from *Kalpana* (1948). Copyright of Cineteca di Bologna, Italy.

The film

If many Hindi films, especially in the first decades after the advent of sound, are essentially 'operatic' – in which a medley of songs and dances (as many as a staggering 72 in 1932s *Indrasabha*) are loosely stitched together by a storyline periodically invoked through dialog and action – *Kalpana* is perhaps best appreciated as a long dance performance similarly interrupted by a quasi-autobiographical storyline that, unless one is familiar with Shankar's life, can be confusing to follow, as well as by satirical and allegorical set-pieces that comment (often obliquely) on then-contemporary events and trends. The acting is, at best, highly mannered, and Shankar's flat delivery of lines and static poses seem especially awkward. Although Amala Shankar, as his main love interest, is more spirited, it is clear that neither of these talented artists was really comfortable expressing feelings through verbal language. It is dance that is the lifeblood of this film.

Framed as the unsuccessful pitch of a screenplay by an idealistic writer (Shankar, made-up with gray hair, spectacles, and a Gandhi cap) to a jaded studio owner, the film unfolds as the life story of one Udayan ('arising', the Sanskrit version of Uday's name), an artistic genius who dreams of serving the nation. In childhood, escaping a deadening village school to stage dance performances with friends, including the headstrong girl Uma, Udayan finds a benevolent mentor in Uma's father, shows skill at painting, and (now grown up and played by the middle-aged Shankar) departs for the pilgrimage city of Banaras for further artistic education. There he assembles a dance troupe that includes the Muslim youth Noor (who, as Udayan's best friend, makes a passing nod to communal harmony) and a group of talented sisters from a respectable family – whose playful camaraderie with adolescent boys and willingness to appear on a public stage probably alludes to then-current discourse about 'purifying' dance of its traditional association with courtesans and making it suitable for middle-class girls. The resulting show, starring Udayan, who performs a famous Shankar piece based on the mythology of Shiva and also demonstrates a sinuous arm and hand technique that is captured in an expressionist montage, is followed by a quarrel with the theater owner over profits and his apparent accidental murder. The young artists flee into the countryside, which is in the grip of drought and famine, to which Noor soon succumbs. While trying to save him, Udayan encounters a deranged village girl, Kamini ('desirous', played by Lakshmi Kanta), who recovers to become his dance student and, eventually, the jealous second female figure in a love-triangle with his former childhood playmate and future dance partner and wife, Uma ('mother', an epithet of Parvati, played by Amala Shankar, whom Uday had married in 1942).

Post-famine, Kamini brings Udayan to Bombay – a city, as he petulantly announces, 'filled with all the filth of Europe and America' – and introduces him to the city's Westernized elite, to whom he pitches his idea for a cultural center that will revive traditional Indian arts. An industrialist's boast about his new factory leads Udayan into an apparent reverie presenting portions of one of Shankar's most famous ballets, 'Labour and Machinery', in which massed male and female workers execute machine-like movements in a shadowy industrial set – seemingly inspired by Fritz Lang's *Metropolis* (1927) – and then are led in revolt by a proletarian hero (Shankar, of course). Awaking, Udayan insults his would-be patrons and flees the cocktail party in disgust, only to be pursued by one 'decent', *khadi*-clad industrialist who hands him a check for 50 lakh (five million) rupees to start his center, reminding him that 'rich people can also be human beings'. The fact that rich human beings – including the principal patrons of Shankar's erstwhile Almora Centre – can also be British, is as carefully elided here as was the foreignness of much of his artistic education and early performance career, via the film's substitution of holy Banaras for decadent London and Paris.

The establishment of the Himalayan *Kalakendra* ('cultural center'), which the remainder of the film celebrates, is heralded by a montage of newspaper headlines and models of its intended components, triumphantly announced by a voiceover narrator: 'Experimental radio station! Library! Museum! Gymnasium! National theatre!' Its scope is further suggested by brief vignettes of Udayan lecturing on neuroanatomy; rows of dhoti-clad boys chanting Sanskrit mantras; students in painting classes; and physical training that includes boys wrestling and girls boxing. An apparent student performance offers glimpses of another famous Shankar ballet, in which dancers garbed as wooden marionettes (*kathputli*) perform to a song that declares, 'We have been asleep for centuries, dancing like wooden puppets' – that the sword-wielding puppet masters are coded as bearded, turbaned Muslims seems to unconsciously incorporate one of the tropes of Hindu nationalism. Other performance pieces – such as a satire on modern higher education by black-robed graduates in mortar-board caps, and a pitiable appeal for national unity from an emaciated Mother India clad in a tattered sari – are inserted, often abruptly, into the storyline.

Two subplots concern crises that apparently threaten the center: Kamini and Uma's rivalry for Udayan's affections, and its need for funds once the initial gift has been exhausted. The former, perhaps alluding to Shankar's many amours but also seemingly intended as an allegorical conflict between materialism (Kamini) and spiritual artistry (Uma), has many confusing ups and downs, including attempted murder and fantasied suicide, but ends with Uma's marriage to Udayan, staged as the danced union of Parvati and Shiva in a shimmering *devaloka*. The latter occasions a debate in which Kamini proposes making a film to earn money; Udayan rejects this and instead proposes mounting a massive 'spring festival' (*vasant-utsav*) that will showcase their new national theater and bring together Indians of all classes as well as practitioners of all the country's dance traditions.

This grand spectacle, which comprises most of the film's second half, incorporates more examples of Shankar's solo and ensemble choreography along with ethnographic footage of Indian tribal and South-East Asian dancers, vignettes about the arrogance and licentiousness of princely rulers (the film was made just as most of them were facing accession to newly independent India and Pakistan), the continuing fight between Kamini and Uma and the angst it provokes, and scenes of a cheering audience in an orientalized version of a European opera house. Despite having been forced to crawl into this structure through a knee-high archway (because, as an usher announces, 'in the temple of art, both king and pauper must bow their heads'), the princes are eventually charmed by female dancers, who, in one remarkable sequence advocating women's liberation, strut proudly down a gangway wearing only blouses and skirts – the absence of the requisite *dupatta* constituting the equivalent, in the Indian context, of appearing topless. Donations pour in, apparently insuring the continued life of Udayan's Centre. His would-be cinematic life story does not fare so well, however: the bored producer abruptly cuts the writer's narration short, announcing that the script lacks commercial appeal, and has the writer thrown into the street. There, alone under a lamppost, he bewails the fact that, in the present benighted state of his country, 'my *kalpana* (fantasy) will remain only a *kalpana*'.

The legacy

Among the several ironies that surround *Kalpana* is the fact that the script of this dance-centered film – telling the story of the non-making of a dance-centered film – explicitly rejects cinema as a corrupted and corrupting art form ('it is doing our country more harm than good', Udayan opines, in response to Kamini's proposal that they make a film) and instead champions a revived 'national culture' to be taught in precisely the kind of ashram-like academy that had (in fact) been dissolved by Shankar in 1944, in order to devote himself to filmmaking. In a further irony, the dance academies that would actually prove enduring in post-Independence India would largely reject Shankar's syncretic style in favor of 'pure' strains of reinvented regional traditions (Bharatnatyam, Kathak, Manipuri, Odissi, etc.), and yet his eclectic vision would be enthusiastically adopted by the very industry that he had critiqued. Indeed, viewing *Kalpana* makes clear that Bombay film choreography and (what Usha Iyer aptly calls) 'dance musicalization', especially during its celebrated 'golden age', owed a great debt to the *kalpana* and innovation of Uday Shankar.

This is evident in big-budget films that prominently featured dance and dancers – such as V. Shantaram's *Jhanak Jhanak Paayal Baaje* ('The anklebells ring', 1955). Perhaps the most celebrated Hindi film about dance (a box office hit, also honored with four Filmfare Awards and the President's Gold Medal), it features a series of dreamlike mini-ballets that are no less hybrid than those in *Kalpana* and that sometimes draw on the Khmer and Thai-influenced costumes and jewelry favored by Shankar's Paris-nurtured 'oriental' esthetic. Shankar's influence is evident, too, in semi-art films, such as the underappreciated masterpiece *Jagte Raho* ('Keep awake', Sombhu Mitra, Amit Maitra, 1956) – a dreamlike allegory of dystopian urban life unfolding during a single night, that ends with a Shankar-esque apotheosis into a morning hymn (*Jago Mohan pyaare*, 'Wake, darling Krishna'), that features Nargis bearing a pot of water – echoing a scene in *Kalpana* in which Uma, to the same *bhajan* lyric, offers puja for Udayan's spring festival.

There are Shankaresque echoes, too, in the semi-autobiographical *Kaagaz ke Phool* ('Paper flowers', 1959) by Guru Dutt, whose own artistic trajectory began as a dancer at Shankar's Almora Centre. His story frame – of a dying director, rejected by the cynical magnates of an industry that once lionized him, and reveling in a long flashback that recounts his career – suggests *Kalpana's* frame and embedded narrative, and Dutt is also justly famed for his choreographic approach to dreamlike musical sequences. Shankar's stamp is even more visible on the famous balletic dream sequence of Raj Kapoor's hit, *Awara* ('The tramp', 1951). A late add-on by Kapoor to K. Abbas's dark screenplay, this nine-and-a-half-minute segment – featuring six sets, four songs, and scores of dancers – was, at the time, reputedly the most expensive musical number ever produced. It was choreographed by Simkie (Simone Barbiere), Shankar's longtime French partner and a teacher at his school, and its corps of dancers was supplied by Shanti Bardhan, another ex-Almora student. Its vision of the protagonist Raju's internal world moves between a hell and heaven that hybridize Christian imagery of fire and devils with Hindu temple spires and Shaivite statuary, to the accompaniment of music that combines raga-esque sitar and tabla passages with frenzied orchestral ones evoking (among other things) Mussorgsky's 'Night on Bald Mountain'. Anyone who has seen *Kalpana* can easily recognize the *Awara* sequence's debt, both choreographically and cinematographically, to Shankar's hybrid vision.

Figure 2. Seibi Lee as Hanuman, with vanara troops in a Leela Dance Collective production of 'Son of the Wind'. Photo by Margo Moritz.

This vision has likewise been reaffirmed in the art form that (according to *Kalpana*) Shankar loved best: live ensemble dance performance – both in the rethinking of 'classical' styles that has been ongoing in India since the 1980s, and in the contemporaneous efflorescence of such innovation among dance schools and companies in the Indian diaspora. This was exemplified by the remarkable performance with which the Sonoma State program concluded: 'Son of the Wind', a spectacular retelling of *Ramayana* episodes centered on Hanuman, mounted by the pupils of Pandit Chitresh Das (1944–2015), a Bengali Kathak guru who established a school in San Francisco in 1979. The Leela company, an outgrowth of this school, features many of Das's senior students, and their lavish production – their first independent choreography since their guru's death – is a tribute to his love for large-scale story ballet (a love shared with his senior neighbor and friend during his childhood in Kolkata, Uday Shankar). As a *Ramayana* scholar who also enjoys dance, I was struck both by the production's sophisticated conception (incorporating several strands of Rama-epic lore, both 'classical' and 'folk') and by the professionalism of its execution by an all-female cast of 17 dancers (Figure 2). Given that traditional *līlā* performances of epic stories in India generally feature exclusively male casting, even in female roles, the gender reversal here was striking, especially given the predominant martial mood (*vīra rasa*) of most of the episodes – though the dancing was so powerful and effective, the costuming and makeup so beguiling, that I entirely forgot about gender during the show. With its technical brilliance, emotional power, and reverent yet creative reinterpretation of sacred epic, 'Son of the Wind', staged by American women of a variety of ethnic backgrounds, was world-class transnational dance theater that celebrated Indian performance traditions even as it innovated within them and challenged cultural stereotypes. In my imagination (*kalpana*), Uday Shankar was looking down from the upper balcony, and (as in much of his film) smiling benignly.

Disclosure statement

No potential conflict of interest was reported by the author.

References

Beaster-Jones Jayson. *Bollywood Sounds: The Cosmopolitan Mediations of Hindi Film Song*. New York, NY: Oxford UP, 2014. Print.

Booth Gregory. *Behind the Curtain*. New York: Oxford UP, 2008. Print.

Dissanayake Wimal, and Malti Sahai. *Sholay, A Cultural Reading*. New Delhi: Wiley Eastern, 1992. Print.

Erdman, Joan L. *Who Remembers Uday Shankar?* Revised version of paper delivered at the annual conference of the Society of Dance History Scholars. 1997. Web. 28 April 2017. <https://mm-gold.azureedge.net/new_site/mukto-mona/Articles/jaffor/uday_shanka2.html>.

Munsi, Urmimala Sarkar. "Imag(in)ing the Nation: Uday Shankar's *Kalpana*." *Traversing Tradition: Celebrating Dance in India*. Eds. Urmimala Sarkar Munsi and Stephanie Burridge. London: Routledge, 2011. 124–150. Print.

Prasad Madhava. *Ideology of the Hindi Film, A Historical Construction*. New Delhi: Oxford UP, 1998. Print.

Purkayastha Prarthana. "Dancing Otherness: Nationalism, Transnationalism, and the Work of Uday Shankar." *Dance Research Journal* 44.1 (2012): 68–92. Print.

Filmography

Awara (The Vagabond). Dir. Raj Kapoor. R. K. Films, 1951.
Indrasabha (Indra's Court). Dir. Jamshedji Framji Madan. Madan Theatre, 1932.
Jagte Raho (Keep Awake!). Dirs. Amit Maitra and Sombhu Mitra. R. K. Films, 1956.
Jhanak Jhanak Payal Baaje (The Anklebells Ring). Dir. V. Shantaram. Rajkamal Kalamandir, 1955.
Kaagaz Ke Phool (Paper Flowers). Dir. Guru Dutt. Guru Dutt Films, 1959.
Kalpana (Imagination). Dir. Uday Shankar. Uday Shankar Production, 1948.
Metropolos. Dir. Fritz Lang. Universum Film, 1927.

Dance Musicalization: Proposing a choreomusicological approach to Hindi film song-and-dance sequences

Usha Iyer

ABSTRACT
How do dancing bodies influence the music composed for them? Does the gestural repertoire of the on-screen performer impact the musical performance of the playback singer? How might a focus on dance provide new models for theorizing the Hindi film song-and-dance sequence? Through a focus on the dancing body, this article calls for a reconsideration of the process of 'song picturization,' a term commonly used in the Bombay film industry to reference the practice of recording the song first and then "adding" visuals to it. Using the example of the dancer-actress, Vyjayanthimala, it argues that in the case of certain dancer-actors, a reverse process of 'dance musicalization' may be at work, where the performer's dance vocabulary and bodily comportment precede and influence the song. A choreomusicological analysis accords equal importance to the 'sounding body' of the dancer-actor as to the bodies that produce the film's music, leading to the conceptualization of film music as produced through a multi-bodied 'choreo-musicking body.'

On a dusky Bombay evening, I sit with my father, listening to his personally curated cassette tape compilation of songs by his favorite male playback singer, Talat Mahmood.[1] Yet again, as one of his best-loved songs, 'Jalte hain jiske liye' ('These lamps in my eyes burn for you') from *Sujata* (1959) comes on, my father expresses his annoyance that this poignant *ghazal* is sung through the prosaic medium of a telephone and carps peevishly at one of Mahmood's finest songs being 'wasted' on the up-and-coming actor, Sunil Dutt, with his simpering smile. 'Oh, only Dilip Kumar could have done justice to Talat in that song', he declares. As a result of what he deems a banal song picturization, his verdict is that this song, which perfectly showcases the mellifluous cadences of Mahmood's voice, is better *heard* than *watched*. My father's cinephilic response points to issues of crucial import for the study of the Hindi film song-and-dance sequence regarding the importance of song picturization for the appreciation of film music, and the 'matching' of bodies and voices to produce the perfect dual star text of playback singer and on-screen performer (Majumdar 191). Pondering his judgment about 'Jalte hain jiske liye' (even as for me the point of cathexis in that song is the actress Nutan's ability to cry so movingly on screen, the tears welling up in the first cutaway to her and finally running down her cheek in the next), I wonder aloud if such a purely aural engagement ('better heard than watched') is possible with *dance* numbers. Tellingly, this is not a category that many serious-minded, old-school Hindi film music aficionados like my father would pay much heed to. It prompts me, however, to think about what we hear and see when we engage with songs as compared with dance numbers, and what this might suggest about modes of production and reception. Even when we listen to rather than watch, for example, dance numbers like 'Hoton pe aisi baat' (*Jewel Thief*, 1967), 'Choli ke peeche kya hai' (*Khal Nayak*, 1993), or 'Dard-e-disco' (*Om Shanti Om*, 2007), our memory is likely to conjure up *images* of the dancer-actors' movements, in this case, Vyjayanthimala's vigorous movements and swirling red skirt, Madhuri Dixit's rhythmically heaving bosom, and Shah Rukh Khan's sinuous gyrations respectively. These wide-ranging examples raise questions asked less often of the Hindi film song-and-dance composite form (and indeed of musical numbers in other cinematic contexts): is our spectatorial engagement with dance numbers and song sequences qualitatively different? How do on-screen dancing bodies impact the music composed for them as well as our reception of this music? Much of the analysis of song-and-dance numbers has focused on music, mise-en-scène, the relationship of the musical number to the narrative, and has treated the song-and-dance sequence as a combined entity. In this article, I explore one way in which a focus on dance in the popular Hindi film song-and-dance sequence can provide new models for theorizing this cinematic attraction.

Through a focus on the display and mobilization of the dancing body, I call for a reconsideration of the process of 'song picturization,' a term commonly used in Hindi film production and in studies of this industry to reference the practice of recording the song first and then 'adding' visuals to it. While 'song picturization' suggests the primacy of the song as driving the image and our relationship to it, the proposal advanced here is that in the case of certain dance numbers or famed dancer-actors, a reverse process, where a desired dance vocabulary precedes and influences the conceptualization of the song, may instead be at work. While scholars have discussed song picturization as a central practice in the production of song-and-dance sequences (Majumdar, Booth, Dyer), this article proposes an alternate mode – of 'dance musicalization' – to address differences in production and reception modalities when a dancer-actor is featured in a film or a musical number. Employing choreomusicological theory, historical accounts of dancer-actors' influence on musical composition, and spectatorial responses to the music-dance composite, I argue that the inclusion of dancer-actors may alter the music composed in popular Hindi films so that it responds to their dancing skills and bodily comportment. This may impact the choice of music composer, playback singer/s, song lyrics, broad musical influences (western, Indian, classical, folk etc.), the structure of the musical composition (melody, beat, vocals and instrumentation, solo and chorus sections), and thus the affective figurations of the composed music. The larger aim of attending to dance in this manner is to trouble the binary of music and dance in the song-and-dance sequence, whether in terms of expressive propensities or processual temporalities (i.e. what comes first).

A dance-centered taxonomy of song-and-dance sequences

The various typologies that theorize the function of musical numbers in popular Indian cinema may be extended to consider how the dynamic figurations of the body wrought by cinematic dance forms produce unique constructions of narrative, stardom, and gender.[2]

Calling specific attention to dance (which includes a consideration of movement vocabulary, music, star bodies, mise-en-scène, cinematography, editing) is critical to understanding Hindi cinema's production and reception processes and economies. A dance-centered taxonomy of song-and-dance sequences that I have proposed elsewhere charts the differences between 'song sequences' (do not include dance at all), 'song-and-dance sequences' (may feature a range of dance movements), and 'pure dance sequences' (dance accompanied by instrumental music and no sung lyrics).[3] While any attempt at classification runs the risk of being read as producing stable and fixed categories, the intention of this taxonomy is not to solidify the often-fluid forms of musical numbers into restrictive categorizations, but by outlining some common and recurrent modalities, to help elucidate the production logics and spectatorial pleasures of popular Hindi cinema.

Within the category of song-and-dance sequences, the taxonomy proposes two broad sub-categories: the 'production number' and the 'narrative number,' both featuring physical movements that may be designated as dance. The narrative number is integrated to various degrees with the film narrative in terms of the semantic content of the song, the spaces in which the number is performed, the characters performing it, and the movement vocabulary employed by these characters. In this type of song-and-dance sequence, bodily movement is meant to express inner emotions, and may range from languid movements like swaying or skipping along rhythmically to intermittent gestural communication and choreographed dance steps. However, movements in the narrative number tend to be 'free-flowing' and are not always strictly and continuously synchronized and coordinated with the melody and rhythm of the song. In the interest of historical and narrational coherence, and because it features the dancer-actress, Vyjayanthimala, who is a central figure for these claims, this article will cite examples from the Hindi film, *Kathputli* (Puppet, 1957).[4] In the narrative number, 'Manzil wahi hai pyaar ki rahi badal gaye' ('The journey of love is the same but the travelers have changed'), the male protagonist, Loknath (played by Balraj Sahni), is seated at a piano within the domestic space of his living room, while the film's heroine, Pushpa (played by Vyjayanthimala) sways intermittently but does not perform dance 'steps' that are strictly coordinated with the song (Figure 1).[5] Where an actress not particularly known for her dancing skills would stand gracefully by the piano or restrict herself to a twirl or two, Vyjayanthimala's *Bharatanatyam*-trained dancing body refuses to stay still in this undemanding narrative number, with the resultant impression of her body, head, and eye movements being in spectacular excess of the song's expressive demands.[6] Loknath, like most leading men until the 1970s and 1980s, resolutely stays at the piano and sings.[7] The narrative number, more generally, is choreographed to appear as a spontaneous expression of inner emotions in a space not designated as one for paid performance.

In contrast, the production number is structured around a display of dancing bodies, highlighting the experiential rather than the narrational pleasures of the text. In the production number, the dancing is overtly choreographed, often frontally presented to an internal audience, and marked by distinctive moves that are strictly and continuously coordinated with the melody and rhythm of the song. Unlike the self-enclosed world of the narrative number (that often lends itself to romantic solos or duets), the production number is marked by a mode of looking where the performer explicitly invites and often returns the gaze of the internal as well as external audience, and is thus overtly coded as a performance. The production number is markedly set off from the narrative by a system of visual and aural brackets created by the dramatically altered movement vocabulary and

Figure 1. Romantic narrative number – 'Manzil wahi hai pyaar ki rahi badal gaye'. Source: DVD image grab, copyright of Shreerangam Productions, India.

audio-visual spectacle of a dance performance. In the spectacular final dance number in *Kathputli*, for example, Pushpa performs an intricately choreographed dance on the theater stage to percussive rhythms and the song, 'Bol ri kathputli dori kaun sang baandhe' ('Tell me, oh puppet, who holds your strings'). In contrast to Vyjayanthimala's loosely choreographed movements in the narrative number, 'Manzil wahi hai pyaar ki', here we encounter the full force of her dancing talent as she performs a *Kathakali*-inspired routine, the classical dance form's movement vocabulary occasioning the use of the percussive rhythms of the *chenda* drum of Kerala.[8]

A further taxonomic category of importance to the argument for dance musicalization is that of 'pure dance' sequences, which are not accompanied by a sung composition and hence do not convey the semantic content of a song's lyrics but function primarily to display the performer's dancing skills. This may be likened to the concept of *nrtta* in Indian classical dance, where certain dance segments are choreographed to show off the physical skills of the dancer and serve as *alankara* or ornamentation. These segments in the Indian classical dance repertoire that demonstrate high valuation of ornamentation and embellishment are not without their affective modality; the demonstration of dance skills produces *rasa*s or spectatorial affects of awe, delight, pleasure, and amazement (Ram 164). In popular Hindi cinema, 'pure dance' sequences are often found in films featuring dancer-protagonists, for example, the courtesan, Indrani's (Sadhona Bose) *Manipuri*-inspired court dance in *Raj Nartaki* (Court Dancer, 1941),[9] the stage dancer, Jimmy's (Mithun Chakraborty) rehearsal of his disco moves to recorded music in *Disco Dancer* (1982), the backup or background dancer, Mili's (Urmila Matondkar) gyrations on the beach to the percussive 'Spirit of *Rangeela*' (*Rangeela*/Colorful, 1995), or the vigorous 'dance-off' between two professional dancers, Nisha (Karisma Kapoor) and Pooja (Madhuri Dixit), in *Dil toh Pagal Hai* (The Heart is Crazy, 1997).

In categorizing musical sequences according to the presence or absence of dance, this proposed taxonomy points to differences in the *semantic* content of the dance number (including references to the external world, invitations to gaze upon the dancing body, and a generalized address) and of the song sequence (expression of personal emotions, interiority, address to beloved/offspring/god etc.). Crucially, the taxonomy also reveals distinctions in the *musical* structure and *sonic* quality of the dance number (rhythm-based, percussive, includes chorus sections for background dancers) and the song sequence (melody-based, typically displaying less orchestration, featuring solos or duets). These divergences point to temporal and motivic structures in dance and music so that narrative numbers' emphasis on melody and lyricism fulfills their function in expressing inner feelings, while production numbers' foregrounding of rhythm, a faster tempo, and extended instrumental sections allow for *nrtta* or 'pure dance' display. The qualities of the music and the comportment of on-screen bodies are thus closely imbricated and calibrated to generate the affective propensity of each type of musical number.

Song picturization

Differentiating between song sequences and dance numbers complicates the term, 'song picturization.' Gregory Booth describes the term as 'used most frequently by the Indian press to identify both the process of adding visual images to a song and the resultant product' (143). Neepa Majumdar notes that the use of the term song picturization to describe the production of song sequences 'shows a certain tendency toward defining the image in the terms set out by the song' (180). In their analyses of the Hindi film song sequence, Booth, Majumdar, and Richard Dyer point out that since the term 'song picturization' indicates that songs are recorded first and then 'picturized,' this suggests the primacy of the song, which sets the agenda for the visuals (Dyer 43). In the context of the American film musical, Rick Altman highlights the genre's ability to reverse what he calls the 'normal' image-sound hierarchy of classical Hollywood cinema, arguing that in the musical number, sound generates the movement within the image and the image becomes subordinate to sound as tempo and melody lead the dancers' movements as well as the editing decisions (230).

The formal reversal of the image-sound hierarchy produces ideological reversals of narrative and spectacle, which scholars of music and dance have read as moments with liberatory potential. For Sangita Gopal, the phrase 'song picturization' reverses the primacy enjoyed not only by the image in relation to sound but also the diegesis in relation to the soundtrack:

> Entrusted with putting into visual terms the world evoked by the song, the film narrative had to create 'situations' into which the song could be inserted and picturized. As such, the songs did not emanate from the story world but had to be *accommodated* by it. (809)

Adrienne McLean, in her discussion of Rita Hayworth's dance numbers in *Gilda* (1946) and *Affair in Trinidad* (1952), argues that the primacy of song over narrative in the musical number allows for the insertion of dance, which in turn allows the female body to speak in a register of its own choice: 'For where music rules, dance can enter, to join in enlivening the passive, still, inactive female image through … the "dimensionalizing force" of the body in motion' (5). While the interruptive force of song-and-dance sequences upon the narrative indeed allows for a radical rupturing of hegemonic structures of cause-and-effect-driven narrative and of gender performance, I'd like to examine further the presumed process of song picturization, which raises a number of questions for scholars of music and dance.

In *Music in Contemporary Indian Film: Memory, Voice, Identity*, Jayson Beaster-Jones and Natalie Sarrazin note: 'Many scholars of Indian film have analyzed the picturization of song sequences with minimal analysis of the musical features' (8). Through attention to dance, the aim is to look more closely at musical features even as we examine how dance exists not only in the realm of image but also of sound, through its relations with beat and rhythm.

Dance musicalization

While the procedural logic of song picturization may apply to most non-dance song sequences and to narrative numbers where, say, a romantic duet is first recorded and then the director, choreographer, cinematographer, and others determine what the characters on screen are to do with themselves while the song plays out, for many production numbers that foreground dance moves, it is the movement vocabulary planned for the sequence that influences the kind of song to be recorded. Thus, in the production stages of films starring accomplished dancer-actresses such as Vyjayanthimala or Madhuri Dixit, for example, filmmakers may often decide to include one or more dance-heavy production numbers to showcase these actresses' talent, which in turn may prompt them to commission songs to match the desired movement vocabulary. In a television show on dancer-actresses, *Baaje Payal*, film producer and director Mohan Kumar exclaims, 'If we didn't exploit [*sic*] Vyjayanthimala in one or two dances, which is her strong point, it would be our *badnaseebi* (folly),' while another producer-director, J. Omprakash, remarks of Vyjayanthimala, 'Having a dancer as an actress is great for a producer as music is much better and there is grace in the dance picturization'. The improvement in a film's *music* as a result of it featuring a dancer-actress suggests that dance vocabulary significantly influences the music of a film, often calling for enhanced rhythmic structures to accompany the dance. *New Delhi* (1956), which features Vyjayanthimala as a professional dancer, for example, creates a number of narrative situations to put on display the actress's considerable dancing skills, and the songs to which she dances foreground qualities such as rhythm and speed, and include extended non-vocal, instrumental sections to complement the 'pure dance' segments of the performance. As Janaki Devi, a South Indian professor of music and dance, Vyjayanthimala performs an *allaripu* item from the *Bharatanatyam* repertoire, set to percussive instrumentation and *bols* or rhythmic enunciations. Later in the film, the Tamil Janaki Devi play-acts as Mohini, a girl from the Northern state of Punjab, in what may be read as a cross-regional, North–South double role. Sure enough, a key aspect of this role play, when the actress in question is Vyjayanthimala, is a performance of the dance of that state, in this case, the folk-dance form of *Gidda*. By depicting Vyjayanthimala as a south Indian *Bharatanatyam*-trained dancer who can also adeptly perform the vigorous moves of *Gidda*, the film reinforces its message of national integration centrally through dance (classical and folk) and the accompanying music. It wouldn't be a stretch to surmise that it is Vyjayanthimala's ability to convincingly perform both types of dance forms that motivates the inclusion of diverse musical idioms from Punjab and Tamilnadu in the film's soundtrack.

Commenting on Hollywood's Fred Astaire-Ginger Rogers series of dance films, Steven Cohan observes that the musical scores, often written by leading Broadway talents such as Irving Berlin, were composed to showcase certain set dance routines:

> Astaire in a solo, the two stars in a challenge dance, Astaire in a speciality dance, the two stars in a romantic duet, the two stars in a novelty dance incorporating them into a big production number on the Big White Set that tries to compete with Berkeley's style. (9)

'So formulaic does the pattern become,' Rick Altman observes of the numbers' sequencing, 'that by *Top Hat* a routine is established which is rarely varied throughout the remainder of the series' (164). Dancer-actors define a 'routine' of spectacle that engenders a different mode of production and reception, propelled by the display of the formidable skills of the moving, on-screen body. I therefore suggest that a process of 'dance musicalization' – where a particular type of desired dance vocabulary precedes and influences the conceptualization of the song – may substitute 'song picturization' in many Hindi film *production numbers*. In these instances, we may witness a displacement of 'the priority of the song as a musical object, rather than as a visual object' (Booth 143) since the visual attraction of dance dictates the aural dimension of the song in the case of many production numbers. In terms of reception as well, dance musicalization may offer an interpretive framework to understand why we remember certain numbers, such as, 'Hoton pe aisi baat' and the other dance numbers mentioned earlier, as audio-visual composites rather than only as aural attractions. Dance influences the mode of production as the dancing star body authors to a significant extent the film's narrative as well as its making, and in turn this on-screen dancing body produces a mode of reception where, as spectators, we find ourselves compelled to move to the music, whether by tapping our feet, nodding our heads, getting on a dance floor, dancing in a wedding *baraat* procession, or, in the case of reality television shows, competing to approximate the original choreographic composition. One of the functions of delineating a dance-centered taxonomy is indeed to point to this difference in the embodied spectatorship of song sequences and dance numbers, each producing its own spectatorial comportment and affective intensity.

Dance, stardom, and authorship

While leading actresses of the 1950s such as Nargis, Meena Kumari, and Nutan did have women-centric films especially designed to showcase their acting abilities, the dancer-actress wielded authorship of a different nature on account of her particular skills, which engendered a distinctive mode of performance, with altered relations between spectacle and narrative. Returning to producer-director J. Omprakash's assertion that working with a dancer-actress like Vyjayanthimala leads to an improvement in the film's music, we may presume that Vyjayanthimala's dancing skills are likely to lead to the conceptualization of folk and classical dance numbers, which in turn influence the musical compositions in the film, as we saw in *New Delhi*. One could conjecture, for example, that energetic, percussion-heavy, folk-music-based songs like 'Bakad bam bam baaje damru' ('The drum goes bakad bam bam') in *Kathputli* and 'Chad gayo paapi bichua' ('A scorpion has climbed over me') in *Madhumati* (1958) were composed to showcase Vyjayanthimala's effervescent dancing skills. In some cases, films come to exist only to celebrate the skills of the dancer-actress. Lekh Tandon, director of *Amrapali* (1966), in which Vyjayanthimala plays the eponymous Hindu courtesan, remarks, 'I made Amrapali only because of Vyjayanthimala being such a great dancer and because of the choreographer Gopi Krishna. Without them, I wouldn't have made the film at all' (Baaje Payal). The film is overtly marked with Vyjayanthimala's authorial stamp, featuring a series of dazzling production numbers designed to show off her classical dance skills, the raison d'etre of the film. Reviews, like this one of *Nagin* (1954), reiterate that the narratives in many Vyjayanthimala films are mere scaffolds for her resplendent dancing: '*Nagin*'s story seemed more like a flimsy excuse to string along a series of melodiously composed Hemant Kumar [songs, performed] by a sinuous Vyjayanthimala. She had eight scintillating Lata solos to put across on screen – each was a hit' (Raheja). Clearly, *Nagin*'s attractions seem to lie in its music and dance, with mention made only of the music composer, playback singer, and dancer-actress, suggesting as well a powerful connection between the workings of these three. Indeed, music and dance were so critical to the film that 'the last four songs, two reels of musical climax, were [shot] in colour' (Rao 32). The presence of the dancer-actress in this instance produces an impetus for technological changes (only song-and-dance sequences being shot in color, for example), production innovations (cinematography, makeup and costume, sets and props, editing), the significance of certain industry personnel (music composers, playback singers, choreographers), and, through the concept of 'dance musicalization,' I argue, the type of music composed for the film.

Erin Branningan notes of Rita Hayworth that she was one of the few female musical stars to take the lead in numbers that emphasized dance over song and that in the musicals following those she made with Astaire, she performs more solos than duets (150). It is with a dancer-actors in particular that dance is rendered more important than song, and production number solos than narrative number duets, which changes the articulation of heterosexual coupling accordingly. Where, in a typical male-centered narrative, what Ravi Vasudevan terms 'para-narrative units,' such as song, dance, and comic sequences, create parallel pleasures to the central narrative (31), in a female-centered dance film, the para-narrative unit of the song-and-dance sequence, and in particular, the production number that explicitly invites the spectatorial gaze upon the dancing body, deeply problematizes the work of the narrative. *The Encyclopaedia of Indian Cinema*'s entry for *Kathputli* – 'A Vyjayanthimala vehicle, the film consists of expensively staged dance sequences loosely strung together' (350) – reflects the difference in narrative organization when a dancing star and production numbers are the primary attractions. *Kathputli*'s narrative construction is indeed in the service of Vyjayanthimala's scintillating production numbers, with only half-hearted attempts to resolve the miscommunication between her character Pushpa, her husband, Shivraj, and the theater director, Loknath. A conventional 'happy ending' is tagged on in the final minutes of the film. However, this remains a noticeably weak attempt to neutralize inadmissible conflicts and desires – especially those of Pushpa, for public performance and for Loknath – which entirely exceed this hasty resolution. The film, in its lack of dedication to the narrative demands of Indian domestic melodrama, including to heterosexual romance, reveals that its central investment is to put on display its leading lady's dancing abilities. Indeed, the film features only one romantic narrative number ('Manzil wahi hai pyaar ki,' discussed above), whose suggestions of a budding romance between Pushpa and Loknath are never pursued by the film. Thus, often in films starring dancer-actresses like Vyjayanthimala the para-narrative unit of the dance number 'floats free of the business of narrative' (Vasudevan 50), refusing to be integrated into the conventional exigencies of the male-centric plot, and opens up the popular cinematic narrative to other configurations of spectatorial and performative pleasures, including a markedly different aural landscape produced through an emphasis on dance.[10]

A choreomusicological approach to song-and-dance sequences

Shammi Kapoor – the 'swinging sensation,' and one of the few dancing heroes of the 1960s – relates an anecdote about the recording of the song, 'Tareef karoon kya uski' ('How shall I praise her') in the film, *Kashmir Ki Kali* (1964) where the playback singer, Mohammed Rafi was worried about too many refrains that repeated the first line. Kapoor reminisces, 'I showed Rafi-saab how I was going to sing the song, and I said that in my gestures, I would find a different way of singing the first line every time it came. And I told him to sing it the same way too' (Rajadhyaksha 59). Kapoor's anecdote points to the specialized knowledge of the body and of their personal gestural repertoire that dancer-actors in particular possess. This somatic knowledge extends into a special engagement with sound and music in the song-and-dance sequence. Sherril Dodds and Susan C. Cook employ the phrase, 'bodies of sound' to theorize the intrinsic and mutually constitutive relationship between music and dance, bodies and sound:

> The idea that neither the music nor the dance occupies a position in which one determines or dominates the other underpins our enquiry. Instead, we conceive a mobilization of meanings that come into play through the reciprocal exchange between popular music and dance. (1)

Attention to the practices of moving and sounding bodies and to the linkages between the sensorial planes of sound and movement alerts us to how dancing bodies are instrumental in the creation, transmission, and reception of music.

Choreomusicology, a portmanteau word combining choreology and musicology, provides a useful theoretical framework to study the choreomusical relationships underpinning song-and-dance sequences. Rather than the old binary of parallelism and counterpoint, choreomusicologists recommend approaching music and dance as a composite form where the two sensory planes are seen as being in a state of mutual implication or possession (Jordan 47). Let us turn to the production number, 'Bakad bam bam baaje damru' ('The drum goes bakad bam bam') from *Kathputli* to ascertain what insights a choreomusical reading may provide (Figure 2).[11] In this song-and-dance sequence, Vyjayanthimala performs a dancing double role, as it were, playing up the *nrtta* or decorative gestural elements of a peacock heralding the rain, set to instrumental music, and showcasing expressive *nritya* and *natya* elements in her role as the dancing rural belle, lip-synching to the noted playback singer Lata Mangeshkar's voice.[12] In the third shot of the sequence, featuring a long shot of Vyjayanthimala in the dancing peacock role, the instrumental music begins with two clangs to which she raises high one foot after another (in the manner of the *mayurigati* or peacock gait), followed by a musical shift to a more tinkling *santoor*-produced sound as she executes a circular body movement (a modified *bhramari*) and then leaps to a stop (*utplavana*) as the music also pauses.[13] This is followed by a horizontal neck movement (*sundari* or *attami* in the *Abhinaya Darpana*) to two percussive beats. In her discussion of choreomusicology, Stephanie Jordan discusses how, through somatic engagement, dance and the body can influence musical experience and thinking about music. 'Rhythm is an immediate point of contact between the two art forms. As a phenomenon, it can, after all, enter through both the eye and ear,' she remarks (52). In 'Bakad bam bam baaje damru', we perceive rhythm aurally through the instrumentation (strings, drums, *santoor*), but equally, visually through Vyjayanthimala's leaping, swirling, and staccato neck movements. Indeed, this entire opening section sets to instrumental music serves to showcase Vyjayanthimala's well-known facility with the *Bharatanatyam* movement vocabulary and especially foregrounds the desired

Figure 2. Production number – 'Bakad bam bam baaje damru'. Source: DVD image grab, copyright of Shreerangam Productions, India.

components of *nrtta* exposition, which include *angasuddha* (clarity and firmness in the rendering of line), *tala suddha* (precision in relation to beat), *lasya* (grace), and *tandava* (vigor, strength, and speed of footwork and other gestures).

Tala suddha or precision in relation to beat or to time is especially key to considering rhythm choreomusically. Dancer-scholar Shobana Jeyasingh remarks, 'Through footwork it is possible to pattern time in such a minute and detailed way that on one level the dance is the percussive structure of the music' (186). Indeed, as 'bodies of sound,' dancing bodies produce music most explicitly when they engage in percussive footwork, clapping, leaps and the like. In the ninth shot of 'Bakad bam bam baaje damru', Vyjayanthimala makes her second entry – this time as the village belle – with a close-up of her feet. The music changes from the strings and percussion of the earlier section to a mellifluous flute-driven melody as we see the village belle's feet step forward delicately and then tap the ground four times, emphatically reinforcing the percussion (*damru*/drum) that joins the flute. The change in footwork is braided with the instrumentation, and indeed it is the tapping of the ground with the foot that accentuates or makes *audible* to us the *damru* that is referenced in the song. But dancers are not only music-makers with footwork and leaps; contact with a surface is not always necessary to produce sound. Gestures can also have their aural dimension, produced through an interaction with space, and 'cine-choreographies' like sweeping camera movements or slow motion produce aural effects as well.[14] The next three shots in 'Bakad bam bam baaje damru' are instructive on this point. Beginning with the close-up of the feet of the village belle, when the sonic *damru*/drum and visual foot taps are introduced, as if echoing the upbeat rhythm of the image and sound, the camera tilts up slowly to a high angle long shot, taking in Vyjayanthimala's entire dancing body. The music, dance, and camera movement are braided together; as the flute-led melody develops (in a circular musical movement), Vyjayanthimala rotates her head sideways and circles her arms around her torso four times to the beat. Her circular dance movement appears to swivel the camera upward rhythmically as a third participant in this choreomusical *ménage à trois*. She changes the dance step only after the camera is stable and static at a high angle position. Finally, as we arrive at the sung *mukhda* or opening phrase, an uncharacteristically long one-and-a-half minutes after the song has begun (underscoring this musical number's purpose of putting on display Vyjayanthimala's *nrtta* skills), the imbrication of music, dance, and cinematography are in evidence again as, in a slightly low angle shot, the village belle rises rhythmically to the beat of the 'bam bam bam' of the song, and portrays through *mudras* or gestures the beating of the *damru* (drum) and the dance of the *mayur* or peacock. Onomatopoeic lyrics like 'bam bam bam' and 'jhan jhanake ghunghroo' (the sound of anklets) reflect the intertwined choreomusical foundation of dance numbers as they perform the function of the *nattuvangam* (metal cymbals) in *Bharatanatyam* that sets the rhythm for the *nrtta* sections, or the spoken *bols* in *Kathak* to which the rhythmic footwork or *tatkar* is performed.[15] The inclusion of these onomatopoeic lyrics buttresses the argument for dance musicalization as it suggests the specificities of lyrical composition for dance numbers.[16]

A choreomusical analysis of 'Bakad bam bam baaje damru' encourages us to think of music and dance as not just 'call and response' but as deeply imbricated with each other and with the cinematic apparatus. The opening shots of this production number illustrate how dance moves reiterate key musical structures and elements such as pulse and rhythm, and how musical phrasing is accentuated through dance gestures. Adopting this choreomusicological approach, we may appropriate the term song *picturization* as reflecting dance's power to *visibilize* music. In many instances, this enables a reversal of the audio-visual terms of engagement so that we begin to *see* music and *hear* dance. 'This is not music you can know alone, you have to know it with the dance,' remarks dance practitioner-theorist, Jade Power Sotomayor, of the Mexican Son Jarocho folk form. In the embodied music-making of Hindi film production numbers and pure dance numbers, the visual attraction of dance often dictates the aural dimension of the song.

We only have to *hear* a song without watching the accompanying picturization, or *watch* a dance without the accompanying music to appreciate the effect of choreomusical synchrony in some numbers while recognizing that others don't lose from lacking the visuals (such as 'Jalte hain jiske liye' for my father) or the music (for example, the innumerable soundless GIFs of Bollywood dance moves circulating on the internet).

Conclusion: The choreomusicking body

Matthew Rahaim, in his study of gestures and voice in Hindustani music, employs the term, 'musicking body' to understand the body that comes alive in the moment of musical performance. While his focus is on the gestural repertoire of the *Hindustani* vocalist or musician, in the realm of Hindi film music, where the voice and the body are split between the playback singer and the on-screen performer, respectively, the on-screen dancing body provides the gestures that combine with the off-screen voice and instrumentation to embody melodic ideas. Rahaim aims to 'highlight the consubstantiality of voice and body by transcribing bodily action, no less than vocal action, as music' and asserts that melodic action is made dynamic through 'the immaterial curves' the musician's body traces in the air (xi). A choreomusicological approach to the Hindi film song-and-dance sequence enables us to advance the notion of a 'choreomusicking body' as composed of a conjoining of the playback singer's voice, the on-screen performers' gestural repertoire, the music composer's composition, as well as the bodies of the often-nameless musicians who produce the instrumental soundtrack for the number.

This reconceptualization of the production of film music through the multi-bodied choreomusicking body deepens our analysis of the ideological work of the musical number in popular Hindi cinema. One may push further, for example, the theorization of the 'dual star text' and the work of Lata Mangeshkar's voice in 'managing' the potentially dangerous circulation of the actress's body in public spaces (Majumdar, Srivastava) by considering the difference in the reception of Mangeshkar's voice when she sings for a dancer-actress like Vyjayanthimala and for an actress like Nutan, who is not particularly known for her dancing abilities, and of whom it has been written: 'She exudes very little physicality. The body does not seem to matter. No wonder it was rare to see Nutan dance on screen, despite being a trained Kathak dancer' (Joshi 14). The Mangeshkar-Nutan star text is associated with song sequences featuring little to no dance movements (often set to S. D. Burman's slow, melodious compositions) while the Mangeshkar-Vyjayanthimala star text is best known for its vigorous production numbers (often set to C. Ramchandra's brisk and robust dance-music). Using the choreomusicking body as an analytical framework helps us note how the heroine's on-screen comportment has the potential to alter the reception of a playback singer's voice, which in turn determines aesthetic judgments about the quality of acting and music. Nutan, hailed as a sensitive actress, was also Mangeshkar's favorite on-screen body for her voice (Joshi 14). The singer notes of Nutan: 'her presentation of the song on the screen used to be very natural. The gestures and emotions that take place while singing a song used to be enacted by her to perfection' (rediff.com), suggesting a closely imbricated 'musicking' body, where Mangeshkar sees her voice as perfectly complemented by the composure of Nutan's non-dancing body. This consubstantiality of voice and body is not as evident in Mangeshkar's comments on Vyjayanthimala: '[she] performed most of the dance oriented roles in films and complemented the dance with her acting skills. … Her dancing skills and my songs in the movies *Kathputli, Nayi Dilli* and *Madhumati* were highly appreciated by the audience' (rediff.com). Mangeshkar's separation of her voice from Vyjayanthimala's dancing body and of dancing from acting (a binary that informed many reviews of Vyjayanthimala's films – is she a 'serious actress' or merely a 'dancing star')[17] prompts us to examine hierarchies of *musical* value between these categories of performance: are song sequences and narrative numbers considered musically superior to production numbers? Such a hierarchy is familiar to us from the world of classical Indian music, where concert music is more highly regarded than music accompanying dance (similar to concert music vs. ballet music in the western context).[18]

A choreomusical analysis allows us, on the other hand, to tell the story differently. Shikha Jhingan notes how playback singing allowed on-screen stars the freedom 'to work on their performance with a clear referent, the recorded song, using the disembodied voice of the singer to enhance their own performance, emoting according to the tonal and expressive registers of the pre-recorded voice'. A choreomusical approach proposes a reverse inquiry: do playback singers base their singing upon on-screen bodies? How does the gestural repertoire of the on-screen performer impact the musical performance of the singer? Did the gloriously expressive body of Hindi cinema's favorite vamp, Helen, prompt the playback singer, Asha Bhosle, to include trilling laughter and whispered sighs in her vocalization of Helen's baroque production numbers? So far, this has been discussed as a cultural articulation of modes of femininity through the figures of the raunchy vamp, the demure heroine, and the pious playback singer.[19] However, a choreomusical analysis that accords equal importance to the 'sounding body' of the dancer-actress as to the bodies that produce the music, illuminates, for example, the skill, talent, competence, and range of motion in voice and body required to bring alive the otherwise-disparaged dancing vamp figure through trained dancing bodies, playback singers that specialize in rhythmic harmonies, and composers and musicians who render the song *danceable*.

The theorization of Hindi film song-and-dance sequences must take into consideration the *combinatoire* of expression produced through the choreomusical exchanges of music and dance as well as playback singers and on-screen bodies and recognize the singularity of dance as a means of picturization. Analyzing how gesture, voice, and music work together to embody melodic ideas allows for a proliferation of methodological approaches to the study of the song-and-dance sequence that may do justice to the manifold affective responses we have to listening to songs (without the video – on the radio or on our phones), watching song-and-dance sequences on their own, watching them as part of the film narrative, or dancing to/with them. A combination of industry observations, spectatorial speculation, and choreomusicological approaches inform my proposal to include 'dance musicalization' in our discussion of the song-and-dance sequence so we may move beyond the unidirectional logic suggested by the process of song picturization and begin to understand the multiple logics mobilized in the assembly and reception of these spectacular attractions.

Notes

1. In popular Indian cinema, since the 1940s, playback singing has been the preferred mode of musical performance, with the playback singer first recording the song, which is then lip-synchronized by the on-screen actor. Commerically available film song compilations may be categorized by playback singer, on-screen star, music composer, decades, or themes (for example, 'Romantic hits of the 70s,' 'Haunting Melodies of Lata Mangeshkar' etc.).
2. See Arnold (178); Gopalan (129–35); Gopal (41), *Conjugations*; Chandavarkar (18); Ranade (7).
3. Iyer (132–36).
4. I mainly discuss dancer-actresses in this article as women were the primary performers of dance numbers in popular Hindi cinema until the 1990s.
5. This narrative number may be viewed here: https://www.youtube.com/watch?v=1RF8Dcg2PqA.
6. *Bharatanatyam is a* South-Indian classical dance form, among the first to be canonized as 'classical' by the Sangeet Natak Akademi (The National Academy for Music, Dance and Drama). In addition to a vast gestural vocabulary, *Bharatanatyam* is characterized by the *araimandi* (half-squat) stance, and the execution of geometric movements in a given time cycle. Vyjayanthimala was trained in the dance form from a young age and continues to perform as a classical *Bharatanatyam* dancer.
7. The popular Hindi film's gendering of music and dance is evident in film critic, Partha Chatterjee's nostalgia for a time when heroes did not engage in the vigorous gyrations of post-1980s stars like Govinda: 'In the good old days, dancing was not considered a masculine

pursuit and the likes of Dilip Kumar, Dev Anand and Motilal, of an earlier generation, would have taken exception to the very suggestion that they did more than a few rudimentary steps in their films as an accompaniment to the songs they picturized' (197).

8. *Kathakali* is a South-Indian classical dance form that originated in the region now designated as the state of Kerala, and is among the eight canonized classical dance forms. It is predominantly performed by men whose face paint and costume indicate the mythic or epic characters they represent.
9. *Manipuri* dance is a canonized classical dance form from the North Eastern state of Manipur that predominantly depicts religious themes, especially the *Raas Lila* or the dance of Krishna and Radha.
10. A similar lack of investment in narrative cohesion with strongly 'motivated' musical interludes may be seen in the films of other dancer-actresses from the 1930s to the present, such as, Sadhona Bose, Sitara, Helen, Padmini, Silk Smitha, Madhuri Dixit and others.
11. This production number may be viewed here: https://www.youtube.com/watch?v=Cwyxpyd6eM4.
12. These terms draw from the medieval performance treatises, the *Natya Shastra* and the *Abhinaya Darpana*. *Nrtta* refers to 'pure dance' movements that are not intended to convey a particular meaning to the audience but rather to demonstrate the dancer's skills. *Nritya* is expository dance meant to convey a narrative or an idea to the onlooker through *abhinaya* or expression. *Natya* is a more theatre-related category where *nrtta* and *nritya* are both utilized, but in addition, the element of drama is introduced through the use of the spoken word and other conventions of the stage (Khokar 58).
13. These Sanskrit terms describing dance movements are taken from the classical dance lexicon codified in the twentieth century, which draws from the *Natya Shastra*, the *Abhinaya Darpana*, and other performance treatises.
14. Erin Brannigan uses the term 'cine-choreography' to analyze how cinematic techniques produce new forms of choreographic practice: 'The variety of movements featured in dancefilm are produced through the cinematic process and can be of any nature: the movement of a body part, crowd, object or graphic detail, and may be animated by outside forces such as natural elements or technological manipulation. It is these movements that create the *cine-choreographies* that constitute filmic performance in dancefilm' (ix).
15. *Kathak* is a North-Indian classical dance form, one of the eight dance forms canonized as 'classical' by the Sangeet Natak Akademi (The National Academy for Music, Dance and Drama). In addition to a vast gestural vocabulary, it is marked by elaborate footwork and spins of the body.
16. One may cite here the example of the repeated onomatopoeic phrase 'dola re dola' (swaying of the body) in *Devdas* (2002) or phrases like 'payal ki chan chan' (the tinkling of anklets) and 'kangne ki khan khan' (the clinking of bracelets) that proliferate in the Hindi film song-and-dance number more generally.
17. A *Star and Style* feature on the actress' career reflects this prejudice: 'In the wake of "Devdas" came films like "Naya Daur," "Sadhana," "Madhumati" and "Paigham" rounding out Portrait No. 2 as the heroine who could no longer be shrugged off casually as a "dancing star" (5).
18. Consider here as well the higher status accorded by the industry to Mangeshkar's dulcet 'narrative-number voice' over her sister, Asha Bhosle's flamboyant 'production-number voice'.
19. See Majumdar; Mazumdar; Mehta; Basu; Gehlawat for discussions of aural and on-screen femininity, and how this was negotiated through the offscreen persona of Lata Mangeshkar and various on-screen bodies that conformed to or subverted the norms of ideal femininity.

Disclosure statement

No potential conflict of interest was reported by the author.

References

Altman, Rick. *The American Film Musical*. Bloomington: Indiana UP, 1987. Print.

Arnold Alison. "Popular film song in India: a case of mass-market musical eclecticism1." *Popular Music* 7.2 (1988): 177–188.

Basu, Anustup. ""The Face that Launched a Thousand Ships": Helen and Public Femininity in Hindi Film." *Figurations in Indian Film*. Eds. Anustup Basu and Meheli Sen, 139–157. London: Palgrave Macmillan, 2013. Print.

Beaster-Jones, Jason, and Natalie Sarrazin, eds. *Music in Contemporary Indian Film: Memory, Voice, Identity*. New York, NY: Routledge, 2016. Print.

Booth, Gregory. "Religion, Gossip, Narrative Conventions and the Construction of Meaning in Hindi Film Songs." *Popular Music* 19 (2000): 125–145. Print.

Brannigan, Erin. *Dancefilm: Choreography and the Moving Image*. New York, NY: Oxford UP, 2011. Print.

Chandavarkar, Bhaskar. "Growth of the Film Song." *Cinema in India* 1.3 (1981): 16–20. Print.

Chatterjee, Partha. "A Bit of Song and Dance." *Frames of Mind*. Ed. Aruna Vasudev, 197–218. New Delhi: UBS ' Distributors, 1995. Print.

Cohan, Steven. "'Feminizing' the Song-And-Dance Man: Fred Astaire and the Spectacle of Masculinity in the Hollywood Musical." *Screening the Male: Exploring Masculinities in the Hollywood Cinema*. Eds. Steven Cohan and Ina Rae Hark. New York, NY: Routledge, 1993. 46–69. Print.

Cook, Susan C., and Sherril Dodds, eds. *Bodies of Sound: Studies Across Popular Music and Dance*. New York: Routledge, 2016. Print.

Dyer, Richard. *In the Space of a Song: The Uses of Song in Film*. Abingdon: Routledge, 2012. Print.

Gehlawat, Ajay. *Twenty-first Century Bollywood*. Abingdon, Oxon: Routledge, 2015. Print.

Gopal, Sangita. "The Audible Past, or What Remains of the Song-Sequence in New Bollywood Cinema." *New Literary History* 46.4 (2015): 805–822. Print.

Gopal, Sangita. *Conjugations: Marriage and Form in New Bollywood Cinema*. Chicago, IL: U of Chicago P, 2011. Print.

Gopalan, Lalitha. *Cinema of Interruptions: Action Genres in Contemporary Indian Cinema*. London: BFI, 2002. Print.

Iyer, Usha. "Stardom Ke Peeche Kya Hai?/What Is behind the Stardom? Madhuri Dixit, the Production Number, and the Construction of the Female Star Text in 1990s Hindi Cinema." *Camera Obscura: Feminism, Culture, and Media Studies* 30.3 90 (2015): 129–159.

Jeyasingh, Shobana. "Getting Off the Orient Express." *The Routledge Dance Studies Reader*. Eds. Alexandra Carter and Janet O'Shea. New York, NY: Routledge, 2010: 181–187. Print.

Jhingan, Shikha. "The Singer, the Star and the Chorus." India-Seminar, 2009. <http://www.india-seminar.com/2009/598/598_shikha_jhingan.htm>.

Jordan, Stephanie. *Moving Music: Dialogues with Music in Twentieth-century Ballet*. London: Dance Books, 2000. Print.

Joshi, Namrata. "Nutan." *Women in Indian Film*. Ed. Nasreen Munni Kabir. Delhi: Zubaan Books, 2008. Print.

Khokar, Mohan. *Traditions of Indian Classical Dance*. Delhi: Clarion Books, 1984. Print.

Majumdar, Neepa. *Wanted Cultured Ladies Only!: Female Stardom and Cinema in India, 1930s–1950s*. Urbana: U of Illinois P, 2009. Print.

Mazumdar, Ranjani. *Bombay Cinema: Archive of the City*. Delhi: Permanent Black, 2007. Print.
McLean, Adrienne L. ""It's Only That I Do What I Love and Love What I Do": "Film Noir" and the Musical Woman." *Cinema Journal* 33.1 (1993): 3–16. Print.
Mehta, Monika. *Censorship and Sexuality in Bombay Cinema*. Austin: U of Texas P, 2011. Print.
"PIX: Lata Mangeshkar on Nutan, Mumtaz, Madhuri." Rediff.com, 31. Dec. 2012. Web. 22 Aug. 2015.
Rahaim, Matthew. *Musicking Bodies: Gesture and Voice in Hindustani Music*. Middletown, CT: Wesleyan UP, 2012. Print.
Raheja, Dinesh. "Vyjayanthimala: Bollywood's Dancing Queen.' Rediff.com, 2002. Web. 15 May 2013.
Rajadhyaksha, Ashish. *The Sad and the Glad of Kishore Kumar*. Mumbai: Research for Cinema Studies, 1988. Print.
Rajadhyaksha, Ashish, and Paul Willemen. *Encyclopedia of Indian Cinema*. London: British Film Institute, 1999. Print.
Ram, Kalpana. "Being 'Rasikas': The Affective Pleasures of Music and Dance Spectatorship and Nationhood in Indian Middle-class Modernity." *Journal of the Royal Anthropological Institute* 17.s1 (2011): S159–S175. Print.
Ranade, Ashok. "The Extraordinary Importance of the Indian Film Song." *Cinema Vision India* 1.4 (1980): 4–11. Print.
Rao, V.A.K. Ranga. "She brought Lustre to the Silver Screen." *Sruti* 314 (Nov. 2010): 31–36. Print.
Sotomayor, Jade Power. "The Fandango Fronterizo: Moving Borders and Son Jarocho's Speaking and Space-Making Bodies." Lecture at the Stanford Colloquium on Dance Studies, 2016.
Srivastava, Sanjay. "Voice, Gender and Space in Time of Five-Year Plans: The Idea of Lata Mangeshkar." *Economic and Political Weekly* (2004): 2019–2028. Print.
Vasudevan, Ravi. "The Melodramatic Mode and the Commercial Hindi Cinema: Notes on Film History, Narrative, and Performance." *Screen* 30.3 (1989): 29–50. Print.
"Vyjayanthimala." Star and Style, 15 Jun. 1966. 4–5. Print.

Filmography

Affair in Trinidad. Dir. Vincent Sherman. Columbia Pictures Corporation, 1952. Film.
Amrapali. Dir. Lekh Tandon. Eagle Films, 1966. Film.
Baaje Payal. Doordarshan, 2002. Television.
Court Dancer. Dir. Modhu Bose. Wadia Movietone, 1941. Film.
Dil toh Pagal Hai. Dir. Yash Chopra. Yash Raj Films, 1997. Film.
Disco Dancer. Dir. Babbar Subhash. B. Subhash Movie Unit, 1982. Film.
Gilda. Dir. Charles Vidor. Columbia Pictures Corporation, 1946. Film.
Jewel Thief. Dir. Vijay Anand. Navketan, 1967. Film.
Kashmir Ki Kali. Dir. Shakti Samanta. Shakti Films, 1964. Film.
Kathputli. Dir. Nitin Bose, Amiya Chakrabarty. Shreerangam Productions, 1957. Film.
Khal Nayak. Dir. Subhash Ghai. Mukta Arts, 1993. Film.
Madhumati. Dir. Bimal Roy. Bimal Roy Productions, 1958. Film.
Nagin. Dir. Nandlal Jashwantlal. Filmistan, 1954. Film.
New Delhi. Dir. Mohan Segal. De Luxe Films, 1956. Film.
Om Shanti Om. Dir. Farah Khan. Red Chillies Entertainment, 2007. Film.
Rangeela. Dir. Ramgopal Varma. Jhamu Sughand Productions, 1995. Film.
Sujata. Dir. Bimal Roy. Bimal Roy Productions, 1960. Film.
Top Hat. Dir. Mark Sandrich. RKO Radio Pictures, 1935. Film.

Romance, piety, and fun: The transformation of qawwali and Islamicate culture in Hindi cinema

Pavitra Sundar

ABSTRACT
This article charts the trajectory of the qawwali, one of the foremost markers of Islamicate culture in Bombay cinema. Between the 1940s and 1980s, the film qawwali was a secular, romantic genre celebrating the wit and artistry of a singer-poet wooing his or her beloved. With the success of Nusrat Fateh Ali Khan and A. R. Rahman, the genre enjoyed a comeback in the 2000s, but in the form of 'dargah' qawwalis. What comes into view in this second cinematic incarnation of the genre is not romance but Muslim men's religiosity. 'Item-numberesque' qawwalis of the last decade continue the erasure of gendered courtship rituals once associated with 'classic' film qawwalis. As I map shifts in the genre's narrative functions, performance styles, and picturization over six decades, I connect them to broader transformations in discourses of nation, religion, and identity as well as the business of film- and music-making in India.

Introduction

This article charts the trajectory of the qawwali in Bombay cinema. Like the ghazal, this Sufi poetic form has a long, syncretic history in South Asia. For decades, both genres have served as pre-eminent musical markers of 'Islamicate culture' in Hindi cinema (Kesavan 256). In this piece, I demonstrate that the qawwali goes from being a secular, romantic genre in films of the 1940s through the 1980s to a more serious, devotional form in the early 2000s. The classic film qawwali emphasized the wit and artistry of the singer-poet wooing his or her beloved. It celebrated gendered conventions of romance, even as it used a spiritual idiom to do so. In its second incarnation, the qawwali is less about worldly romance and more about Muslim (men's) religiosity. As with the waning of the ghazal form in Bombay cinema, this transformation of the qawwali effects a de-estheticization of Islamicate culture on screen. The irony, of course, is that the revival of the film qawwali occurs because of two Muslim men's artistic prowess off-screen: music-director A. R. Rahman and world-music star Nusrat Fateh Ali Khan. An appreciation of Islamicate artistry diminishes as qawwalis get used to index a coming-of-age moment on screen, a moment when a lost man finds purpose and community. The last decade has also seen the rise of item-numberesque qawwalis. These star-studded, eminently danceable numbers re-embrace the genre's historical functions as a vehicle of romance. Something changes, however, as commodified and spectacular dancing bodies come to the fore. With the itemization of the genre, the social graces and elaborately gendered courtship rituals associated with the genre in its mid-twentieth century screen iterations are rendered obsolete. Listening, either for pleasure or piety, gets devalued. In the process, gender, romance, and Islamicate culture are articulated anew. As I map these shifts in the genre's narrative functions, performance styles, and picturization, I argue that the changing fortunes of the qawwali in Bombay cinema speak to broader transformations in discourses of nation, religion, and identity as well as the business of film- and music-making in India.

Classic film qawwalis

From the 1940s through the 1960s, qawwalis were primarily used in Muslim socials and historicals, film genres that told stories set in an Islamicate milieu. One of the earliest uses of a qawwali as a song sequence comes in *Zeenat* (1945) where a group of women sing 'Aahein na bharin, shikwein na kiye' (Bhattacharjya). 1960 appears to be the high point for the genre, with *Barsaat Ki Raat* (1960), *Chaudhvin Ka Chand* (1960), and *Mughal-e-Azam* (1960) all hitting the theaters that year. While each of these films included qawwalis that remain popular today, *Barsaat Ki Raat* stands out in my story. The film tells of the trials of a penniless and lovelorn poet Aman (Bharat Bhushan) who pens qawwali lyrics that he and his accomplices sing on stage. Later masala films of the 1970s and early 1980s also give us qawwalis rendered by Muslim characters or in Muslim social settings. In *Amar Akbar Anthony* (1977), for example, Akbar Allahabadi (Rishi Kapoor) is a qawwali singer who famously woos his lover Salma Ali (Neetu Singh) in the song 'Parda hai parda' ('These veils [between us]'). This song is an occasion for public romance and an attempt by Salma's father to block that romance. Akbar's other songs 'Shirdiwale Sai Baba' ('Sai baba of Shirdi') and 'Tayyab Ali pyaar ka dushman' ('Tayyab Ali, enemy of love') also mobilize qawwali elements. While there is little that is explicitly sacred in what I am calling 'classic' film qawwalis, they do maintain many aspects of traditional qawwali performances.

Sacred performances in a Sufi dargah (shrine) are usually led by one or two primary qawwals accompanied by a male chorus and musicians on the harmonium, tabla, dholak, and/or sarangi:

> Qawwals have distinctive voices with a very wide vocal range and, in particularly intense moments, will hold long notes at a high pitch and improvise a rapid vocal melisma (sequence of notes). The accompanying ensemble claps the beat along with the instrumentalists and contributes its collective voice in responsorial singing, especially in moments when singing/chanting a particularly powerful line of poetry that is repeated indefinitely. (Beaster-Jones 117)

Film qawwalis approximate these musical conventions and the general division of labor between the lead singer and chorus. But with Mohammed Rafi and Manna Dey rather than professional qawwals rendering playback for most of these songs, the sound of the voice in the classic film qawwali is quite distinct from that heard in sacred settings. Not only do we get women singing qawwalis in films, the men's vocal style 'are more akin to crooning rather than a chest-based voice production' (Zuberi and Sarrazin 168). The look of the singers on screen, though, is similar to their ritual counterparts. Men are shown in 'Muslim-style attire (skull caps and high-collared *sherwani* coats) gesticulating [and clapping] in traditional shrine-qawwali style' (Manuel 384). While women are not traditionally qawwali singers, they are marked on screen as Muslim by their angarakhas (courtesan-style tunics) and churidars, dupattas, veils (sometimes skull caps), and jewelry.

The traditional qawwal and his troupe attempt to lead the assembled gathering to a state of spiritual ecstasy. For the audience, listening is the route to the divine: 'What makes music essential to Sufism is sama', the central ritual of "listening" to mystical songs – poems set to music – as a means of spiritual advancement' (Qureshi, 'Sufi Music' 107). But it is not music per se, but the poetic text that the singer performs, that is important. Like artistic genres in the Bhakti tradition, qawwali uses poetic lyrics in Urdu, Farsi, classical Hindi, and Punjabi that speak in allegorical terms of the devotee's union with the divine (Bhaskar and Allen 16). Concerned with the 'wrong' effect that music may have on listeners, the Sufi oral tradition specifies that:

> for sama' music, texts are primary; musical features may enhance, but may never obscure them. At the same time, sama' music also articulates *zikr*, the ceaseless repeated name – and thus remembrance – of God. On this basis, the accentuational emphasis of drumming and of hand-clapping has been accepted as a positive feature of sama' rhythm. (Qureshi, 'Sufi Music' 109)

These intricacies of Sufi philosophy and performance are critical to my argument. As I demonstrate below, the rhythmic intensity and poetry of qawwali make it well suited for Hindi cinema. However, that cornerstone of Sufi qawwali practice – listening – is transformed in the process.

The lyrical porosity between wordly and divine love and the repetitive, rhythmic nature of the genre make the qawwali eminently suitable for Hindi film songs. Classic film qawwalis capitalize on the simultaneously sacred and worldly connotations of the lyrics, even if the setting of the performance is resolutely secular. They urge us to appreciate the wit, wisdom, and artistry of singer-poets. As such, they draw on, and extend, the secularization of the genre that has occurred over time in South Asia through concerts, intimate salon performances, and competitions (Qureshi, 'His Master's Voice' 82). Well into the 1970s, qawwalis were rendered on screen not by ritual singers associated with a dargah but a hero or heroine in love. These characters are presented as singer-poets engaged in staged performances in which two groups trade poetic verse. We, along with the internal audience in these songs, are positioned as appreciative listeners, as esthetes. And we listen not so much for spiritual insight, but for poetry and romance. In films as diverse as *Mughal-e-Azam*, *Dil Hi To Hai* (1963), and *Amar Akbar Anthony*, the mise en scene highlights the secular, esthetic nature of the performance. The venue is very clearly established as a theatrical space (with a raised stage) or a *mehfil*, a space where people have gathered to be entertained by the qawwali performance. Frontal and tracking shots accentuate the sense that we are watching a staged show. The hero and heroine are the leaders of each group; the addressees are the leader and members of the other group as well as the audience. The relationship between the singer and his or her audience is established by the response shots of the listeners on- and off-stage and in the way the two groups take turns singing lyrics that carry the conversation forward. Both fun and festive, this is a scene of esthetic pleasure.

Moreover, it is often the case that one group of singers is composed of men and the other of women. The witty banter back and forth suggests a competition between the two groups. Each couplet is a challenge to the other group. This is, then, a playful 'battle of the sexes.' The songs may stage a playful seduction or a competition over a shared love interest. As such, these qawwalis enact a heterosexual romantic courtship ritual in public. They are very clearly about worldly romance, with ample references to the charged exchange of looks (*nazar*, *darshan*, and *purdah*), even when they are, in traditional qawwali idiom, also appealing to the divine. A famous example is 'Tere mehfil mein' ('In your gathering') from *Mughal-e-Azam*, which has two women, Anarkali (Madhubala) and Bahaar (Nigar Sultana), facing off in a qawwali contest as they vie for the attention of Prince Salim (Dilip Kumar). The two women embody two divergent traditions of the qawwali: the witty competitive performance for love, often rendered more playfully than it is here, in Bahaar's performance, and the yearning for spiritual union with the beloved, embodied in Anarkali's performance (Bhaskar and Allen 18–19). Some qawwalis stage a gentle mocking of heterosexual romantic conventions. Think, for instance, of *Chaudhvin Ka Chand*'s 'Sharmake yeh kyon sab pardan-ashin' ('Why do these shy veiled women') where two groups of women mimic a conversation between men and women on the question of purdah, aware that there is a man spying on their festivities. Gendered play is front and center in 'Chali chali' ('[She] leaves') from *Bluff Master* (1963) which has the hero Ashok, played by Shammi Kapoor in drag, dueling with his love interest Seema (Saira Bano).

I turn now to the climactic qawwali of *Barsaat Ki Raat*, 'Na to caravan ki talaash hai' ('Neither in search of a caravan') to demonstrate some of the classic features discussed above.[1] Our protagonist is Aman Hyderabadi (Bharat Bhushan), a singer-poet who pens qawwali lyrics for a living. He steps on stage midway through this song to support the qawwali family with whom he is affiliated – the patriarch Mubarak Ali, daughters Shama and Shabab, and son-in-law Chand Ali – in a duel with another qawwali maestro Daulat Khan. While this song is ostensibly set in the Ajmer Sharif dargah, the famed resting place of the Sufi mystic and leader Moinnudin Chisthi, it is impossible to identify this location from the mise en scene. From the very first shot, this song (like the other qawwali sequences in the film) establishes the setting as staged *mehfil*, with the two groups sitting across from each other on raised platforms facing the audience. We also get several long shots and tracking shots of men in the audience clapping and shaking their heads in appreciation. The direction of the singers' gazes and the 'horizontal' camera movement – alternating medium shots of the performers as well as tracking shots that travel back and forth between the two groups and the audience (including radio listeners) – never let us forget that this is a high-stakes literary and musical competition.

The lyrics of the song speak of love that transcends borders, weaving in references to such classic romantic figures as Laila-Majnoon, Radha-Krishna, Sita, and Meerabai. Together these references highlight the fact that history of the qawwali on the subcontinent is one of cultural and religious syncreticism. While the genre is emblematic of Islamicate culture on screen,

> there are no distinctively Muslim aspects of qawwali, which freely or loosely uses melodies based on Hindustani rags, as well as tunes associated in other contexts with Hindu occasions. … Hindu devotees and visitors are commonly estimated to constitute around one third of those who attend Chishti shrines, especially during 'urs festivities when qawwali is featured. Further, Sufiana qawwali has traditionally accommodated Hindu performers. (Manuel 380)

This fluidity and syncretism is well-demonstrated in the way this qawwali deploys the Hindu folk-mythological *panaghat-lila* (woman waylaid at the well) theme at the end of the qawwali. The speaker in these stanzas is a gopi who laments the difficulty of getting water from the well as Krishna bothers her. Even as these lines are a plea for maintaining social decorum and the honor of the gopi, the broader mythological references are to love that breaks social boundaries. The song 'asserts that love for God transcends organized religions, the differences between Hindu and Muslim, and indeed caste' (Pauwels 18–19). As if to underline this argument, Sahir Ludhianvi's lyrics switch rapidly from Urdu to Punjabi to Braj, even borrowing from a well-known qawwali thought to be composed by the thirteenth-century mystic Amir Khusro Dehlavi, 'Bahut kathin hain dagar panaghat ki' ('The road to the well [the path of love] is very rough') (Pauwels 19 and 29, n. 25). The tune of the opening couplet recalls a Punjabi qawwali by the seventeenth century Sufi poet Bulleh Shah, called 'Mera ae charkha nau lakha' ('My spinning wheel [life] is priceless'), famously performed by Nusrat Fateh Ali Khan.[2] The allegorical final qawwali of *Barsaat Ki Raat* broadcasts Aman and Shabnam's (Madhubala) forbidden love over the radio, drawing her as well as her livid father to the performance space. Thus, 'Na to caravan ki talaash hai' goes a step further than celebrating cultural and religious syncretism. Its *panaghat-lila* reference, in particular, cements another important function of the qawwali, which is to critique rigid social and religious boundaries.

As we move away from the 1960s, we get lots of qawwalis in non-Islamicate, secular contexts (e.g. weddings or parties). The characters singing are often not Muslim and there is often nothing Islamicate about the film genre, the song situation, or the space – nothing, that is, apart from the musical genre. 'Pal do pal ka saath hamara' ('Our time together is brief') for example, is set on board the fated train of the film's title (*The Burning Train* [1980]). A number of late 1970s and 1980s qawwalis are in the villain's den with a courtesan or a male qawwali troupe performing for the brotherhood. Zuberi and Sarrazin write that in these songs 'devotion and zeal are re-packaged in rockstar-like movements.' They go on to claim that 'by the 1990s and 2000s, the genre was highly sexualized and became almost unrecognizable from its original roots, traditional decorum, or values' (170). While this is true to some extent, I want to be careful to distinguish between the classic qawwalis and the post-2000s ones. As diverse as they are, qawwalis in films between the 1940s and 1980s are united in their foregrounding of romance and secular performance (more so than on faith). This emphasis on love and courtship was overshadowed when the musical genre enjoyed a resurgence in the early 2000s.

Nusrat Fateh Ali Khan, A. R. Rahman, and the Sufi vogue

While the qawwali did not entirely disappear from Bombay cinema in the 1980s, there were few hit film qawwalis in this period, making the 'return' of the form in the early 2000s quite dramatic. The history of qawwali outside of Bombay cinema – that is, in other performance venues and media – is a critical part of this narrative. Ghulam Farid Sabri and his troupe (later known as the Sabri Brothers) were among the first qawwals to receive not only national but international recognition. Sabri's musical innovations and pioneering world tours in the 1970s gained him a following of Sufis and Muslims on both side of the India–Pakistan border (Qureshi, 'His Master's Voice' 88). But it was Nusrat Fateh Ali Khan's ascendancy on the world music stage in the late 1980s and 1990s that ignited the Sufi vogue still current in Indian media.

Hailing from a family of professional qawwals, Nusrat Fateh Ali Khan was well established in Pakistan before he became an international star. He was, and continues to be, widely recognized as having introduced important innovations while maintaining a traditional repertoire and classically oriented style (Qureshi, 'His Master's Voice' 89). In 1985, he participated in the WOMAD traveling world music festival organized by Peter Gabriel and was subsequently signed on to the Real World Records label. Western film audiences were introduced to his virtuoso singing through his collaborations with Gabriel on his soundtrack (and 1989 album) for *The Last Temptation of Christ* (1988) and *Natural Born Killers* (1994), and with Eddie Vedder of Pearl Jam fame in *Dead Man Walking* (1995). Also important was his work with Michael Brook on two experimental albums *Mustt Mustt* (1990) and *Night Song* (1996), both released by Real World (Jacoviello 324). Khan's 'rhythmic improvisational style' gave qawwali a place in 'trendy, cosmopolitan, world music culture, whose audiences respond strongly, pulling the music away from its textual base' (Qureshi, 'His Master's Voice' 94). Thus, even as musical prowess and 'authenticity' are valued in the world-music arena, the specifically spiritual dimensions are eclipsed, especially for non-Sufi and non-South Asian listeners. Be that as it may, Nusrat Fateh Ali Khan's success, both in the subcontinent and abroad, opened doors for other Sufi and Pakistani artists.

Peter Manuel links the flourishing of Sufi music in India in recent years to two developments: the growth of the Indian middle- and upper-class in the post-liberalization period (early 1990s on) and the concomitant rise of Hindutva politics. In response to the latter,

> liberal elements of the newly flourishing bourgeoisie have cultivated a fresh interest in and celebration of the syncretism and composite aspects of Indian culture and music; they have also promoted a renewed commitment to secularism (which in the Indian context implies tolerance and religious pluralism rather than opposition to religion). (Manuel 379)

This then explains the 'Sufi performance arts vogue' (382), the interest not only in group qawwali performances such as that of Nusrat Fateh Ali Khan's troupe and the Sabri Brothers, but also in solo renditions of Sufiana poetry in various languages (Abida Parveen is the leading figure in this genre) and Sufi rock, a genre inaugurated by the band Junoon (lead singer Salman Khan).[3] A whole host of singers, with very different musical backgrounds and expertise, have been part of this boom in Sufi music – so much so that singer Shubha Mudgal, herself a part of this phenomenon, notes wryly, 'The fad has become a way to legitimize a new kind of Hindi pop; pop singers just put "Maula" [Lord] or "Ali" in and call it Sufi music' (qtd. in Manuel 389). Some observe that this fad constitutes little more than tokenism and exoticization, promising little change for actual singers at Sufi shrines or Muslims in Indian society (391–92). Less cynically, we might argue that these various forms of Sufi music serve a crucial political purpose in that they articulate a critique of political and religious orthodoxy (Abbas 632). After all, as Manuel himself notes, in the midst of rising fundamentalism, the (qawwali) dargah scene – both in real-life and on screen – stands as a 'resilient island of communal harmony' (381).

The visual and aural presence of Sufism in Hindi films increased substantially with the success of A. R. Rahman in the 1990s. One of Rahman's contributions as he shifted Hindi (and Tamil) cinema's musical vocabulary was the re-introduction of qawwalis. When he first catapulted to fame, Rahman's Sufi faith was very much a topic of conversation in the media. The story of his (family's) conversion to Sufism is famous, as is his own piety. Whereas previous qawwalis in Hindi cinema were mainly secular romantic duets, many of Rahman's songs returned film qawwalis to their sacred settings. This is something that not even the handful of Hindi films that used Nusrat Fateh Ali Khan's voice did. Rahman often employs his own distinctive voice in his qawwalis or qawwali-esque songs, as is evident in 'Piya Haji Ali' (*Fiza* [2000]), 'Al Maddath Maula' (*Mangal Pandey* [2005]), 'Khwaja mere khwaja' (*Jodhaa Akbar* [2008]), and 'Kun faya kun' (*Rockstar* [2011]) Other qawwali-inspired or Islamicate songs he composed in his early years as a Hindi music director include 'Ishq bina' ('Without love,' *Taal* [1999]) and 'Kehna hi kya/Kannalane' ('What can I say/My love,' *Bombay* [1995]), and perhaps most famously 'Chaiyya chaiyya' (*Dil Se* [1998]).

Dargah qawwalis

What is striking about this new crop of qawwalis is the very different song situations out of which they emerge and the different settings and ethos they articulate compared to the qawwalis discussed earlier. 'Dargah' qawwalis are not limited to a particular film genre. Still used to articulate a syncretic ideal, qawwalis often appear in films that are about Hindu–Muslim unity in one way or another, such as *Veer-Zaara* (2004), *Mangal Pandey*, and *Bajrangi Bhaijaan* (2015). But where the emphasis in classic qawwalis was on romance and Islamicate culture – on literary and artistic sophistication in the Muslim socials and historicals – now the emphasis is on faith and on Muslim devotional practices. This is most evident in the mise en scene and camerawork of the song sequences.

In songs as diverse as 'Aaya tere dar par' ('Arrived at your doorstep,' *Veer-Zaara*), 'Arziyan' ('Requests,' *Delhi-6* [2006]), and 'Bhar do jholi' ('Fill my bag,' *Bajrangi Bhaijaan*), we see that the performance space has shifted from the theater or salon to more hallowed locale.[4] We typically get a roving camera that cranes high up to give us a sense of the contours and scale of the dargah or mosque in which the song is set. This is very different than the flat, frontal esthetic of the older, staged performances. Here, the monumentality of Islamicate architecture and the space of communal worship takes precedence over the relationship between the qawwal and the internal audience.

Dargah qawwalis attempt to evoke a cinematic experience of sama' by visualizing the practice of listening to qawwalis in a sacred space. Take, for example, 'Arziyan,' which is ostensibly set in Jama masjid, an iconic mosque in Delhi. The song opens with a 38-s long high-angle shot looking down at row upon row of people performing namaz. It then cuts to a close-up of a devotee's face and hands as he prays. More shots of the grand exterior and of unnamed men communing and praying alongside each other follow. Finally, a minute into the song, the camera lands on our hero Roshan (Abhishek Bachchan), a diasporic Indian exploring his family's roots. The song thus diminishes the star appeal and importance of the hero, focusing instead on the vast prayerful community (Bhattacharjya). A good tourist, Roshan watches respectfully as others engage in ritual practice. He listens to and records the qawwali troupe singing at the mosque. The leaders sing in the voices of Javed Ali and Kailash Kher, singers known for their Sufiana timbre and style. As is often the case with dargah qawwalis, 'Arziyan' is a montage sequence, covering shifts in time and space. Images of Roshan's friends and family members, some of them engaged in Hindu rituals, flash across the scene as the singers intone the lines 'More piya ghar aaya / Maula mere Maula' (My beloved has come home / O master). The structure of the sequence thus shifts attention away from the qawwali performance itself and to the actions and feelings of the protagonist in that space.

Rockstar's 'Kun faya kun' ('[He said] Be and it is') likewise uses the opening montage of the song to depict the hero JJ/Jordan's (Ranbir Kapoor) struggles up until the time he joins the community of the faithful at the Nizamuddin dargah. His journey within the dargah is itself articulated in stages, as he goes from being a homeless person seeking refuge in the shrine to being a curious observer of the rituals and qawwali performance, to being an engaged audience member, and finally to participating as a musician and believer. The gestures and eye movements of the singers and audience indicate that this is a homosocial appeal to the divine. Recall how different this is from the lateral exchanges of looks (from the men's group to the women's and back) in the classic qawwalis. Halfway into the song we witness a moment of spiritual enlightenment. The camera moves rapidly from a long shot of Jordan singing with the qawwali troupe to a low-angle medium shot that centers him, eyes closed, lost in the song. As his voice and movements get more intense, the camera moves back again and cranes up swiftly to give us a high-angle view, as if god were looking down on him. The shots that follow repeat this vertical structure, accentuating visually the relationship between the qawwal and his divine interlocutor. The camera dwells on his face, his astonishment at the spiritual realization this music has brought him.

'Khwaja mere khwaja' does something similar. This qawwali is staged for the emperor and his wife (Hrithik Roshan and Aishwarya Rai) and their respective retinues, in *Jodhaa Akbar*. While the song employs a frontal esthetic that recalls the classic qawwalis, it does so to draw attention to the whirling dervishes' religiosity. There are relatively few shots of the imperial audience. The singers' closed eyes as well as their upward gestures and glances indicate that they are addressing not their patron so much as god. A sequence of alternating low-angle and high-angle shots form the climax of the performance, indicating a connection between the men and god. As the dervishes rise and start rotating in place, Akbar closes his eyes and tilts his head up; a flash of light in the sky indicates the heightened state he reaches in that moment. He then rises and joins the dervishes' whirling. The intensity of Akbar's spiritual experience is thus compared to Jodhaa's bhakti, her devotion to Krishna articulated elsewhere in the film (Bhaskar and Allen 161–2).

Crucially, in most dargah qawwalis, the hero is *not* the primary qawwal. He is no longer presented as a singer-poet who composes brilliant lyrics to woo his beloved. In fact, the beloved addressee is more clearly a divine figure here. The hero is part of the internal audience for the song – often because he arrives at the scene of the qawwali performance in the dargah and is drawn in. As the hero finds himself and a group that validates his existence and his pain, he gets cast as a pious figure. Romance gets elided and so do women, both as singers and as audience members. This is particularly startling given how instrumental women were in the classic qawwalis discussed earlier. Thus, what was once a playful, heterosexual romantic interaction becomes a serious, devotional experience that mostly occurs in the company of other men. There are, of course, precedents for this type of qawwali in Hindi cinema. 'Sajde mein hai sar' ('My head is bowed [in prayer]') from *Mirza Ghalib* (1954) and 'Maula Saleem Chisthi' from *Garm Hawa* (1973) come to mind here. In both films, however, it is the women's experiences of love that are the subject of the qawwali. The lyrics of the songs provide commentary on the woman's plight; the picturization in each case focuses on her sorrow.

Another A. R. Rahman composition, 'Piya Haji Ali' from *Fiza*, provides an instructive counter-point to the masculine homosociality of most other dargah qawwalis. This sequence is similar to the other in that we get free-wheeling camerawork that defines the space of Mumbai's famous Haji Ali dargah, its sea front location, and the many men and women who visit the shrine daily. What makes this distinct, however, is the centrality of the women in this song. The song opens with images of a group of male qawwals seated in an enclosed, raised platform within the dargah; classical maestro Ustad Ghulam Mustafa Khan and his son Ghulam Murtaza Khan, and A. R. Rahman provide the vocals (Bhattacharjya). Most of the song picturization focuses on the hero's mother Nishatbi (Jaya Bachchan), sister Fiza (Kareena Kapoor), and love interest (Shabana Raza/Neha Bajpayee) who coming looking for their beloved Amaan (Hrithik Roshan) and for some sense of solace in the dargah. What they find in Haji Ali are memories of his laughing, teasing self. The hero himself is largely missing. Following Priya Kumar, we might read this as an implicit commentary on the absence of the hero in this peaceful, syncretic, and religious space. The song is a lament that the space of solace available to the women is not accessible to the hero given the broader social context that associates Muslim masculinity with violence and terrorism. It also stands in sharp contrast to the hyper-inscription of masculinity in the dargah in other film qawwalis. It is worth remembering that despite its mainstream address, *Fiza* is an atypical film. Priya Kumar calls it a 'Muslim minoritarian' film (178); Ira Bhaskar and Richard Allen count this among 'New Wave Muslim Socials' (91). These categories indicate that Khaled Mohammed's film is doing something different than most mainstream films in its representation of Muslim characters and their lives. To some extent, 'Piya Haji Ali' overlaps with 'Maula Saleem Chisthi' in *Garm Hawa*, one of the first new wave Muslim socials. The long shots in that qawwali also articulate the monumentality of Muslim sacred space in which it is set (the Ajmer shrine). While the visual emphasis there is on the monument itself, not as much on individuals praying, it too does not feature a hero as singer-poet. The qawwals are in silhouette or in shadow, so we do not see them singing. Like 'Piya Haji Ali,' it, too, is a montage sequence that has a pensive, documentary feel.

Bhaskar and Allen see this shift to dargah qawwalis as a positive development, for it undermines the association of Islam with terrorism in popular media, both in India and around the world:

> In Islamicate films of the contemporary moment, the foregrounding of the Sufi saint's *dargah* and the qawwali performance associated with that space evoke an emotional, devotional, and ideological realm that counters negative responses to Muslim communities. (17)

They go on to mention the significance that the Haji Ali dargah in Bombay takes on in films like *Fiza, Salim Langde Pe Mat Ro* (1989), and *Mammo* (1994) through its 'evocation of an Islam different from the one associated with terrorism' (17–18). I am less sanguine about these dargah qawwalis. The settings and song situations of these more contemporary qawwalis emphasize two ideas. First, these songs render Sufism the 'good' kind of Islam, tolerant and hip, sanctioned by Hindi cinema and by such venerated figures as Nusrat Fateh Ali Khan and A. R. Rahman. My reading dovetails with Peter Manuel's insight that the elite in India has embraced Sufi performances as a way to push back against the Hindutva-ization of the public and political sphere. Moreover, in these examples, Sufism comes to represent *Islam* more than a syncretic religious philosophy and practice. Second, dargah qawwalis emphasize religious identity and practice. While they highlight a passionate, tolerant kind of spirituality, the emphasis in these songs is still on religion and that is potentially problematic. That the qawwali becomes a masculine and homosocial genre in films of the early 2000s has important implications for the representation of Muslim masculinity. Muslim identity, particularly that of the hero, becomes about *religion* and not about culture, language, or literary and artistic sophistication. Benign and tolerant as they appear, dargah qawwalis animate cinematic representations of the 'good' Muslim man by drawing on entrenched notions of difference and impassioned religiosity associated with Islam the world over. Thus, a musical genre meant to project an open and secular notion of India, in fact demonstrate the limits of discourses of national tolerance and religious syncretism.

Qawwalis as item numbers

The past decade has also seen the rise of item-numberesque qawwalis. Sometimes called fusion or rock/pop/techno qawwalis, these recent iterations of the genre accentuate the 'trance-dance associations and substitute[e] traditional instrumentation with synthesizers, hyped-up bass, and other sampled sounds' (Zuberi and Sarrazin 173). Not surprisingly, these songs and their remixed versions become favorites in clubs. Like other Sufi-inflected film songs, many item-numberesque qawwalis use earthy, heavy voices and styles of singing to invoke a Sufi ethos. Some use Islamicate iconography and Urdu lyrics aplenty, but dispose of other musical features of the qawwali. Think, for instance, of the Sufi lyrics and gestures of the male dancers in 'Chaiyya chaiyya' (*Dil Se*). Also, not all contemporary qawwalis are picturized as item numbers. But whether it is an elaborate courtship fantasy such as 'Tumse milke' ('Having met you,' *Main Hoon Na* [2004]), a philosophical dargah sequence like 'Ya Ali' (*Gangster* [2006]), or a seductive mujra such as 'Kajra re' ('Kohl-rimmed eyes,' *Bunty Aur Babli* [2005]) or 'Dil mera muft ka' ('My free heart,' *Agent Vinod* [2012]), this type of qawwali articulates a different relationship to gender and Islamicate culture than its predecessors did. Like the classic qawwalis, these sequences are staged scenes of earthly (heterosexual) desire, but they are presented in far more spectacular fashion. More frenzied and elaborately choreographed, they amplify the historical functions of the genre while giving it the sexual energy of item numbers. The qawwali is no longer a seated affair. While these new qawwalis maintain the frontal, staged emphasis of the older ones, dance and visual choreography come to the fore. The lyrics of these qawwalis may be as evocative as ever, but the subtle turn of phrase, the poetry, that was a mark of Islamicate genres is no longer key. These are qawwalis to be watched and danced to, and not 'just' listened to – that is, they move us in other ways.

Take for instance, 'Kajra re,' the Shankar-Ehsaan-Loy composition hailed as marking the 'reinvention of the qawwali' (Taneja). One of the biggest hits of 2005, the song relied on the star power of Aishwarya Rai (in a cameo performance as a bar dancer), Amitabh Bachchan, and Abhishek Bachchan. The mise en scene is equally impressive. In a video about the making of the film, art director Sharmishta Roy describes the set she designed for 'Kajra re' as 'kitschy … with an old-world charm … a combination between Indian architecture and a Broadway show' ('Making Of The Film | Bunty Aur Babli'). The cinematography and choreography make it difficult to keep our eyes off Aishwarya Rai:

> [She] wears a tiny choli (blouse), and a flowing skirt down to her knees. Her dress is more evocative of a street or village dancer than that of a courtesan in that she shows skin and her legs are bare. While her clothes signify lower class status and a gypsy life, traditionally coming with allusions of a free sexuality, unbounded by middle class norms of behaviour, she seems more a dancer rather than a prostitute by profession. … The camera in *Kajra Re* has picked up music-television-style moves in that it zeroes in on body parts, unlike older dance numbers that stay with whole or half body shots and shots of the face. The camera lingers up and down the body. (Nijhawan 106)

The sexualization of Rai in this sequence is evident. It is not just her outfit and dance moves that center her as a desiring and desirous body; the gaze of the camera is as critical to this construction. As Rai performs her signature dance moves (choreographed here by Vaibhavi Merchant), she and her back-up dancers maintain a frontal esthetic. But whereas classic cinematic qawwalis used frontality, intercutting, and tracking shots to establish the relationship among the dueling qawwals and between the singers and their appreciative audience, item numbers like 'Kajra re' use these devices to keep us glued to the spectacle of dancing bodies. This being a mujra, the relationship between the courtesan/bar dancer and her clients – mainly, the cop Dashrath Singh (Amitabh Bachchan) – is clearly articulated through alternating close-ups of the stars' eyes. Both Singh and the conman Rakesh Trivedi (Abhishek Bachchan) are drawn to Rai's character, and they constitute the second party in this qawwali. Other men in the bar remain on the sidelines, in the shadows, except when they serve as the back-up party. That is, when the camera attends to them, it is to show them clapping and dancing behind the two male stars.

In merging the roles of the internal audience and performer thus, 'Kajra re' diminishes the role of *listening*. This is an important divergence not just from the traditional qawwali form (where the goal is sama') but also its more secular cinematic counterparts. As discussed above, classic qawwalis emphasized lyrical artistry and the relationship between qawwals and their listeners (be they on- or off-stage). Dargah qawwalis emphasize the transformative experience of listening to qawwalis in (masculinized) spaces of Muslim religiosity. What is at stake in those post-2000s qawwalis is one's relationship with the divine, evident in characters' upward gestures and gazes as well as camerawork emphasizing sacred spaces and communal worship. In its contemporary item-number garb, the Hindi film qawwali tends to highlight not listening or praying so much as desirous dancing. The camera no longer dwells on the appreciative internal audience. It is as if the spectacularity and star power of these 'qawwalis on acid' – director and choreographer Farah Khan's term for her qawwali 'Tumse milke' ('Main Hoon Na | Making') – have made visual consumption and participatory dancing more important than listening. Indeed, *Main Hoon Na* cuts swiftly from a college scene of men ogling at a woman to their fantastical ode to her. The qawwali gives us two sets of dancing stars: Shah Rukh Khan and Sushmita Sen, and the younger couple played by Zayed Khan and Amrita Rao. There is no audience within the song; everybody is a performer. In 'Dil mera muft ka,' the Kareena Kapoor item number in *Agent Vinod*, the dancers do facilitate listening: they plant a microphone in the flowers they tie to the villain's wrist. This allows the cop (Saif Ali Khan) to listen in on the villains' conversation – not to the dancers. Violence and villainy are also center-stage in 'Ya Ali,' where the qawwali is the soundtrack to internecine gangster battle (Sarrazin 194). To be sure, there are precedents for spectacularity in qawwalis in 1970s masala films (as well as in earlier films).[5] But the commodification of dancing bodies and the devaluing of listening that happens in its wake in recent films is of a different order.

Conclusion

I want to end with two recent qawwalis that demonstrate that the classic film qawwali and all it represented are no longer tenable. The first, 'Senti-wali Mental' (*Shaandaar* [2015]), is a competition between the bride's and the groom's parties, as part of pre-wedding festivities. While the establishing shot wows us with the grand interior of the theater, it is followed by one in which the wedding planner JJ (Shahid Kapoor) comments on the opulence and wastefulness of the rich. As beautiful and grand as it is, this is a space that rings hollow. With just 20 people in a theater that could hold 2000, this is a space emptied of the adoring crowds so crucial to the classic qawwali. Apart from family members cheering their respective relatives on are two groups of people sitting in the distance, following the lead of a conductor in coattails. This audience's clapping, we realize, is orchestrated. The very first verse of the qawwali confirms that despite the familiar setting and Islamicate mise en scene – a group of men and women seated across each other on a big stage, draped in colorful, sparkling outfits, scarves in hand – we cannot expect an endearing courtship ritual. What follows is a mean-spirited battle of the sexes. Much to the surprise of the women on stage, the groom Robin (Vikas Verma) and his party open with a verse that paints women as shallow, crazy, and self-absorbed. 'Pyaar ho gaya, bhai' (It's love, brother), quips JJ on hearing the men's opening gambit, but sisters Alia (Alia Bhatt) and Isha (Sanah Kapoor), the bride, recognize Robin's misogyny. They respond by deriding men for their blundering and stupid ways as well as their sex drive, which the women are careful to distinguish from romance. The barbs get sharper with each exchange, culminating with the fitness-obsessed Robin insulting women, and the bride Isha in particular, for being fat. With the women completely demoralized, it is up to other men – the father of the bride Bipin Arora (Pankaj Kapoor) and JJ – to step in and save the day. This scene is oddly similar to the climax of the *Barsaat Ki Raat* qawwali discussed above, 'Na to caravan ki talaash hai.' In that song, the lovelorn Shama is unable to go on singing because her love is unrequited, and this compels Aman to take over and continue the musical conversation about love as transcendent. In the *Shaandaar* qawwali, by contrast, it is the men's cruel put-down (rather than love) that silences the sisters and draws the patriarch into the fray. It is as if the more refined and respectful – not to mention artistic – exchange staged in the classic qawwali does not work in the contemporary moment. The *Shaandaar* qawwali thus marks an important shift in cinematic representations of gender, romance, and Islamicate culture. At the same time, through the oblique reference to *Barsaat Ki Raat*, 'Senti-wali mental' reveals (and rehearses) the gendered conventions of the classic cinematic qawwali. In both songs, men are cast as saviors; they are heroes deserving of women's undying love.

The comedy group AIB (All India Bakchod) takes this critique a step further in 'Creep qawwali' (2015), a viral video that is as much a send-up of the classic film qawwali as an ad for the dating app TrulyMadly. It shows two groups of women facing off in a musical contest to determine which of their stalkers is the creepier of the two. All the musical, visual, and gestural signs of the cinematic qawwali are put to work in this song. Two women, each with a group of back-up singers, trade witty verses about gendered romantic norms – or, in this case, the violation thereof. Dressed in lavish, color-coordinated angarakhas, they perform synchronized gestures to the sounds of the tabla, harmonium, and rhythmic clapping. Static camerawork, intercutting between the two parties, and a frontal esthetic emphasizes the conversation and competition between the two seated groups. But, where classic qawwalis celebrated gendered conventions of romance, AIB's version satirizes those very conventions. The creep's infelicitous and grammatically incorrect language, his sleazy pick-up lines ('I deliver your pizza / Will you deliver my baby?'), and his violation of the women's personal and online space make him the worst suitor possible. In fact, like the women in *Chaudhvin Ka Chand*'s 'Sharmake yeh kyon pardanashin,' these singers know that the creep is watching them surreptitiously. In both songs, the camera reveals the voyeur, endorsing the women's critique of male aggression in the name of love. Thus, if love in the classic qawwali is a spiritual quest that knows no boundaries, the AIB parody renders it as sexual harassment. And even as it turns out that the two women are singing about the same man (one Mr. Suresh Kumar) the problem extends far beyond this individual stalker. Both groups sing of how the internet and their neighborhood are full of such men. These women complain, but do not need rescuing by other men; they rely on each other for support. Ending on a note of female solidarity, 'Creep qawwali' gestures to a cinematic precedent that has faded out of view in recent years, that of women singing qawwalis (among) themselves and offering a distinctly gendered take on romance, modesty, and propriety.

In reading 'Senti-wali mental' and 'Creep qawwali' as symptomatic of the fate of the genre in recent years, I posit that the problematic gender politics of the genre are ever more visible today. Contemporary item-numberesque qawwalis are more than just glamorous versions of the qawwalis of yesteryear. They depart from the homosocial, more pious overtones of the dargah qawwalis by returning women to the scene, primarily as objects of male attention. They also return rambunctious, romantic men to the genre. But, the transformation of performance practices and the relationship between qawwal and audience – the emphasis on dancing rather than listening for artistic or spiritual edification – suggests an altogether different configuration of gender, love, and Islamicate culture. The itemization of aural and visual signs of Islamicate culture is of a piece with the waning of the figure of the *tawaif* and the ghazal form. Despite making room for women singers specializing in Sufiana music in the playback realm, Hindi cinema struggles to craft a complex and nuanced picture of Muslimness on screen. Outside of Muslim new wave films, Muslim religiosity continues to be an exceedingly gray and bearded affair. As qawwalis begin to look and sound like every other fast-paced, spectacular item number, they disrupt older lexicons of the genre. Where once the sensuousness and eroticism of the film qawwali was located in its lyrics, it is now articulated visually, as a commodity spectacle. All in all, the qawwali as a cinematic genre can no longer sustain the romantic ideals of the past. Item-numberesque qawwalis urge us to shed the nostalgia attached to the genre. But they also make that task immensely difficult. They move us, both literally and emotionally, in powerful ways, implicating us in both the sensuous pleasures and the complex gender, sexual, and cultural politics of the genre.

Notes

1. This song is sometimes referred to by the refrain of the final couplets, 'Yeh ishq, ishq hai' ('This is love, love'). See, for instance, Heidi Pauwels' essay on the panaghata-lila theme.
2. Another qawwali in the film, 'Jee chahtha hai' ('The heart desires') includes a similar, albeit briefer, turn to a traditionally Hindu idiom at the end of the song.
3. Junoon's lead singer is not to be confused with the Bollywood star of the same name.
4. This last is a film version of Sabri brothers' famous qawwali 'Bhar do jholi'.
5. Staged numbers like 'Parda hai parda' (*Amar Akbar Anthony*) and 'Hai agar dushman' ('If there is an enemy [in society],' *Hum Kisise Kum Naheen* [1977]) had the performers decked out in colorful clothes and deployed veils, sequins, lanterns, and roses to great effect. Some qawwalis were performed by courtesan characters, and were thus designed to be spectacular and seductive *mujras*. Examples include 'Tere mehfil mein,' the famous qawwali competition in *Mughal-e-Azam*, and the Rekha and Amitabh number, 'Pyaar ke rang se' ('With the color of love') from *Kasme Vaade* (1978).

Disclosure statement

No potential conflict of interest was reported by the author.

References

Abbas, Shemeem Burney. "Risky Knowledge for Risky Times: Political Discourses of *Qawwali* and *Sufiana-kalam* in Indian-Pakistani Sufism." *The Muslim World* 97 (Oct 2007): 626–39.

Beaster-Jones, Jayson. *Bollywood Sounds: The Cosmopolitan Mediations of Hindi Film Song*. Oxford: Oxford University Press, 2015.

Bhaskar, Ira, and Richard Allen. *Islamicate Cultures of Bombay Cinema*. New Delhi: Tulika Books, 2009.

Bhattacharjya, Nila. "Qawwali." Personal communication. 27 Mar. 2017.

Jacoviello, Stefano. "Nusrat Fateh Ali Khan: The Strange Destiny of a Singing Mystic. When Music Travels…." *Semiotica* 183.1/4 (2011): 319–41.

Kesavan, Mukul. "Urdu, Awadh and the Tawaif: The Islamicate Roots of Hindi Cinema." *Forging Identities: Gender, Communities and the State in India*. Ed. Zoya Hasan. Boulder, CO: Westview Press, 1994. 244–157.

Kumar, Priya. *Limiting Secularism: The Ethics of Coexistence in Indian Literature and Film*. Minneapolis: University of Minnesota Press, 2008.

Manuel, Peter. "North Indian Sufi Popular Music in the age of Hindu and Muslim Fundamentalism." *Ethnomusicology* 52.3 (Fall 2008): 378–400.

Nijhawan, Amita. "Excusing the Female Dancer: Tradition and Transgression in Bollywood Dancing." *South Asian Popular Culture* 7.2 (Jul 2009): 99–112.

Pauwels, Heidi. "'The Woman Waylaid at the Well' or Paṇaghaṭa-līlā: An Indian Folk Theme Appropriated in Myth and Movies." *Asian Ethnology* 69.1 (2010): 1–33.

Qureshi, Regula. "His Master's Voice? Exploring *Qawwali* and 'Gramophone Culture' in South Asia." *Popular Music* 18.1 (Jan 1999): 63–98.

Qureshi, Regula. "Sufi Music and the Historicity of Oral Tradition." *Ethnomusicology and Modern Music History*. Eds. Stephen Blum, Phillip V. Bohlman, and Daniel M. Neuman. Urbana: University of Illinois Press, 1993. 103–120.

Sarrazin, Natalie. "Devotion or Pleasure? Music and Meaning in the Celluloid Performances of *Qawwali* in South Asia and the Diaspora." *Muslim, Culture and Identity in the Muslim World: Performance, Politics and Piety*. Ed. Kamal Sahi. London: Routledge, 2014. 178–199.

Taneja, Nikhil. "From Melody to Dev D." *Hindustan Times* 31 Dec. 2009. <http://www.hindustantimes.com/music/from-melody-to-dev-d/story-eYCER1lxIpKEY6z7tjja5L.html>.

Zuberi, Irfan, and Natalie Sarrazin. "Evolution of a Ritual Musical genre: The Adaptation of Qawwali in Contemporary Hindi Film." *Music in Contemporary Indian Film: Memory, Voice, Identity*. Eds. Jayson Beaster-Jones and Natalie Sarrazin. New York, NY: Routledge, 2017. 162–175.

Filmography and Discography

Agent Vinod. Dir. Sriram Raghavan. Eros International and Illuminati Films, 2012.

Amar Akbar Anthony. Dir. Manmohan Desai. MKD Films, 1977.

Bajrangi Bhaijaan. Dir. Kabir Khan. Eros International and Salman Khan Films, 2015.

Barsaat Ki Raat. Dir. P. L. Santoshi. Shri Vishwa Bharati Films, 1960.

Bluff Master. Dir. Manmohan Desai. Subhash Pictures, 1963.

Bombay. Dir. Mani Ratnam. Aalayam Productions, 1995.

Bunty Aur Babli. Dir. Shaad Ali. Yash Raj Films, 2005.

Chaudhvin Ka Chand. Dir. Mohammed Sadiq. Guru Dutt Films, 1960.

"Creep Qawwali." TrulyMadly and All India Bakchod, 2015. Web. 29 Aug. 2017. < https://www.youtube.com/watch?v=gEC0pKHJKNM>.

Dead Man Walking. Dir. Tim Robbins. PolyGram Filmed Entertainment and Working Title Films, 1995.

Delhi-6. Dir. Rakeysh Omprakash Mehra. UTV Motion Pictures and Rakeysh Omprakash Mehra Pictures, 2006.

Dil Hi To Hai. Dir. P. L. Santoshi and C. L. Rawal. Rawal Films, 1963.

Dil Se. Dir. Mani Ratnam. India Talkies and Madras Talkies, 1998.

Fiza. Dir. Khalid Mohamed. The Culture Company and UTV Motion Pictures, 2000.

Gangster. Dir. Anurag Basu. Bhatt Productions, 2006.

Garm Hawa. Dir. M. S. Sathyu. Unit 3 MM, 1973.

Hum Kisise Kum Naheen. Dir. Nasir Hussain. Nasir Hussain Films, 1977.

Jodhaa Akbar. Dir. Ashutosh Gowariker. UTV Motion Pictures and Ashutosh Gowariker Productions, 2008.

Kasme Vaade. Dir. Ramesh Behl. Rose Movies, 1978.

"Making Of The Film | Bunty Aur Babli | Part 2." Yashraj Films, 2009. Web. 29 Aug. 2017. < https://www.youtube.com/watch?v=eybtH0RosG0>.

Main Hoon Na. Dir. Farah Khan. Red Chillies Entertainment, 2004.

"Main Hoon Na | Making | Tumse Milke Dilka Hai Jo Haal / Qawwali Song." Red Chillies Entertainment, 2016. Web. 29 Aug. 2017. <https://www.youtube.com/watch?v=y4gtawLmZ7c>.

Mammo. Dir. Shyam Benegal. National Film Development Corporation, 1994.

Mangal Pandey. Dir. Ketan Mehta. Kaleidoscope Entertainment and Maya Movies, 2005.

Mirza Ghalib. Dir. Sohrab Modi. Minerva Movietone, 1954.

Mughal-e-Azam. Dir. K. Asif. Sterling Investment Corporation, 1960.

Mustt Mustt. Perf. Nusrat Fateh Ali Khan. Prod. Michael Brook. Real Worlds Records, 1990.

Natural Born Killers. Dir. Oliver Stone. Warner Bros., 1994.

Night Song. Perf. Nusrat Fateh Ali Khan. Prod. Michael Brook. Real Worlds Records, 1996.

Rockstar. Dir. Imtiaz Ali. Shree Ashtavinayak Cine Vision and Eros International, 2011.

Salim Langde Pe Mat Ro. Dir. Saeed Akhtar Mirza. National Film Development Corporation, 1989.

Shaandaar. Dir. Vikas Bahl. Dharma Productions and Phantom Films, 2015.

Taal. Dir. Subhash Ghai. B4U Entertainment, 1999.

The Burning Train. Dir. Ravi Chopra. B. R. Films and United Producers, 1980.

The Last Temptation of Christ. Dir. Martin Scorcese. Universal Pictures and Cineplex Odeon Films, 1988.

Veer-Zaara. Dir. Yash Chopra. Yash Raj Films, 2004.

Zeenat. Dir. Syed Shaukat Hussain Rizvi. Eastern Pictures, 1945.

A.R. Rahman and the aesthetic transformation of Indian film scores

Jayson Beaster-Jones

ABSTRACT
Orchestral scores in Hindi cinema have been virtually ignored both by fans and scholars: they have received little attention from Indian music and film critics and are only infrequently a subject for commentary. Despite the lack of respect for film scores, however, music director A.R. Rahman carefully crafted his scores to generate musical narratives that operate in tandem with film narratives. In order to illustrate how Rahman's film scores of the late 1990s and early 2000s marked an inflection point for background music in later Indian films, this article compares the background scores of the films *Taal* (1999) and *Swades* (2004). The article traces the development of musical themes in these films and Rahman's later shift in compositional approach, suggesting that later composers in mainstream and *hatke* cinema deployed new tactics in their film scores, such as the development of musical themes unrelated to the song melodies composed for the film. These changes in background scoring practices provide new incentives for audiences to attend to musical sound in the narrative, heralding the commercial success of multiplex films of the 2010s, even as they blurred the boundaries between film song and film score.

Orchestral scores in Hindi cinema have largely been overlooked by scholars of Indian film, perhaps because of the spectacular nature of Indian film songs and their social importance in/through circulation in the Indian music industry. It is relatively rare for film scores to be distributed on physical or digital media, although there are some notable exceptions, such as the inclusion of one or two instrumental or remixed versions of film songs on the soundtrack, or the almost unheard of release of the background score as a separate recording. Most often, these versions are not evaluated on their own merits because they are viewed by film music distributors (and the audiences themselves) as being extraneous to the more common practice of distributing song-based soundtracks. Likely for similar reasons, background scores receive little attention from Indian music and film critics and are only infrequently a subject for commentary.

In other published works (Beaster-Jones, *Bollywood Sounds*, xiii), I have suggested that the individuals involved in film production make a clear separation between film song and film music (background scores), with the former being far more important in the grand scheme of things: music directors are paid far more than score composers and composers themselves are seen within the industry as largely being interchangeable, a mentality also shared by many Hollywood film producers. I would like to nuance this perspective here by pointing out the melodic interrelationships between song and score, such that music directors like A.R. Rahman have come to incorporate portions of songs in the background score, and vice versa, in the creation of a musical narrative of Indian films.[1] Like other music directors, Rahman regularly incorporates recognizable song melodies into his score as a way of indexing the characters and their emotional states in the film narrative. What is less common, however, is that Rahman's scores regularly develop other melodies that do not appear in the song soundtrack and he also incorporates melodies from the musical interludes of songs into his scores in order to expand the larger musical narrative in ways that parallel cinematic practices in other parts of the world. Consequently, since these melodic themes in the score do not have lyrics or a vocal melody attached to them, they are more likely to go unnoticed or unheard by audiences.

In this essay, I investigate the role and relative importance of background scores in two Hindi films that are suggestive of largescale changes in post-liberalization films. My argument here is that A.R. Rahman created a new sensibility for background scores in Hindi cinema, such that they became a more central component of the film narrative vis-à-vis earlier periods of Hindi cinema. In other words, Rahman's film scoring suggests a shift away from the melodramatic mode of scoring used by composers in the 1970s–1990s. Moreover, in the first decade of the 2000s, mainstream film music composers began to change their approach to film scoring to include new compositional techniques, such as the greater use of musical silence to emphasize moments of powerful dialog or narrative revelations, as well as the development of a parallel set of musical themes unrelated to the song melodies composed for the film. Through a comparative analysis of the background scores to *Taal* (1999) and *Swades* (2004), I argue that Rahman's film scores of this period marked an inflection point for background music in Indian films, encouraging audiences to more carefully attend to the aural narrative (soundtrack, writ large) of films. I conclude this essay by arguing that Rahman's film scoring practices likely enabled new cinematic sound practices in films of the 2010s as Indian film directors have come to experiment with new styles of filmmaking.

Background scores in Hindi cinema

Although I have made this point elsewhere (Beaster-Jones, *Bollywood Sounds*, xiv), it is worth reiterating the distinction between 'film music' (*saṅgīt*) and 'film song' (*gīt*) as categories of music in Indian cinema. While many scholars and fans use these terms interchangeably, people involved in music production place them in discrete categories based upon their distinct roles within the film. From this perspective, 'film music' is the incidental background music – also called the 'film score' – which helps to generate the underlying context and mood of scenes of variable lengths in a film. While they might incorporate the human voice and/or chorus, scores only rarely contain lyrics because they are designed to undergird particular scenes. In other words, rather than be the focus of attention, film music may or may not include a clear melody, defined harmony, rhythm, and so forth.[2] By contrast, I use the term 'film song' to refer to foregrounded music in the film narrative. Songs tend to have conventional song forms – typically the *mukhda-antara-interlude* form – and they have lyrics performed by playback singers that are lip synced by actors in the film. Generally speaking, film songs are the only music that appear on the soundtracks distributed by music companies in India, and songs are used to promote the film on radio, television, and the Internet. This is not the case for film music, which is typically only heard as a component of particular scenes, but is typically not distributed on the soundtrack. Thus, even though orchestral scores have been present in Indian cinema since at least the 1940s, they are not regularly distributed like Hollywood scores.[3]

While there is an established canon of writing on Hollywood film scores, there is almost no writing on Indian film scores.[4] This dearth of discussions of film scores is predominantly because songs have captured the attention of film scholars, reviewers, and fans due to the visual spectacle of song picturization, and because songs are distributed by the Indian music industry in ways that background scores are not. It is exceedingly rare for music from background scores to be distributed on film soundtracks on its own, although as I will illustrate here, music of the background score sometimes makes its way into the recorded soundtrack through covert inclusion in the musical interludes of song sequences. In other cases, where instrumental and/or remixed versions of the key songs from a film are included on a soundtrack, these tracks are rarely mentioned by music scholars and reviewers, likely because they are believed to serve as a kind of 'filler' for soundtrack recordings (see Morcom). Although they are a necessary component of commercial Indian cinema, background scores similarly receive minimal attention from audiences and remain largely unheard and unremarked upon. Score composers themselves are marginalized within the filmmaking process, often being commissioned to compose music for film cues without having an opportunity to consult with film director or music director (Tubby, personal correspondence, July 2016). In addition, my composer interlocutors rarely failed to mention that the Filmfare Award for Background Score is considered in the technical categories (e.g. cinematography, choreography, costume design) rather than the artistic categories (e.g. film direction, music direction, best actor), which indexes its peripheral status within the filmmaking community. For this reason, it is common for music directors to subcontract another composer to write the film score, as score composition is simply not worth the time.[5]

As far as the background score in Hindi cinema is concerned, composers derive inspiration from a number of sources. For instance, melodies derived from songs written for the film make frequent appearances. These melodic themes are used by filmmakers as a way of indexing characters and situations, and most especially, emotion in the film narrative. In addition, because songs are released long before the film, filmmakers can assess which songs have become popular before the film release and these melodies can be worked more deliberately into the film score (Tubby, personal correspondence, July 2016). As such, the most effective film scores have synergies with the music of songs, even if the score and songs might be composed by different individuals who are not formally collaborating. Another source of inspiration for themes used in the score draws from classical Indian aesthetic theory (*rasa* theory) which is a codified system of affect that has systematic performative indexes in the Indian classical arts.[6] While some composers have certainly utilized this code, particularly in cinema of the 1930s to the 1960s, I suspect that film music composers have drawn as much inspiration from international musical tropes as they do from Indian musical conventions. Indeed, like certain music directors, Indian film music composers are often criticized for copying (or drawing inspiration from) music from particular scenes of Hollywood films, even the music undergirding these scenes are mediated by local musical-cinematic convention.[7] What is not often acknowledged, however, is that Hindi film editors, like their counterparts in Hollywood, frequently utilize 'scratch music' (i.e. prerecorded music that conveys the approximate musical mood of the scene) when editing films. As such, editors frequently require that composers stay true to the emotional context of music they have selected and only minimally modify the musical content.[8]

Despite the marginal status of the field of background score composition in Indian films, the music director A.R. Rahman has a reputation for a deep engagement with the background scores of the films for which he composes the songs.[9] This attention to musical details of the film score was relatively unusual for scores of the 1990s. I will not dwell here on biographical details of Rahman or his general compositional style in this essay, as there is more much written about him than any other Indian composer.[10] It is worth noting, however, that Rahman had a long period of apprenticeship with the Tamil music director Ilayaraja, who himself has long been known for the high quality of his orchestral scores, film songs, and his ability to compose from a palate of Indian instruments and Western orchestra. It is also well-known that Rahman is perhaps the only Indian music director who has been able to successfully crossover into Hollywood, having scored the music for a number of international films, most notably *Slumdog Millionaire* (2008), the compositions for which he took home two Academy Awards. These days he seems to be working on almost as many Hollywood projects as Indian projects, in addition to maintaining a busy schedule of live performances.

While Rahman has been an international celebrity as a music director for the last decade, much of his characteristic sound and approach to background music is evident in his early film scores. For example, I have written about the film *Bombay* (1995) and the many lives of the 'Bombay Theme' (Beaster-Jones, "Violence"). Here I want to expand the discussion of Rahman's film scoring practices to other films, along with the covert inclusion of *film music* on his song soundtracks.[11] As far as establishing his career in Hindi language cinema (as opposed to South Indian films dubbed into Hindi), *Taal* is perhaps the most important film in Rahman's early career. While he certainly garnered mainstream attention with *Roja* (1994), *Taal* cemented his status as a top-tier music director, one who was able to transcend his early success, as compared to other successful music directors of the 1990s who had a couple of superhit films, then otherwise faded into obscurity. While *Taal* did not win an award for its background score, it did win Rahman a Filmfare award for the Best Music Direction in 2000 and was the top grossing Bollywood soundtrack in 1999–2000. In addition, *Taal* was well-received internationally, and it was one of the very few Hindi films reviewed by Roger Ebert and the first Hindi film to break into the top 20 in the United States (Govil 76).[12]

After a discussion of *Taal*, I discuss Rahman's development of melodies in his film *Swades* (2004). I selected *Swades* for analysis because it won the Filmfare Award for Best Background Score in 2005, one of four such awards that Rahman has received in the last two decades.[13] Moreover, it is one of the very few Hindi films in which the background score was released as an entirely separate album from the song soundtrack. After providing a brief summary of the narrative themes in the film, I trace the musical themes, paying particular attention to the melodies that provide insights into the hero's affective state. These themes, I will show, are also connected to themes otherwise hidden in the musical interlude of the song 'Yeh Taara Woh Tara' [This star that star], thus providing additional insights into the tangled interactions between film song and film score in Indian cinema.

Analysis of *Taal*

In *Taal*, a scion of a rich industrialist, Manav Mehta (Akshay Khanna), encounters village belle Mansi (Aishwarya Rai) during a family excursion in Himachal Pradesh to finalize a 600 crore rupees business deal by Manav's father, Jagmohan Mehta (Amrish Puri). In the first half of the film, the hero is saved from falling off a cliff by the heroine, but not saved from falling in love with her. Mansi and her father, Tarababu (Alok Nath), run a village school teaching traditional music and arts: they are poor, but socially valued members of Indian society. Manav pursues Mansi and she indicates her reciprocal love through, among other things, drinking from his Coke bottle and embroidering his scarf with Manavsi (a portmanteau of their names). Once the business deal is finished, Manav returns home to Mumbai but is unable to convince his family that Mansi would be a proper addition to the extended family. Mansi and her father, Tarababu, travel to Mumbai to initiate a match, but unfamiliar with the local customs of the super-rich in the metropolis, did not make an advance appointment. Through the sister-in-law's design, they are left outside waiting for hours in order to show them their place in Mumbai's social hierarchy. Once they are able to make into the house and point out the Mehta family's hypocrisy, as well as their own frustration for being ill-treated, a verbal altercation leads to Tarababu striking Jagmohan and being thrown out of the house.

Shortly after leaving the house, Mansi and Tarababu encounter a troupe led by Vikrant Kapoor (Anil Kapoor) rehearsing a song and dance routine to a remixed version of one of Tarababu's *pahāṛī* folk songs. Fresh from their experience in the Mehta household, Mansi and her father are receptive to Vikrant's pitch (his 'Rules of Success') that Mansi join his troupe as a star performer, albeit with the stipulation that she dedicate herself to work and not have any romantic involvements. Despite Manav's apology on behalf of his family, Mansi joins the troupe and has a meteoric rise to success, ultimately winning an MTV Award and an international competition. Manav continues to pursue her, showing up at various events, despite Vikrant's attempts to deter him. The contractual stipulation that Mansi not get romantically involved does not, apparently, apply to Vikrant and he proposes marriage to her. She accepts. Manav eventually lands in the hospital with serious burns after trying to save the Manavsi scarf from the fire engulfing his family cottage. This near death experience spurs Manav to reconcile with his father, then Jagmohan to reconcile with Tarababu, which then puts pressure on Mansi to reconcile with Manav, which she only does on her wedding day after Manav has been severely beaten by police.

In most ways, the film narrative of *Taal* follows the Bollywood cinematic conventions of the 'family film' (Dwyer, *All You Want*; Ganti, *Bollywood*) insofar as it highlights generational romantic conflicts among the super wealthy that require parental assent in order to resolve the romantic conflicts. Like other family films of the 1990s, there are strongly patriarchal dimensions to the narrative. Indeed, the narrative resolution can only occur after the conflicts surrounding the wounded prides of the fathers are resolved. *Taal* also falls into the genre of Hindi films that features actors/dancers on the stage in diegetic performances, which helps to explain its larger than usual number of songs in this period. Unlike other films of this genre, however, the film narrative represents actors and musicians in rehearsal in behind the scenes moments that are at once self-reflective glimpses into the off-screen lives of performers, as well as self-conscious representations of the work required to make these performances happen. Ostensibly, what they produce in the film are stage shows, but would not be a stretch of the imagination to see that they are also depicting the labor of song–dance sequences for films. Finally, the film provides a fascinating meta-commentary on the neocolonial tendencies of the Indian music industry, as musicians in capitalist centers appropriate music from the folk margins, rebrand it, and incorporate it in the culture industries in ways that leave the original artists cut out of commodity circuits. That said, the filmmakers conspicuously elide the fact that the Indian film industry itself has always been voraciously neocolonial in mediating folk songs for use in film songs.

Taal background score

Musically speaking, the soundtrack contains an unusually large number of tracks for this era of film song, including two different versions of the best-known songs 'Ishq Bina Kya Jeena' [What is life without love?] and 'Taal Se Taal Mila' [Meeting of the rhythms]. In addition, as I indicated earlier, it also contains two tracks of film music: 'Beat of Passion (Title Music)' and 'Raga Dance (Music)'. As is frequently the case in Hindi films, the first half of *Taal* focuses upon character and relationship development and generates the conflict which is resolved in the second half of the film. Musical themes are similarly developed in the background score of the first half of the film, then indexed again at moments of conflict and resolution. References to song melodies and the lyrical text that comes along with 'Taal Se Taal Mila' and 'Ishq Bina Kya Jeena' are used consistently to indicate Mansi's internal struggle over her choice to pursue a stage career with Vikrant. Based upon my discussion with the score composer Tubby discussed earlier, I would anticipate that it is not coincidental that these two melodies predominate as the filmmaker would have had an opportunity to playtest the melodies in radio and television promotion of the film. Indeed, the other song melodies appear with much less frequency and are much less important to the musical narrative in the film score. In the context of a distinction between film music and film song, it is striking that the themes that I have dubbed 'Manav's Theme' and 'Mansi's Theme' appear as much as or more in the background score than any of the song-based themes. Moreover, compared to the discussion of *Swades* below, Manav's and Mansi's themes appear much more evenly throughout the film (Figure 1).

Despite being a distinctive melody that is developed throughout the film, the melody that I am calling 'Mansi's Theme' (Figure 2) does not make its way into the song soundtrack recording that was distributed in advance of the film. Uncharacteristically for a melody in the background score, the theme is performed by a female vocalist singing 'saiyyon aava' (Come, my beloved) in a dialect of Hindi that uses vocal ornamentation gesturing to North Indian folk practices. The synthesizer drone undergirding this theme is a standard compositional approach that Rahman uses to meld different musical styles, particularly in his early films. The harmony below this theme never cadences, that is, it keeps the harmonic tension created through dissonant intervals, which suggests that her desire is never fulfilled. Each instantiation of 'Mansi's theme' evokes desire from the heroine's perspective, even as the reverb used in the recording of this melody evokes the Himalayan landscape.[14] 'Mansi's Theme' is also the first recognizable melody that we hear after the title track, when Manav gazes down into the valley that contains Mansi's familial home. It appears again at Manav and Mansi's first meeting as she saves him from falling to his death down a cliff. Following from the convention in Hindi cinema in which the hero and heroine of the film meet and

Time in Film [h:mm:ss]	*0:00:00 0:20:00*	*0:20:00 0:40:00*	*0:40:00 1:00:00*	*1:00:00 1:20:00*	*1:20:00 1:40:00*	*1:40:00 2:00:00*	*2:00:00 2:20:00*	*2:20:00 2:40:00*	*2:40:00 3:15:00*
Score Melodies									
Mansi's Theme	0:08:31	0:20:22 0:53:37			1:30:47				2:54:42
Manav's Theme	0:12:47	0:24:26 0:32:11	0:44:36 0:52:45 0:54:23			1:40:53 1:44:21	*2:14:20	2:25:23	
Song Melodies									
Beat of Passion	*0:00:30								
Kariye Na	*0:02:50								
Taal se Taal	*0:14:27	0:20:52 0:26:32 0:30:24	0:52:05						
Ishq Bina		*0:35:55		1:04:38			2:13:29	2:27:05	
Raga Dance					*1:23:30				
Na Mi Samajh					*1:37:39	*1:40:19 1:41:51			
Ramta Jogi							*2:05:19		2:42:07 2:47:51
Nahin Samne							*2:14:20		
Ishq Bina [alternate]								*2:28:28	2:53:19
Taal Se Taal [western]									*2:57:17

Figure 1. Themes appearing in the *Taal* background score.
Notes: As a way of spatially representing when themes appear in the film, the columns represent 20 min intervals. Asterisk by a time represents the song sequence.

exchange their first electric gaze, so too the background sound fades away as the hero and heroine experience the shock of recognition that they are destined to be together.

'Mansi's Theme' then disappears for another 30 min in the film, until the moment that Jagmohan, realizing that Manav and Mansi's love affair is blossoming, announces imperiously that the family is returning to Mumbai. At this point, the affect of the melody is transformed to reflect Mansi's sense of loss, and the uses of the theme in the second half of the film are cued when she has to decide whether to pursue love or stardom. The final rendition of 'Mansi's Theme' appears at the very end of the film when Manav and Mansi are finally reunited and the heroine's desire has been fulfilled: its importance to the film narrative is cemented as hero/heroine run to each other in slow motion in the final scene of the film.

Close analysis of the melody that I am calling 'Manav's Theme' (Figure 3) provides additional insights into the development of musical scores in Hindi cinema, as well as

Figure 2. Rough transcription of 'Mansi's Theme'.

Figure 3. Transcription of Manav's Theme.

insights into the changes that Rahman wrought in musical-cinematic discourse. Like the heroine's theme, 'Manav's Theme' is also established early in the film and follows Manav and Mansi throughout the character development phase of the narrative. The theme ties them together as a couple at various key moments in the film, including a sensual yoga session, one of the few on-screen kisses in post-Independence Indian cinema, and Manav himself playing the theme on piano in his family home. 'Manav's Theme' appears frequently in the background score of the film, and like 'Mansi's Theme', it does not belong to its own song in the soundtrack of the film. The melody does make a brief appearance, however, in the opening musical interlude of the song 'Nahin Samne Tu' [You are not before me] which is the last complete song in the film. By this point, the theme has already been strongly associated with Manav and another strong example of the covert inclusion of film music in the soundtrack of a film song in ways that index specific moments and emotions within the film. Indeed, had this been a Hollywood original soundtrack (OST), these musical themes would have been included on the soundtrack as their own compositions. However, because this is a Bollywood score, they were not.

Swades (2004)

Swades is a film that addresses the persistent social issues that arise from the continued operation of India's caste hierarchy, as well as the ethical responsibilities of India's diasporic populations to help develop the motherland. As such, the filmmaker (Ashutosh Gowariker) seems to be targeting audiences living in India and abroad. Indeed, while the film flopped in the Indian box office, it continues to remain a cinematic touchstone for audiences living outside of India.

In the film, Mohan (Shah Rukh Khan), an Indian expatriate living in the United States as a NASA engineer, returns to India to bring his nanny, Kaveri (Kishori Ballal), to the United States to live the remainder of her old age in comfort. On his return to Delhi, he learns that his nanny has left a nursing home and returned to her natal village. By chance, he encounters his childhood playmate, Gita (Gayatri Joshi), who recognizes Mohan as he looks for a map in a bookstore owned by a friend in Delhi. Grasping his intentions, she deliberately gives him incorrect directions to the village without revealing her identity to him. Depicted as a Westernized Indian, Mohan rents a mobile home to travel, thus creating a portable sanitized space for himself, even as he refuses to drink the local water. While wandering lost, he encounters a Sufi *pīr* who directs him to the village while they sing the duet 'Yun hi chala' [Move like this]. Upon arriving at the village, he finds Kaveri who welcomes him home, but stalls him in his request for her to join him in the United

States. While staying in his mobile home in the center of the village (rather than in any of the houses, a form of separation), additional villagers are introduced, including Mela Ram (Daya Shankar Pandey) who desires Mohan's help in opening a *dhābā* in the United States, the local postmaster-wrestler Nivaran (Rajesh Vivek), and Gita's younger brother Chikku (Master Smith Seth), each of whom receive their own musical theme (see below). These characters introduce Mohan to village life and the operation of the local panchayat. Mohan subsequently learns that Gita has found her calling and returned to the village as a teacher from Delhi, but her school is under threat of the village panchayat who will repurpose a portion of her school for grain storage if she is unable to find more pupils. Mohan is thus persuaded to help increase enrollment at the school among the local families who are not sending their school-aged children. He in turn enlists Mela Ram and Nivaran to help him convince families to use the local school facilities. It is at this point that the filmmaker begins to explore the larger theme of caste, as some families express discomfort at their upper- and mid-caste children sharing the space of the school with lower caste children. By contrast, lower caste families are unable to see the purposes of education as they anticipate their children will follow their hereditary caste professions. Dalit families are forbidden from even working in the village. Mohan receives intense pushback from the upper caste families who argue that as an outsider who has a dubious status as a Hindu and as an Indian, he has no right to moralize about caste prejudice in the village.

Midway through the film, a traveling film company comes to the village to screen the classic 1973 Hindi film *Yaadon Ki Baarat*, with the central screen separating the castes: lower caste audiences have to watch the film backward from the rear of the screen. The Dalit family has to watch the film from a distance. When one of the regular power outages hits the village and the film becomes unwatchable, Mohan in his role as a NASA engineer sings 'Yeh Taara, Woh Taara' [This star, that star] as he reveals to the villagers the wonders of the night sky and the roles of individual stars in the constellations. At a significant moment of the song, the screen partitioning the upper and lower castes is brought down and all of the children begin to mingle with each other. As I will discuss below, Rahman uses melodies from musical interludes in this song as significant themes of the background score with their own development in the film narrative in ways that parallel the use of melodic themes in *Taal*. As Kaveri postpones her decision to leave, so too Mohan postpones his return to NASA. And, as the romance narrative between Mohan and Gita begins to blossom, Kaveri sends Mohan on an errand to collect rent from one of the agricultural tenants of Gita's family land. After a long trip, Mohan arrives to learn that the family of Haridas, the tenant, has been shunned by his village and is unable to support his family because he attempted to shift away from his traditional caste occupation in order to pursue an opening in farming that the market provided. In retaliation for his perceived impudence, the local village cut off the irrigation he would need to farm and refused to purchase the meager crops he managed to harvest. This moment, combined with a later encounter with a small boy selling water to railway passengers, forces Mohan into an activist frame in the rest of the film.

On the day of Dussehra, a moment when some of the lower caste villagers begin to send their children to school, Mohan is forced into a debate about the comparative merits of the perceived American 'culturelessness' and Indian *sanskriti*, in which Mohan argues that adherence to caste prejudices is one of the cultural practices that continues to impede Indian development. As Mohan grapples with his relative Indianness, the film cuts to a village performance of the Ramlila, at the end of which Sita (played by Gita) is rescued from

Ravana by Ram and his army. At this point, Mohan realizes his calling to bring light into darkness, then engages the villagers in creating a small scale hydroelectric project to provide continuous power (light) to the village.[15] Eventually, Kaveri elects to stay in India, and Mohan wraps up his career at NASA in order to bring his engineering skills to the village.

Swades background score

If the music and thematic development for *Taal* exemplifies Rahman's approach to film scoring in the first decade of his career, then the music of *Swades* embodies his approach to film scoring at the beginning of the second decade of career. That is, following from the recognition that Rahman had been receiving from audiences after the success of Oscar-nominated *Lagaan* (2001), the score of *Swades* appears to be oriented as much to audiences abroad as they are to new middle class audiences in India. This shift in scoring foreshadows the success of *Slumdog* and Rahman's eventual career shift to Hollywood films. Accordingly, while the background score of *Swades* shows many similarities with *Taal*, the thematic development within the score brings to bear many tools that were latent in Rahman's earlier scores, but are more consistently applied here. As such, Rahman's approach to *Swades* creates the enabling conditions for new approaches by other composers in later films, particularly for filmmakers attempting to move away from the narratives of conventional Hindi cinema.

As in other Hindi films, there are a number of musical ideas associated with particular characters and/or their emotional states at the moment that come from a variety of sources and musical conventions. Musical themes connected to the songs composed for the film are one of these sources. For example, the song 'Saawariya' [Beloved], which appears midway through the film and is lip synced by the actor playing Gita operates as a musical sign of her gradually falling in love with Mohan. Interestingly, the theme appears early in the film when Gita and Mohan interact for the first time in the Delhi bookstore, and in so doing, it foreshadows the relationship they are to develop in the film. The melody appears a few times after the song performance in the film, which like Mansi's theme from *Taal*, reinforces Gita's affective state within the film and her attachment to the hero. Like *Taal*, the *Swades* soundtrack incorporated a couple of instances of film music that blur this song/music distinction. In the case of *Swades*, however, and comparable to earlier practices, these are instrumental reprises of songs used in the film, albeit performed in a semi-classical style by the bansuri player Naveen Kumar ('Pal Pal Hai Bhaari') and shehnai player Madhukar Dhumal ('Yeh Jo Des Hai Tera'). These melodies are featured throughout the film as a kind of foreshadowing of the relationships that the characters will later develop.

Unlike *Taal*, there are many other themes in the film attached to characters, events, and emotional states that do not find their way into the soundtrack recording of the songs. For instance, Chikku, Mela Ram, and Nivaran each have a theme that is introduced along with their characters that provides insights into the personalities, and which indexes their characters later in the film. The use of pizzicato strings in 'Chikku's Theme', for instance, coupled with longstanding melodic conventions associated with childhood in Indian cinema point to Chikku's playful and mischievous nature. Similarly, the bhangra-inflected style of Mela Ram's 'Dhaba Theme' indexes not only his possible regional affiliations, but also suggests his cheerful, happy-go-lucky personality. Other moments in the film draw from the deep well of musical and sound conventions that carry along intense affective resonances. For example, while Kaveri herself does not receive her own theme, there is a low drone and humming chorus of voices underscoring several moments of the film when the characters discuss Kaveri, and the untimely deaths of Mohan's and Gita's parents. The hummed drone is used as a way of pointing to the *gravitas* of filial piety as an Indian tradition, along with the underlying critique of the decision to place Kaveri in a nursing home in her old age. Similarly, for most of the scene in which Haridas describes his plight, there is an absence of background music in order to emphasize the dialog. However, when he begins crying as he describes the shame arising from his inability to feed and clothe his family, the sound of the sarangi begins to play in the background, amplifying the sorrow of the moment and his feeling of helplessness.[16] Finally, like other Hindi films of this era, there are numerous diegetic references to songs used in other Hindi films and international pop songs that also serve as a component of character development.

As a way of illustrating Rahman's attention to scoring, it is worth discussing the themes attached to Mohan's affective state in the film, several of which are related to his perspective on the social practices of caste in Charanpur village. Each of these melodies is identifiable and distinct, but do not have lyrics written for them. Based upon the way that they are used in the film, I have labeled these themes 'Mohan's Resolve', 'Caste Hierarchy', 'Mohan's Aspiration', and 'Social Progress'.[17] The first three of these themes are introduced in the title sequence which appears approximately 15 min into the film. The title sequence operates like an overture (i.e. an opening song introducing the important themes in Western opera or in musical theater); the last two themes also appear on the film soundtrack as melodies used in the interlude of the song 'Yeh Tara Woh Tara'. Like musical themes in other filmic contexts, these musical cues are subtly and systematically attached to particular contexts within the film and assist in narrative development, albeit in ways that are largely unheard by audiences (Gorbman). As the chart below demonstrates, these themes appear in the background score as consistently as other themes in the film, but are also strategically deployed at key moments within the narrative arc of the film (Figure 4).

'Mohan's Aspiration' (Figure 5) appears most frequently of all of the themes in the film and is strongly associated with his attempts to persuade the villagers to overcome their social conflicts, particularly with regard to the operation of caste within the village. Insofar as it appears in the opening interlude of 'Yeh Taara Woh Taara', it is also connected to Mohan's comparison of social structures to astronomical constellations – that is, an individual star shines alone brightly, but multiple stars are needed to form constellations which have greater overall value. Because 'Yeh Taara Woh Taara' is the first song on the CD and cassette soundtrack released before the film, and because this theme is sung as a vocable (i.e. vocal syllable without lexical meaning) by the playback singer Udit Narayan, it is also the most prominent interlude theme in the film. This melody is also performed by flute and accordion at different points in the film, and Rahman reharmonizes it on occasion as a way to laminate additional meanings/affects onto the melody.

Within the film narrative, 'Mohan's Aspiration' is associated with moments in which Mohan is attempting to convince the villagers to work together to effect a shared social goal and positive social change, particularly with regard to increasing enrollment in the village school. The melody first appears in the opening overture as Mohan opens the windows next to his seat on the flight into India and gazes down upon agricultural land, perhaps as a way of foreshadowing his activist role. Rahman uses the theme in later moments as Mohan presents his cause to the villagers. Musically speaking, the octave leaps in the melody, and rising melodic sequence metaphorically suggest the potential of social progress as part of

Time in Film [h:mm:ss]	***0:00:00 0:20:00***	***0:20:00 0:40:00***	***0:40:00 1:00:00***	***1:00:00 1:20:00***	***1:20:00 1:40:00***	***1:40:00 2:00:00***	***2:00:00 2:20:00***	***2:20:00 2:40:00***	***2:40:00 3:15:00***
Score Melodies									
Mohan's Resolve	0:12:52			1:16:34				2:31:52	2:45:25 2:54:09
Caste Hierarchy	0:12:23			1:17:16 1:18:43 1:19:08			2:19:07	2:32:23	
Mohan's Aspiration	0:14:35			1:19:20	*1:29:31		2:05:00 2:06:49		2:55:02 2:58:04
Social Progress					1:28:56 *1:30:44	1:51:24	2:14:31		
Filial Drone	0:08:28 0:16:23		0:43:07						
NASA Theme	0:01:02 0:03:14 0:11:17							2:31:52	3:01:27
Chikku's theme		0:34:14 0:37:54 0:38:16	0:45:06 0:52:28						
Postman Theme		0:39:05		1:02:08 1:12:46					
Gita's Theme			0:43:54 0:44:29 0:45:34		1:21:01				
Dhaba Theme			0:49:09	1:15:01				2:33:25 2:35:54	
Song Melodies									
Yun Hi Chala		*0:25:0 1 0:33:31	0:57:31	1:12:38 1:13:20				2:30:52	
Yeh Taara					*1:29:31				
Saawariya	0:19:00			1:04:21		*1:55:05		2:36:00	2:58:30
Pal pal	0:16:23 0:18:38		0:59:23					*2:28:00	
Dekho na			0:42:05					*2:37:35	
Yeh Jo Desh									*3:02:14
Yeh Jo Desh (Shehnai)									*3:12:48

Figure 4. Table of musical themes in *Swades*.

Figure 5. Transcription of 'Mohan's Aspiration'.

the broader metaphor of social life and the lessons Mohan has learned working for NASA. The melody is also used as Mohan ruminates on the lesson he learned from his meeting with Haridas. Indeed, the picture of Shah Rukh Khan surrounded by villagers on a boat is the visual image which was central to the marketing of the film on CD/cassette covers and the film poster. The melody also prominently acknowledges the success of his social program at the end of the film when Mela Ram decides to remain in the village to help it operate, rather than pursue life in the United States.

A second interlude melody used in 'Yeh Taara Woh Taara' also has important resonances in the film, as it is associated with moments in which villagers acknowledge the truth of Mohan's pleas for the school and initiate their children's education. I have labeled this melody the 'Social Progress Theme', (Figure 6) as the melody and the harmonic cadences reinforce the characters' understanding of the correct decision. Like 'Mohan's Aspiration', this theme is also reharmonized in different contexts in order to enhance the emotive resonance of the theme within the film.

The filmmaker uses the 'Caste Hierarchy Theme' theme (Figure 7) at a number of key moments of the film, particularly when the lower caste status becomes a disenabling condition for villagers joining the school (i.e. when the Dalit family points out that they are not even allowed to work in the village, much less send their children to the school with the higher castes). Like many of Rahman's pre-2000 compositions, the music creates tension through a repeated melodic sequence coupled with open harmonies and rising bass figure. However, like some of Rahman's post-2000 compositions, this musical figure uses extended harmonies (in this case, a melody based upon the ninth scale degree) in ways that were rare in Hindi film scoring and illustrate Rahman's willingness to fuse techniques in functional harmony with the complexities afforded by Indian melodic systems. Most renditions of this melody in the film incorporate a syncopated drum groove, to which the melodic rhythm provides a counterpoint. Thus, the theme effectively creates tension on melodic, harmonic, and rhythmic bases which, in turn, plays out in the moments of narrative tension in the film.

Finally, the theme that I am calling 'Mohan's Resolve' also appears in the title music of the film as Mohan flies into India. The melody is played most frequently by the accordion in a distinctive syncopated rhythm, as well as a heavy digital delay in a percussive electric piano, each of which points to Mohan's cosmopolitanism. It appears primarily in the second

Figure 6. Transcription of 'Social Progress Theme'.

Figure 7. Transcription of the 'Caste Hierarchy Theme'.

half of the film as a way of underscoring Mohan's will to solve the technological issues that arise as they build their hydroelectric project, but is also used at a particular moment in the film when Mohan asserts his status as a Brahmin, along with his willingness to ignore caste proscriptions by eating food prepared by Mela Ram. Its use in the title music reaffirms the importance of this melody in providing insights into Mohan's character, but like other themes I discussed above, it is not included in the song soundtrack for the film, although it is included in the separate soundtrack of the orchestral score.

Concluding thoughts

I have noted palpable changes in the background scoring in contemporary commercial films, particularly in development of themes and the increase of silence in dramatic moments. In addition, there is an interestingly complicated relationship between song and score in Hindi cinema in which musical and narrative development work hand in hand. As such, I would argue that Rahman's film scores heralded the potential commercial success of *hatke* (different) cinema of the 2010s.[18] They also anticipated the decline of lip synced song sequences in some contemporary Hindi films, even as they blurred the boundaries between film song and film score.

As a way to conclude, it is useful to compare the soundtracks that Rahman wrote for these representative Hindi films and the soundtracks distributed for his international films. For example, the *Slumdog Millionaire* soundtrack incorporates M.I.A.'s song 'Paper Planes', the film songs 'Jai Ho' and 'Ringa Ringa', along with numerous moments from the background score. As such, it largely follows the practices of contemporary Hollywood orchestral soundtracks insofar as it includes a couple of songs that are used in film promotion, but is otherwise centered around moments from the background score that are given their own tracks, with particular attention paid to the end credits song. Compare this to Howard Shore's orchestral scores for *The Lord of the Rings* soundtracks which have some readily recognizable themes and one or two original songs written for the end credits. In the case of *Taal* and *Swades*, which are song-based soundtracks, notwithstanding the separate and very unusual release of the orchestral score of *Swades,* the incorporation of film music is a bit more unusual within the soundtrack conventions of Indian cinema of the time.

In short, I would suggest that Rahman's film scores of the 1990s created the conditions of possibility for what Rachel Dwyer has called 'upper-middlebrow cinema'.[19] This is not to suggest that the music for scores like Gulzar's films of the 1970s–1980s are not an important point for consideration, but their status as art films meant that they lacked the large scale influence in musical-cinematic practice that Rahman's scores have come to reflect. Finally, I am not arguing that the work of writing background scores has even come close to approaching the status of song composition, but that the post-Rahman background score has taken on a slightly higher status in the minds of filmmakers and viewers and is more carefully managed in contemporary films than has been in the past. In so doing, I have illustrated how Rahman's scoring practices developed over the middle part of his career, such that the music he created, in part, facilitated new musical-cinematic practices by later Indian filmmakers.

Notes

1. I am limiting my discussion here to Hindi cinema here because I strongly suspect that Tamil cinema had achieved this state long before the 1990s through the compositions of Tamil-language music director Ilayraja.
2. Kathryn Kalinak notes that this is more or less the function of the musical score in Hollywood films as well. Some composers of Hollywood scores have melodic themes or leitmotifs attached to particular characters or emotions; other scores are less melodically-oriented and center upon harmonic texture and atmospheric sound. As a general rule, composers of Hindi films attend much more to melodic development and pay much less attention to harmony.
3. Moreover, Jeff Smith has noted that even soundtracks for Hollywood orchestral scores have a very small market share as compared to song-oriented soundtracks.
4. For examples of writing on classical Hollywood film scores, see Altman, Gorbman, Kalinak, Chion, Carroll. In the case of Hindi cinema, Morcom has discussed a few classic film scores and Booth has discussed the role of score writing from the perspective of musician's labor.
5. In other cases, music producer Clinton Cerejo noted to me in July 2016, some composers will only agree to work on scoring a film if they also negotiate song composition (personal communication).
6. See Sarrazin.
7. For example, see the YouTube series 'Charcha with Bhurani' that provides many examples, including a segment on theme music (https://www.youtube.com/watch?v=EbQAlk1A4HM). See also http://www.itwofs.com/ for many more examples of the reuse of melodies and musical sounds from a variety of sources.
8. Several contemporary composers noted to me that the music of Hans Zimmer was particularly appealing to film directors and editors and sought to have Zimmer's ethos emerge in their scores, probably because of the vibrant and dynamic nature of his action and superhero film scores, such as *The Lion King* (1994), *Gladiator* (2000), *Pirates of the Caribbean* (2003), and *Inception* (2010). See also Murphy's discussion of Hans Zimmer's role in transforming the sound of contemporary Hollywood film scores.
9. Lest one get too caught up in the romance of the musical auteur, it is worth remembering that like other composers in Hollywood and Bollywood, A.R. Rahman works with a team who assists him with many of the more mundane details of composition such as recording, editing, orchestration, and so on.
10. See Kamini Mathai's biography and Nasreen Munni Kabir's interview with Rahman, among numerous accounts and interviews by broadcast media that are widely available on YouTube and other streaming websites.
11. These moments of film music include "Waltz For A Romance (in A Major)" from *Lagaan* (2001), several tracks included in the *Taal* soundtrack, "Kisna Theme" from *Kisna* (2005), instrumental versions of "Jashn-E-Bahaara" and "Khwaja Mere Khwaja" in *Jodhaa Akhbar* (2008), and "Lakh Lakh Thora" from *Mohenjo Daro* (2016), among others.
12. See http://www.rogerebert.com/reviews/taal-1999.
13. The other awards came for the scores to *The Legend of Bhagat Singh* (2002), *Guru* (2007), and *Jodhaa Akbar* (2008). Rahman has not won such an award after his *Slumdog* success, which coincides with the moment he began working in Hollywood.
14. See also Fiol for discussion on the musical conventions around representing the Himalayas in Hindi cinema.
15. This portion of the film is loosely based upon Aravinda Pillalamarri and Ravi Kuchimanchi's work in the Bilgaon Project. See http://www.indiatimes.com/lifestyle/self/meet-aravinda-and-ravi-the-inspiration-behind-shahrukh-khan-s-movie-swades-249108.html and https://scroll.in/magazine/828148/from-inspiring-swades-to-being-questioned-on-immigration-status-aravinda-pillalamarris-journey
16. See Qureshi on the sound of sarangi as an index of extreme sadness in North India, particularly around issues pertaining to tragedy and death. The sarangi is very much a part of filmic

convention, as well, and has amplified any number of narrative moments in films, most notably in *Sholay* (1975) as Thakur views the sheet-wrapped bodies of his murdered family.

17. The labels for the themes that I use here are distinct from the titles of the cues used in the *Swades* orchestral soundtrack, primarily because I am tracking the movement of discrete musical ideas in the film, rather than the narrative themes in the cues. Accordingly, a number of musical themes that I describe here are repeated in different cues, albeit with different styles, instrumentation, or orchestration.
18. These categories include the films of Anurag Kashyap (e.g. *Dev D*, *Gangs of Wasseypur*), Vishal Bhardwaj (e.g. *Maqbool*, *Dedh Ishqiya*), and Shoojit Sircar (e.g. *Vicky Donor*, *Piku*) whose films are situated between conventional understandings of commercial Hindi cinema and classic understandings of 'art cinema.'
19. This term coined by Dwyer ("Mumbai Middlebrow" 56–7) describes cinema that targets India's new middle classes through film aesthetic that is a self-conscious departure from conventional Hindi cinema, yet does not challenge any presuppositions or realities of this social class. As such, it gestures in the direction of art cinema, albeit in an accessible manner.

Disclosure statement

No potential conflict of interest was reported by the author.

References

Altman, Rick. *The American Film Musical*. Bloomington: Indiana University Press, 1988. Print.

Beaster-Jones, Jayson. *Bollywood Sounds: The Cosmopolitan Mediations of Hindi Film Song*. New York: Oxford University Press, 2015. Print.

Beaster-Jones, Jayson. "Violence, Reconciliation, and Memory: A.R. Rahman's 'Bombay Theme.'" *Music in Contemporary Indian Film: Memory, Voice, Identity*. Ed. Jayson Beaster-Jones and Natalie Sarrazin. New York: Routledge, 2017. 107–119. Print.

Booth, Gregory. *Behind the Curtain: Making Music in Mumbai's Film Studios*. New York: Oxford University Press, 2008. Print.

Carroll, Noel. *A Philosophy of Mass Art*. New York: Oxford University Press, 1998. Print.

Cerejo, Clinton. Personal Interview. 21 Jul. 2016.

Chion, Michele. *Audio-vision: Sound on Screen*. Trans. Claudia Gorbman. New York: Columbia University Press, 1994. Print.

Dwyer, Rachel. *All You Want is Money, All You Need is Love: Sex and Romance in Modern India*. London: Cassell, 2000. Print.

Dwyer, Rachel. "Mumbai Middlebrow: Ways of Thinking About the Middle Ground in Hindi Cinema." *Middlebrow Cinema*. Ed. Sally Faulkner. Abingdon: Routledge, 2016. 51–68. Print.

Fiol, Stefan. "Folk Drums and Tribal Girls: Sounding the Himalayas in Indian Film." *Music in Contemporary Indian Film: Memory, Voice, Identity*. Ed. Jayson Beaster-Jones and Natalie Sarrazin. New York: Routledge, 2017. 133–146. Print.

Ganti, Tejaswini. *Bollywood: A Guidebook to Popular Hindi Cinema*. New York: Routledge, 2013. Print.

Gorbman, Claudia. *Unheard Melodies: Narrative Film Music*. Bloomington: Indiana University Press, 1987. Print.

Govil, Nitin. "Bollywood and the Frictions of Global Mobility." *Media on the Move: Global Flow and Contra-flow*. Ed. Daya Kishan Thussu. Hoboken: Taylor and Francis, 2007. 76–88. Print.
Kabir, Nasreen Munni. *A.R. Rahman: The Spirit of Music*. New Delhi: OM Books International, 2014. Print.
Kalinak, Kathryn. *Settling the Score: Music and the Classical Hollywood Film*. Madison, WI: University of Wisconsin Press, 1992. Print.
Kalinak, Kathryn. *Film Music: A Very Short Introduction*. New York: Oxford University Press, 2010. Print.
Mathai, Kamini. *A. R. Rahman: The Musical Storm*. New Delhi: Penguin Books, 2010. Print.
Morcom, Anna. *Hindi Film Songs and the Cinema*. London: Routledge, 2006. Print.
Murphy, Scott. "A Pop Music Progression in Recent Popular Movies and Movie Trailers." *Music, Sound, and the Moving Image* 8.2 (2014): 141–162. Print.
Qureshi, Regula Burckhart. "The Indian Sarangi: Sound of Affect, Site of Contest." *Yearbook for Traditional Music* 29 (1997): 1–38. Print.
Sarrazin, Natalie. "Songs from the Heart: Musical Coding, Emotional Sentiment, and Transnational Sonic Identity in India's Popular Film Music." *Global Bollywood*. Ed. Anandam Kavoori and Aswin Punathambekar. New York: NYU Press, 2008. 203–219. Print.
Smith, Jeff. *The Sounds of Commerce: Marketing Popular Film Music*. New York: Columbia University Press, 1998. Print.
Tubby. Personal Interview. 19 Jul. 2016.

Filmography

Bombay. Dir. Mani Ratnam. Mus. A. R. Rahman. Amitabh Bachchan Corporation, 1995. Film.
Dedh Ishqiya. Dir. Vishal Bhardwaj. Mus. Vishal Bhardwaj. Vishal Bhardwaj Pictures, 2014. Film.
Dev D. Dir. Anurag Kashyap. Mus. Amit Trivedi. UTV Motion Pictures, 2009. Film.
Gangs of Wasseypur. Dir. Anurag Kashyap. Mus. Sneha Khanwalkar. Jar Pictures, 2012. Film.
Gladiator. Dir. Ridley Scott. Mus. Hans Zimmer. DreamWorks, 2000. Film.
Guru. Dir. Mani Ratnam. Mus. A. R. Rahman. Madras Talkies, 2007. Film.
Inception. Dir. Christopher Nolan. Mus. Hans Zimmer. Warner Bros., 2010. Film.
Jodhaa Akhbar. Dir. Ashutosh Gowariker. Mus. A. R. Rahman. Ashutosh Gowariker Productions, 2008. Film.
Kisna: The Warrior Poet. Dir. Subhash Ghai. Mus. A. R. Rahman. Mukta Arts, 2005. Film.
Lagaan. Dir. Ashutosh Gowariker. Mus. A. R. Rahman. Aamir Khan Productions, 2001. Film.
The Lion King. Dir. Roger Allers and Rob Minkoff. Mus. Hans Zimmer. Walt Disney Pictures, 1994. Film.
Maqbool. Dir. Vishal Bharadwaj. Mus. Vishal Bhardwaj. Vishal Bhardwaj Pictures, 2004. Film.
Mohenjo Daro. Dir. Ashutosh Gowariker. Mus. A. R. Rahman. Ashutosh Gowariker Productions, 2016. Film.
Piku. Dir. Shoojit Sircar. Mus. Anupam Roy. MSM Motion Pictures, 2015. Film.
Pirates of the Caribbean: The Curse of the Black Pearl. Dir. Gore Verbinski. Mus. Hans Zimmer. Walt Disney Pictures, 2003. Film.
Roja. Dir. Mani Rathnam. Mus. A. R. Rahman. Hansa Pictures, 1993. Film.
Sholay. Dir. Ramesh Sippy. Mus. R. D. Burman. Sippy Films, 1975. Film.
Slumdog Millionaire. Dir. Danny Boyle. Mus. A. R. Rahman. Fox Searchlight, 2008. Film.
Swades. Dir. Ashutosh Gowariker. Mus. A. R. Rahman. Ashutosh Gowariker Productions, 2004. Film.
Taal. Dir. Subhash Ghai. Mus. A. R. Rahman. Rajshri, 1999. Film.
The Legend of Bhagat Singh. Dir. Rajkumar Santoshi. Mus. A. R. Rahman. Tips Films, 2002. Film.
The Lord of the Rings: The Fellowship of the Ring. Dir. Peter Jackson. Mus. Howard Shore. New Line Cinema, 2001. Film.
Vicky Donor. Dir. Shoojit Sircar. Mus. Ketan Sodha. Rampage Motion Pictures, 2012. Film.
Yaadon Ki Baaraat. Dir. Nasir Hussain. Mus. R. D. Burman. Nasir Hussain Films, 1973. Film.

Bollywood's variation on the *firanginess* theme: Song-and-dance sequences as heterotopic offbeats

Monia Acciari

ABSTRACT
Song-and-dance sequences have widely been studied as disruptive elements in the narrative of popular Hindi cinema and as quintessential traits of this industry. While the utopic dimension of such musical intervals has largely been theorised, the aim of this article is to expand on this framework to articulate the heterotopic dimension of these interludes. Foucault's concept of heterotopia allows further study of how song-and-dance sequences are elements responsible for communicating both social and cultural aspects. On a similar note, it must be mentioned that the use and representation of foreigners in Indian cinema dates back to its origins, when foreign actresses were often employed in films, replacing local performers. Through historical exploration, this article will specifically investigate how song-and-dance sequences are important 'malleable elements' of the narrative, which are able to articulate identity and to discourse on the representation and articulation of *firangi*ness in popular Hindi cinema.

The history of the fascination that Indian cinema productions have with foreign bodies and cultures dates back to the very beginning of Indian cinema, when mostly British-Jewish and Indo-American actresses populated the silent screens of India, conveying a deeply international flavour right from the start. When it comes to engaging with the history of song-and-dance sequences and the role these 'interruptions' (Gopalan 18) have played in depicting *firangi*ness (foreignness) in popular Hindi cinema, the 1950s and 1960s established an important trend. Song-and-dance sequences from that era viewed the appearance of foreign and non-Indian bodies as a means of providing a marked contrast with the heroine of the films and, as such, as simply a representation of racial and cultural 'otherness'; this characteristic was often used to distinguish social values of appropriateness and unsuitableness, as will be discussed further. Often song-and-dance sequences – natural intervals within the melodramatic story of popular Hindi films – have been used as extraneous interludes that were alien to the development of the narrative, and hence foreign to the plot. This work intends to explore, via filmic text analysis, how song-and-dance routines, which punctuated the narrative of these films as the unaccented offbeats of secondary importance, have evolved over time. In addition, it is important to examine how such musical instances further the representation of *firang*iness[1] in Bollywood cinema; this article proposes an essential historical overview of this phenomenon.[2]

By looking at the past and more recent history of the representation of foreignness in popular Hindi cinema, this work will delineate a trend in the transformation of the representation of *firangi* and the filmic function these narrative instances fulfil in constructing and problematizing the identity of the *firangi*. This started in the 1950s, with the *firangi* as a fetishized transgressive vamp, then progressed in the 1960s to the creation of the 'masked type' form of *firang*iness, and more recently saw the emergence of the redemption-seeking *firangi* type.[3] The aim is to address the sociocultural responsibility held by song-and-dance sequences to update the representation of *firang*iness in popular Hindi cinema. Beginning with a historical overview of salient song-and-dance sequences characterised by their contribution to the notion of foreigner and foreignness over time, the final part of this article will go on to evaluate more contemporary Bollywood songs-and-dances and the current rehabilitation of foreign bodies within the main narrative of the films. I also seek to establish which aspects of foreignness are pronounced and which are suppressed by song-and-dance sequences in recent Bollywood films, to further observe images of 'tailored' foreignness. I will engage with theoretical notions of human geography and specifically with the idea of Michel Foucault's heterotopia alongside filmic text analysis, in order to explore the tension between 'domesticity' and transnationalism in these musical interludes.

By looking at heterotopia, the idea is to address the cultural position these filmic moments occupy, in light of the theoretical support that Foucault's notion offers; heterotopic spaces are defined by the author as 'other spaces' where individuals have little or no intelligible connection with the larger context in which these spaces exist (Foucault 'Of Other Spaces' 25). This notion thus upgrades our interpretation of song-and-dance sequences as merely spaces of desire, to an understanding of them as spaces where *firang*iness is presented more conspicuously. Such an approach seeks to add another layer of complexity to what Sangita Gopal and Sujata Moorti write about such musical intervals. Song-and-dance sequences are socio-political realities and aesthetic experimentation in between realism and utopia (Gopal and Moorti 5). In this light, this article wishes to respond to the following research questions: How have song-and-dance sequences presented the idea of *firangi* across time? Are song-and-dance sequences instances within the narrative that are capable of articulating and feeding specific negative stereotypes while unpacking our understanding of *firang*iness in Bollywood films? To answer these questions, I will be looking at specific song-and-dance performances from the 1950s and 1960s that best typify representation of *firang*iness. By looking at the song-and-dance routine in popular Hindi cinema, the aim is to explore the evolution of these melodic spaces as subversive interventions that enable the representation of *firangiyon* (foreigners) in the filmic text.

Variations on the theme of *firang*iness: Initial annotations

The mingling of traditional traits with the flavour of other international aspects has heavily influenced popular Hindi films and the song-and-dance sequences within them (Gopal and Moorti 4). As Sangita Shresthova reminds us, the use of songs and dances as narrative tools to communicate instances of untold stories and sentiments is part of Bollywood's worldwide appeal (6). The fame of songs working independently from the films they originate in, and their transformation and re-appropriation into broader social contexts as part of discourses on fandom activism (Jenkins and Shresthova), have seen these narrative tools span beyond the film texts themselves and have enabled them to pervade other sociocultural dimensions even beyond the boundaries of India. It is because of this fragmentation – the partial detachment from the original filmic text and shift into new contexts and forms – that these song-and-dance sequences are characterised as having 'ubiquitous dispositions' (Gopal and Moorti 2). Much in the same spirit, Jayson Beaster-Jones writes, specifically with reference to Bollywood songs, that such instances are 'written for moments in the narrative that communicate a complex of musical and extra-musical information' (35). My intervention in this field aims to deepen the understanding of the malleability inherent in these musical intervals, at a cultural level. Hence, the films that have been selected for the analysis in this article matter for three reasons. Firstly, they are recognisable texts, which are important as they testify distinct historical moments in the evolution of song-and-dance sequences in popular Hindi cinema. Secondly, they demonstrate how song-and-dance sequences have a specific function within the narrative of the film. Thirdly, they go beyond the common understanding of song-and-dance sequences as moment of escapism and serve to highlight the filmic function they have in defining foreignness. As such this article will use four films as case studies, to construct and problematise the identity of the foreigner. The films are *Howrah Bridge* (1958), *Gumnaam* (1965), *Love Aaj Kal* (2009) and *Rang de Basanti* (2006). It is therefore important to think about song-and-dance sequences as responsible elements that are able to inform multiple dimensions of a culture and formulate, through an analysis of gestures and movements, the semantics of a society in which modernity and tradition often clash. I suggest that song-and-dance sequences should be regarded as germinal spaces and important 'malleable elements' of a Bollywood film able to instigate new discourses on representation and articulations of *firang*iness.

In an article on Bollywood cinema and its relationship with the West, and the representation of the 'other', Vinay Lal (1998) describes the impossibility for 'outsiders' – what I am framing here as *firangi* – to be an integral part of modern Hindi films; Lal writes:

> There has never been any true outsider in the commercial Hindi film, although as the demands of the ethos of the Indian nation continue to supersede the ethos of Indian civilization, and the boundaries of inclusivity continue to shrink, the outsider will finally have found a place in Indian society. If and when the popular Hindi cinema shows a keen awareness of the outsider, and gives the notion of the 'other' an ontological sanctity, we shall have irreversible proof that in India as in the underdeveloped West … the project of modernity has been, in this most resilient of civilizations, rendered complete. (Lal 233)

However, the problem that Lal's work presents is that of the generalisation of the notion of the foreigner, which lends itself to a more detailed study of the subject. The author explores otherness across diverse films, providing a rather broad idea of the foreigner – pictorialised as the 'universal other' – which does not take into account the geographical, cultural, historical and social connotations of a foreign body. In this light, the objective of my work is, along with expanding the body of literature on this subject, to call for a break from the generalised view of the West and the foreign as the ultimate 'other', which song-and-dance sequences have conveyed until now. This work aims to reappraise the existing argument on the representation of 'otherness' (Kishore, Savwal and Patra) in Indian cinema. Beyond this, it will also move beyond the confines of a dualistic approach – realism or utopia – that framed song-and-dance sequences historically. In this regard, I will propose a third framework for the understanding of these sequences, in order to propose a third dimension: the heterotopic. The aim is to encourage the reading of foreign specificities, overtaking generalisation. In doing so, the intention is to propose a wider critical appreciation of *firangi*ness through the study of its evolution across a variety of song-and-dance sequences. These musical instances within the narrative of the film need to be studied as the filmic components able to shape representations of foreignness in popular Hindi cinema. In order to formulate a renewed frame of interpretation of the filmic index of changing representation of *firangi*, I propose to theoretically engage with the notion of heterotopic spaces, articulated by Foucault.

Heterotopia: The spaces of crisis

Heterotopia is a notion elaborated by French philosopher Michel Foucault that is largely applied to the discipline of human geography. The prefix 'hetero' from the Greek word héteros (meaning other, another and different) is joined with the term 'topia' (meaning spaces); this produces the meaning of 'other space'. Heterotopia is a space where things are different, a space within which individuals exist but have little or no comprehensible connection with one another. The French philosopher used the term to talk about spaces belonging to the human experience that exists outside of utopian and dystopian dimensions. Heterotopian spaces are described as being gaps where *otherness* exists, and functions at physical, psychological and social levels (Foucault, *The Order of Things*; Foucault and Miskowiec). The examples that Foucault proposes are the moment of a phone call or our experience of looking at ourselves in the mirror, writing further that,

> The mirror functions as a heterotopia … it makes this space that I occupy at the moment when I look at myself in the glass at once absolutely real, connected with all the space that surrounds it, and absolutely unreal, since in order to be perceived, it has to pass through this virtual point which is over there. (Foucault, 'Of Other Spaces' 232)

Such an account formulates a complex way of thinking about what is real, and of distinguishing between what is unreal or utopic and what is perceived and accepted.

A space, Foucault explains, plays an important role in framing the presence that bodies have within a specific context and thus the social and cultural value they have in it ('Of Other Spaces' 238). Foucault, defines categories of heterotopia to place these human aspects into perspective. The author highlights that we are still exposed to specific oppositions and defined boundaries, producing a multitude of meanings; such meanings are defined by both the 'bodies' inhabiting these spaces and by their mutual relationship with the overall context. Within the broader discourse that engages with the performance of foreignness in song-and-dance sequences within and beyond Bollywood films, some of these boundaries need to be reviewed. In the process of decoding the 'foreignness' within the diegetic spaces of song-and-dance sequences in popular Hindi films, the interpreting becomes a complex process of cultural reassessment. In order to study such a new relationship, it is important to look at how heterotopias, and broadly heterotopian spaces (which are here referred to as spaces of the song-and-dance sequences within which foreign bodies exist), are able to inform the dynamics of identity formation.

Heterotopia, Foucault reminds us, is a real place, which branches out from a known space (Foucault and Miskowiec 24). Within this frame, sites such as a zoo are examples of heterotopias, as these spaces assemble 'bodies' that are not usually found together. In this article, the spaces of songs and dances, wherein foreignness is embedded, are to be read within the theoretical frame of heterotopia, that is, the moment when foreignness is 'allowed' and even accepted as part of what I would like to dub here 'spaces of crisis'. Song-and-dance sequences are not only moments that break the linearity of the narrative, or insertions of dream-like moments; these sections of the films are also moments of transgression that are suspended and discontinuous from the story. Examples of such transgressive moments are the strategically placed item numbers featuring 'item girls', who were provocative and often foreign. The foreign item girls were used to create an opposition with the idealised moral universe evoked by the plot of the film, and to arouse erotic pleasure on the part of the target audience (Kishore 145). Hence, these interruptions should be studied as spaces of rupture within the narrative, where traditional moral codes are in crisis. Within these set parameters, it is worth interrogating the existence of foreign bodies within popular Hindi films, specifically looking at how such bodies (with their non-Indian traits) are enabled to perform their foreignness.

In 'Of Other Spaces', Foucault argues that heterotopic spaces, in their natural and unusual relationships with other places, suspend, neutralise and reverse the relationships that a particular space has established and constructed with a body and the certain knowledge of the context to which that body originally belongs. Thus, in light of such spatial functions, it is important to evaluate the representation of foreignness transmitted through song-and-dance sequences to observe the historical shift and the cultural signification that these bodies have acquired over time.

Song-and-dance sequences within Bollywood films are observed in this article as borderline spaces in which heterotopias of crisis and deviation form a space of suspension and redefinition of human possibilities and acceptability. Within this theoretical frame, song-and-dance sequences such as 'Mera Naam Chin Chin Chu' in *Howrah Bridge*, 'Jaan Pehechaan Ho' in *Gumnaam*, 'Masti Ki Paathshala' and 'Khalbali' in *Rang de Basanti* and 'Twist' in *Love Aaj Kal* function as germinal spaces in which the evolution of representations of *firangi*ness in popular Hindi cinema can be re-read.

From exotic Helen to 'twisting' blondes: The dancing *firangi* bodies

The use of foreign bodies in Indian cinema to depict heroines, who would present a different kind of personality from the positive, moral rectitude of Indian women, dates back to the origins of this cinema (Acciari, 'Theorizing Liminal Cinema'; Gehlawat; Thomas). After the independence of India, rather than liberalising film censorship, the newly reconstituted Central Board of Film Censors (now Central Board of Film Certification) tightened the control on what should be seen and accepted (Mishra 184). Post-independence, the nationalist project worked to create a unique and renewed Indian identity that by moving away from the colonial past, sought to uphold tradition and morality (Kishore). The industry was faced with emergent representational strategies that would see women being used as positive role models, without sacrificing other pleasures for the audience (Devasundaram 49). With the aim of upholding traditional values via the use of women as symbols of the nation, the Hindi film industry began deploying foreign characters who would provide a contrast with the Hindi heroines and clash with the notion of the woman as muse; this character was the vamp often represented by over-westernised women or non-Indian actresses. It is in the paradigmatic moment of song-and-dance sequences that the performance of foreign bodies contrasts most markedly with those of the Indian heroines. While for the heroine, the song-and-dance sequences were tailored to be integrated and legitimised in the narrative of the film, the foreign bodies were often items of crude entertainment distant from the syntagmatic narrative. In such a display, the disposable bodies of the foreigners had the central purpose of soliciting and intensifying voyeurism. As analysed further, song-and-dance sequences, which employed foreign actresses, led to the emergence of a specific representation and decoding of the West and the production of a series of characteristics that have formed a potential archive of knowledge on *firangi*ness.

The most prominent of the *firangi* bodies of the 1950s and 1960s that needs to be remembered here as being crucial to the evolution of *firangi*ness is the 'flirtatious' Helen, who appeared as an item dancer in numerous Bollywood films. Helen, trained as a cabaret dancer and of Franco-Burmese descent, was defined as the temptress and exotic item dancer contrasting with the positive image of Indian women in the films of this period and throughout the 1970s (Pinto 7–10). Among the notorious song-and-dance sequences that remain connected to Helen is 'Mera Naam Chin Chin Chu' in the film *Howrah Bridge* (1958), which illustrates the eclecticism of a woman who defied the rules of gender in an era when the Bollywood scene was dominated by Raj Kapoor, Dev Anand and Dilip Kumar and, in the 70s, by Amitabh Bachchan. The film is a concoction of mystery and suspense that sees Ashok Kumar as Prem determined to recuperate the family jewels and bring the killers of his brother to justice. The action is interspersed with songs that include an element of attraction and sub-plots (Vasudevan) that break up the narrative and introduce new narratives, which, Lalitha Gopalan claims, constitute a system of interruption. Gopalan argues in fact that 'the most persistent narrative form found in Indian popular cinema includes several interruptions bearing a more or less systematic relationship to the narrative' (19).

In the 'Mera Naam Chin Chin Chu' song-and-dance sequence Helen moves through a variety of looks that range from the perfect East Asian lady wrapped in a fitted cheongsam to a Western woman in a sailor dress, thus showcasing and outlining a variety of identities that define a new set of traits of foreignness. The sequence starts with four men dancing and playing with a small ball; Helen, dressed in an East Asian outfit, dancing and snapping her fingers, runs down the stairs to join the playful group. This early image is cut with other dancing East Asian ladies within a context that has the flavour of post-war indulgence. Helen, with a series of vibrant and hopping steps, changes partners before falling into the arms of one of them, only to finally shy away from him again. Helen moves fluidly across the scene, bouncing between the arms of her various male partners, openly declaring non-commitment.

In a frenetic and whirling final moment, Helen completes her dance in the arms of various partners, between whom she moves intermittently; the game of taking a partner and leaving him builds up a sense of desire and inaccessibility that occurs only within the brackets of a song-and-dance sequence; desire is otherwise unrepresented and improbable within the main narrative of the film. This song-and-dance sequence is composed of a series of gestures, foreign aesthetic features and compositional steps that form, through the interaction of the dancing bodies, a dialect of acceptance and rejection, of closeness and distance that powerfully layers the image of the foreigner in Bollywood cinema. The creation of such an archive of gestures and attributes clashes with the compass of the moral universe that the heroine of the film normally embodies, in which an idealised identity of the nation is underpinned by a fetishisation of chastity. In this light, it should be remembered that these kinds of song-and-dance sequences are arbitrarily inserted and stitched together within the main narrative of the film, but resolve and propel the narrative in crucial ways (Gopalan 67). Helen's vamp persona lends to the reading of foreignness as an (in)accessible body; she is accepted within the body of the filmic text but detached from the actual narrative, thus becoming an accessory item. This image is constructed through the continuous borrowing and re-adaptation of material from non-Indian vocabularies of gesture and expression in Bollywood films.

The borrowing and re-working of Western gestures into popular Hindi cinema were developed further in the 1960s. The culture of 'club songs' has produced an emblematic and problematic representation of the foreigner. While a recognised definition still needs to be formalised and codified, the 'club song' genre finds its climax in 'Jaan Pehechaan Ho' in *Gumnaam* (1965). While being interpreted by the Indian performer Laxmi Chhaya, the song strongly refers to the swinging London of the 1960s and American club culture. The dancers, who are wearing Western-style clothes, gyrate frenetically at the centre of the room, creating a spectacle of Western youth culture. While other song-and-dance sequences are usually sonorous interpolations with recognisable Indian beats and narrative function, the 'offbeat' club songs here are suspended from the narrative, offering no commentary on the characters or storyline. The club songs, while acknowledging the musical youth culture of the 1960s, also created imaginative access to fantasies of the West, in which a specific definition of the foreigner is embedded: that of perdition, liberalisation and transgression. The representation of the foreigner in the 1960s appears to change in form: Indians now wear a mask to achieve a certain degree of foreignness and transgression; however, foreignness is still presented with specific connotations – that of the negative *firangi* (Harris) and the vamp. 'Jaan Pehechaan Ho' is set in a club and, when the doors open, the audience is taken from the outside world into the foreign, permissive world inside the club. The camera moves towards a group of masked men and then moves towards a masked girl in a golden lamé dress, with an aesthetic reminiscent of the 1960s. The frenetic sounds of the drums, guitars and brass ensemble match the dancers' syncopated movements, who sway to the beat of Westernised music. Masked and unrecognisable, the Westernised bodies in the film are not only deprived of an identity but they are also confined to the underground club: a space and world that is in itself alien and foreign. 'Jaan Pehechaan Ho' does not fully serve the purpose of the narrative of the film, but it is able to build a suspended – heterotopic – moment, where the bearers of foreignness are updated from being represented as vamps and seducers, to being empty and anonymous presences extraneous to the narrative. The song produces a variation of the image of the foreign – the masked type – through the Westernisation of the performance. The costumes, the black masks the dancers use to obscure their identity, and the presence of the band Ted Lyons and his Cubs – an Indo-American band that played in some 1960s Bollywood films and was inspired by the Beatles – all make for a performance of the foreign West.

While films of the 1950s and 1960s have offered the opportunity to reflect on the strategies used to represent *firangi* bodies with specific negative connotations, the exploration of more recent films will reveal how such representations have evolved. In addition, the idea is to look at what happens when the *firangi* elements are placed within the narrative of the film, and how the role of song-and-dance sequences is transformed in such a scenario. While the 1950s and 1960s have offered a model of *firangi* representation, more recent films have provided an opportunity to explore other representations of the same phenomenon. An example of a more recent representation of *firangi* bodies in Bollywood cinema is proffered by the film *Love Aaj Kal* (Imtiaz Ali, 2009), an Indian romantic comedy starring Saif Ali Khan as Jai, Deepika Padukone as Meera and English model Florence Brudenell-Bruce impersonating Jo. The film presents a love triangle that sees Jai living in London with Meera. They are a happy couple; however, believing in different values the couple split, and while Meera returns to India and to her former Indian love Vikram (played by Rahul Khanna), Jai remains in London to later pursue his American Dream and move to San Francisco to find employment in the city. Once in the US, he begins dating Jo, a blonde, foreign woman whom he meets in a disco. The song entitled 'Twist', during which the protagonist is invited by an African-American man to join a party that is redolent of an urban burlesque setting show, is the moment when Jo and Jai meet. Reaching the disco-club, the music is irrepressible and young dancers from mixed ethnic backgrounds dance to the rhythm of 'Twist'. Invited by one of the girls of the dance troupe, Jai begins dancing among a large group of Western women, twisting and imitating the movements of the dancers. The camera moves into a nightclub, where a man dressed as a magician and a few women wearing blonde wigs and sequinned black dresses look at Khan mischievously. Heading towards a balcony in the disco-club, he is seen looking at the crowd, while a close up of Jo with a glass in her hand reveals her character approaching the dancing mob. The two protagonists' eyes meet and, in an energetic dance, they rejoice to 'twist' together. Jo walks away and meets Jai in a dark room but, once they are together, she runs away again, building once more a dialectic of attraction and rejection, of accessibility and dismissal. It is only in the darkness of the room that their bodies touch and they look passionately into each other's eyes. This confines a series of flirtatious moments to the context of the dance; since the space remains that of the disco-club, the love between Jo and Jai has sprung up in a context of excess and transgression. Evading the possibility of a kiss, Jo breaks away from their passionate embrace at the edge of the club's balcony and runs away again, only to be recaptured and held to dance and twist again with him. The song's lyrics continue:

Sone Mone Malla Malli Kar Gaye Talli Aankh Waank
Se Lad Gayi, Haan Lad Gayi
Bottle Shottle Kholi Bina
Daaru Shaaru Bin Peethe Hi
Chad Gayi, Haan Chad Gayi
(Beautiful woman, let me drink with her eyes
She's hooked me, yes I'm hooked
The bottle, without opening it
The wine, without drinking it,
I'm still drunk)[4]

While everyone is dancing and moving, the couple meet and become intoxicated by one another. Following a few more energetic moments and a range of people twisting their bodies through dance and acrobatics, the couple stops and walks away from the crowd, hinting at the need for intimacy and solitude. The song 'Twist' is an important moment of reflection on the representation of foreignness. Twist suggests a moment of transgression that moves away from the conventions of a linear life and love encounter; Jai and Jo meet in the darkness of a disco-club – a twist on the convention of courtship in traditional Bollywood cinema, but evidence of an increased permissiveness since 2000. The selection of the Twist as a melodic and dancing style recalls the 1959 American style – the Twist – that historically was understood to be provocative, audacious and rebellious (Knowles). 'Twist' in *Love Aaj Kal* recreates the spirit of rebellion that permeated the 60s as well as a degree of nostalgia for those times. The convergence of these cultural elements bonds the representation of Jo to the well-established grammar of the foreigner; the song-and-dance sequence in 'Twist' adds, literally, a twist to the boy-meets-girl dynamics, where the love story begins in the dark, underground setting of the disco-club. The blonde seducer of dubious morals is later unable to belong firmly to the narrative of the film as a legitimate and accepted body (Kishore); the relationship between Jo and Jai is a forbidden relationship – Jai will return to Meera later in the story – and their relationship is shrouded in the darkness and dubious morality of a nightclub. Although Jo is embedded within the narrative to a greater extent than one might have expected of a firangi in the 1950s and 1960s, happiness is beyond her reach. Though the representation of *firangi*ness might have come some distance, such characters are still prevented from being fully integrated. This is reinforced by the fact that Jo's song-and-dance routines are most frequently located in a nightclub setting, which is itself reminiscent of the type of locations in which *firangi* characters would be most often found in the 1960s.

While the *firangi*ness of Jo is now included within the story, and yet connected to the representations of the 1960s, a further variation on the theme of how song-and-dance sequences produce a pattern of representation on *firangi*ness is seen in *Rang de Basanti* (2006). The plot narrates the story of British *firangi* Sue (Alice Patten), a filmmaker who moves to India to produce a documentary based on her grandfather's diary on Indian freedom fighters. In India, she meets a few new friends and the university student 'DJ' (Aamir Khan). Blonde-haired and blue-eyed, Sue falls in love with DJ, but their love, which includes pre-marital sex and passion, soon comes to an end without 'naturally' transforming this liaison into a recognised and socially accepted engagement. This becomes evident during some of the song-and-dance sequences. In one such sequence, Sue and DJ dance to the lyrics of 'Masti Ki Paathshala' whilst on a night out on a university campus. The song lyrics issue an invitation to be a rebel, to transgress the boundaries of a life made up of duties and rules. While there is a duality to University life, in that these institutions could be seen either as spaces of order or of youthful experimentations, it is the latter that is emphasised here. The lyrics '*Apni toh paathshala masti ki paathshala*', which translates as 'our school is a school of fun', suggests a subversive spirit, which is also evident in the final lyric that calls on the students to 'lose control'. This invitation to let go of the prefixed rules of society provides the perfect backdrop to the flirtation between DJ and Sue, who is lured by his personality. The song's lyrics run:

> Chehre ki kitaabein hai
> Hum woh padhne aate hai
> Yeh surat teri meri
> Mobile library
> Yaaron ki equation hai
> *Love multiplication hai*
> Jisne dilko jeeta hai
> *Woh alpha hai theta hai* (x3)
>
> (We come here to read the faces
> Which are books for us
> The face of you and me
> A mobile library
> There is equation of friends
> Where love is multiplied
> The one who has won the heart
> That is alpha and theta.)[5]

DJ looks at Sue and invites her to join him in a dance that is punctuated by sexually explicit gestures of pleasure and that articulates a performance of their feelings and their vulnerable relationship. This type of public acknowledgement of sexuality clashes with the norms of representation in traditional Bollywood cinema and underlines the extent to which their interracial relationship steps beyond the conventions of Indian society. Far from being a melodramatic and escapist moment of visual pleasure, as other authors have argued (Gopal and Moorti; Sen) of similar melodic intervals in comparable films, this sequence instead stresses the possibility for rupture that song-and-dance intervals offer within the main narrative of the film. The sexualised transgression of DJ and Sue are not set aside to allow for the spectacle of the dance but instead are underscored by both the lyrics and the performances.

Sue clearly forges for herself a unique place as a *firangi* woman within the landscape of contemporary Bollywood. She is embedded within the narrative in a way that was impossible in the 1950s and 1960s. Unlike Jo in *Love Aaj Kal*, she achieves a level of acceptance within DJ's family but does not surrender her disruptive potential or her agency. In this sense, she represents something new and can be thought of as the ultimate evolution of the *firangi*, operating within, whilst also unsettling traditional Indian society.

However, despite these accomplishments she is still denied her happy ending and, as with Jo, ultimately remains an outsider. DJ dies at the radio station as a martyr for the nation, while Sue is prevented by a human barrier from reaching him. She is deprived of the possibility of saving him, loving him or dying with him. This clearly reasserts the position occupied by foreign bodies in popular Hindi cinema, that of denial by traditional society. This does not undo the film's early work in differentiating her from the predecessors of the 1950s and 1960s, it is important to note that foreign bodies are still exiled from the main narrative of the film.

During the aforementioned songs from *Rang de Basanti*, the friends in the group hardly acknowledge DJ and Sue; the couple is left to 'multiply their love' – 'Love multiplication hai' – creating space within these filmic musical instances for their love to blossom. Song-and-dance sequences are heterotopic spaces and a metaphorical cocoon of foreignness, within which, in this case, DJ and Sue's relationship – an interracial liaison – has the opportunity to exist. DJ dances around Sue who, standing immobile, is wound up by the provocative dance of DJ; as a 'rebel', DJ interweaves the language of love and affection with that of desire and passion. Much in the same way, in the song-and-dance sequence 'Khalbali Hai Khalbali' – 'there is commotion' – DJ is dancing with his friends while Sue watches them with a camera in her hand. Just a moment later, when Sue joins in the collective dance, DJ pulls her close to his body and, after a few slow movements and eye contact, they end up kissing, suspended in a heterotopic moment while the rest of their friends continue dancing unconcerned.

This second song-and-dance sequence, 'Khalbali Hai Khalbali', is composed of images of the college friends intercalated with images of their rebellious alter egos during their struggle for freedom. Sue and DJ's kiss and passionate defiance of convention rebelliously challenge the social norms of a traditional society, where *firangiyon* are often depicted negatively (Harris). The repertoire of gestures is enriched to include the explicit expression of sexual desire that not only involves lascivious glances but also draws on an evolving vocabulary of movements: the composition of the dance exudes sensuality and mimics the rhythms of sexual intercourse. While *Rang de Basanti* began a process of rehabilitation of the *firangi* within the entire narrative of the film, both 'Khalbali' and 'Masti Ki Paathshala' song-and-dance sequences have built an exclusive space. DJ and Sue are allowed, where the 'taboo of interracial relationship is broached in strategies and subterfuges' (Joshi 41), to exist within the story and yet, at the same time, to be suspended, as if in a capsule, away from what is traditionally acceptable within the plot of the film. Song-and-dance sequences constitute, in harmony with Foucault's heterotopia, the space where an individual whose characterisation is deviant or divergent from the main context is placed within the story, in order to achieve a representation of a balanced and normalised society. Song-and-dance sequences in *Love Aaj Kal* and *Rang de Basanti*, the most recent films discussed in this article, have built a window of opportunity to rehabilitate *firangiyon*. Jo is allowed to exist within the story, but more than this her entrance in the film is accompanied by the song-and-dance 'Twist', which evokes the moral abandonment and rebellion of the 1960s, providing a nostalgic and legitimised representation of *firangiyon*. The *firangi* Sue, on the other hand, goes one step further in that she is presented as a decent, generous and fair individual who is able to integrate into aspects of local society, at least until the film's final act, which denies her a happy ending in accordance with the ethics of Indian films of the past. The degree of Sue's acceptability within the narrative is higher than her *firangi* forebears. Sue presents the image of a positive girl; she speaks Hindi, is accepted by DJ's mother, is ashamed of her colonial history and seeks redemption through her grandfather's diary. In the song 'Masti Ki Paathshala', Sue is portrayed timidly clapping her hands, while at the beginning of 'Khalbali hai Khalbali', she is seen sitting on the floor watching her friends as they dance, swaying to the beat of the music in a way that is acceptable to traditional Indian standards. These sequences form a heterotopic moment – of detachment and suspension – distinct from the main narrative of the text in which foreignness is often rejected. In spite of hinting at the acceptance of the *firangi* within the narrative, Sue and DJ are only able to live their romance within song-and-dance sequences. Hence, although they have been allowed into the plot, the *firangi* still suffer from a limited sense of integration; while song-and-dance sequences have constructed a habitat for their existence, they have not entirely removed the strictures of the past.

The role that song-and-dance sequences have played in depicting and defining the presence of foreign bodies and more broadly foreignness in popular Hindi cinema has changed considerably over time. From being modes of presenting a negative character or extraneous and alien presences within the filmic text, to exploring the modern diametric opposite of the traditional Hindi woman, song-and-dance sequences have facilitated the formation of patterns of representation of foreignness in popular Hindi cinema. Such models have seen the application of the mechanism of suspension from the narrative and from the filmic context, and the generation of specific portrayals of the *firangi*. While looking at Helen enabled us to think about a series of traits belonging to the *firangi* (which is not necessarily the *gori*), Sue and Jo have uncovered a depiction of the *firangi* that still connects with some level of transgression and otherness, of acceptance and rejection, of openness and closeness from and to the main narrative of the film.

Conclusion

Looking back at Foucault's heterotopic spaces, song-and-dance sequences can be read as a system that opens and closes the connection with the whole narrative – the Foucaultian surrounding – of the film within which the image of the *firangi* is constructed. These moments of interruption created since the beginning of the 1950s and 1960s an imaginary order, constructing a system of crisis with the main narrative of the film, which underlines the mere existence of *firangi* romance and social acceptability essentially within song-and-dance sequences.

These moments of the narrative were able to temporarily fix what was socially unacceptable. Song-and-dance sequences as heterotopic spaces within the narrative enable foreign bodies to be articulated, deferring their social value in favour of a more liberated approach. Song-and-dance sequences are germinal moments able to resolve, within the film, the unresolvable issue of foreignness as *firangi* bodies by defining their role in the film and the space they can occupy in the story. While Gopalan describes song-and-dance sequences as 'delaying the development of the plot, distracting us from the other scene of the narrative through spatial and temporal disjunction and bearing an integral part of the plot' (19), this article has taken a different approach. These sequences are not only moments of suspension in the development of the main narrative, but are also generative spaces in which the multiple possibilities of *firangi* representation can be unfurled.

Bollywood song-and-dance sequences house the tension between the inner and outer scenarios of modernity that the main narrative is unable to accommodate, thus becoming spaces of crisis; specific traits of foreignness are coded within the main text and given expression within song and dance, as 'joyous moments of cultural approval' (Sen 89). More than being a fundamental aspect of the narrative of Bollywood cinema, song-and-dance sequences have acted as moments of mediation and social 're-negotiation' of what is appropriate and what is not within the society. In this regard, the example of Helen is emblematic; she was a foreign body exploited for voyeuristic pleasure, without playing significant roles in the films, and yet the song-and-dance sequences in which Helen appeared were moments of decodification and permission for a certain identity to be performed and accepted. In these roles, we see a further development of this trend mentioned in the character of Jo, who enters the plot of the film from the dark space of a night club (codified as an alien and foreign place in the 1950s and 1960s where *firangi* could exist) to love Jai and perform the ritual of foreignness by a nostalgic dance of rebellion. Sue in *Rang de Basanti* represents another evolution in the language of foreignness; she is allowed into the story to unfold 'historical' redemption. Her performance within 'Masti Ki Paathshala' and 'Khalbali' permit the protagonist to passionately love DJ; however, it should be added that the story of Sue and DJ takes place within the frame of the socially 'secure' space of the university, where complicity dominates the relationship of the group of friends in the story. To conclude, in the films of the 1960s, *firangi* were embedded in alien performances, meaning a complete separation from the plot and with song-and-dance sequences acquiring the status of 'double interruptions' – from the narrative and from what is acceptable. In more recent films, while the plot has accommodated *firangi* within the story, presenting a reformed portrayal of the foreigner that is now permitted but not integrated into the plot, song-and-dance sequences remain reminders of their *firangi*ness. The affirmation of this status, at spatial, temporal and representational levels, has enabled these musical interruptions to the story to become places of Foucaultian heterotopia – of possibility – for the cultural relocation of foreignness in popular Hindi cinema.

Notes

1. The use of the word *firangi* in this article links to the work of Jonathan Gil Harris (2015). He traces the history of the term *firangi,* highlighting that the word originates from the French *franc*, which later turned into the Arabic *ferenji* before reaching its current avatar *firangi*. This word, Harries explains, broadly meant anyone who came from a Christian country, and it is often used in a derogatory manner. In this light, the terms *firangi* and *firangi*ness in this article are used to expose cultural implications of foreign bodies that express pejorative perceptions of social status.
2. The term Bollywood has been well known for a long time; although it has been used in a broad sense for decades as a generic term to describe the commercial Hindi film industry, it is now also a branding term that represents popular artistic productions from India. I limit my usage of the term to refer to the post-1990s popular Hindi cinema industry.
3. The premise behind the development of this theme – the spaces of song-and-dance sequences as being capable of constructing an image of foreignness in Indian cinema – has its origins in my personal experience as a film scholar working on the impact of Bollywood in Italy (Acciari, 'Indo-Italian Screens and the Aesthetic of Emotions' 1–269). Back in 2007, I spent an extensive period of time in Rome, conducting fieldwork and extended interviews alongside participant observation of South Asian communities, in order to gather data regarding the settlement, migration history and film-going practices of these communities. I took part in a local dance-group and attempted a few Bollywood steps through the Apsaras Dance group, led by Italian Valentina Manduchi, a Roman dancer who found, through her school, the means to travel to India to both continue studying and establish working contacts with the popular Hindi cinema industry.
4. The translation of the song is not a word-for-word transliteration but rather gives its gist.
5. The translation of the song is not a word-for-word transliteration but rather gives its gist.

Acknowledgements

I would like to express my deepest gratitude to the organisers of the symposium "The Evolution of Song and Dance in Hindi cinema" for inviting me to be part of this event at Sonoma State University in 2017. I am also indebted to my colleagues at the symposium for their insightful comments on improving my manuscript. I would also like to thank Anugyan Nag for his encouragement and intellectual stimuli. My profound gratitude goes to Professor Justin Smith and Dr. Matthew Jones for their invaluable support and advice in polishing this manuscript, and last but not least, a special thanks to the Cinema and Television History (CATH) research centre at De Montfort University, for funding my trip to the USA and supporting my research in this area.

Disclosure statement

No potential conflict of interest was reported by the author.

References

Acciari, Monia. "Indo-Italian Screens and the Aesthetic of Emotions." PhD thesis, University of Manchester, 2011. Print.

Acciari, Monia. "Theorizing Liminal Cinema: Unsettling the Transnational Spaces of Italian Indian Co-productions." *Journal of Italian Cinema and Media Studies* 4.3 (2016): 387–402. Print.

Beaster-Jones, Jayson. *Bollywood Sounds. The Cosmopolitan Mediations of Hindi Film Song*. New York: Oxford University Press, 2015. Print.

Devasundaram, Ashvin Immanuel. *India's New Independent Cinema: Rise of the Hybrid*. London: Routledge, 2017. Print.

Foucault, Michael. "Of Other Spaces." *The Visual Culture Reader*. Ed. Nicholas Mirzoff. Second. London: Routledge, 2002. 22–27. Print.

Foucault, Michael. *The Order of Things*. 1st ed. London: Routledge, 1989. Print.

Foucault, Michael, and Jay Miskowiec. "Of Other Spaces (Review)." *Diacritics* 16.1 (1986): 22–27. Print.

Gehlawat, Ajay. "The *Gori* in the Story: The Shifting Dynamics of Whiteness in Bollywood." *Twenty-First Century Bollywood*. New York, NY: Routledge, 2015. 66–87. Print.

Gopal, Sangita, and Sujata Moorti. "Introduction." *Global Bollywood*. Ed. Sangita Gopal and Sujata Moorti. Minneapolis, MN: University of Minnesota Press, 2008. 1–60. Print.

Gopalan, Lalitha. *Cinema of Interruptions*. London: Oxford University Press, 2002. Print.

Gowariker, Ashutosh. *Lagaan: Once Upon a Time in India*, 2001. Film.

Harris, Gil Jonathan. *The First Firangis: Remarkable Stories of Heroes, Healears, Charlatans, Cortesans and other Foregners who Became Indian*. Delhi: Aleph Book Company, 2015. Print.

Jenkins, Henry, and Sangita Shresthova. "Up, Up, and Away! The Power and Potential of Fan Activism." *Trasformative Works and Culture* 10.2 (2012). Accessed June 2017. http://journal.transformativeworks.org/index.php/twc/article/view/435/305

Joshi, A. Sarah. "Transgressing the Moral Universe Bollywood and the Terrain of the Representable." *Bollywood and its other(s): Towards New Configurations*, Ed. Vikrant Kishore, Amit Sarwal, and Parichay Patra. Basingstoke: Palgrave Mcmillian, 2014. 41–54. Print.

Kishore, Vikrant. "Bollywood Vamps and Vixens: Representations of the Negative Women Characters in Bollywood Films." *Transgressive Womanhood: Investigating Vamps, Witches, Whores, Serial Killers and Monsters*. Ed. Manon Hedenborg-White and Bridget Sandhoff. Oxford, UK: Inter-Disciplinary Press, 2014. 141–152. Print.

Kishore Vikrant, Amit Savwal, and Parichay Patra. *Bollywood and its Other(s): Towards New Configurations*. New York, NY: Palgrave MacMillan, 2016. Print.

Knowles, Mark. *Tap Roots: The Early History of Tap Dancing*. London: McFarland, 2002. Print.

Lal, Vinay. "The Impossibility of the Outsiders in Modern Hindi Films." *The Secret Politics of Our Desires: Innocence, Culpability and Indian Popular Cinema*. Ed. Ashis Nandy. London: Zed Books, 1998. 228–259. Print.

Mishra, S. "Negotiating Female Sexuality." *Belly Dance Around the World*. Ed. C. McDonald and B. Sellers-Young. Jefferson, NC: McFarland and Company, 2013. 181–196. Print.

Pinto, Jerry. *Helen: The Life and Time of a H-Bomb*. London: Penguin, 2006. Print.

Sen, Biswarup. "The Sounds of Modernity: The Evolution of Bollywood Film Song." *Global Bollywood: Travels of Hindi Song and Dance*. Ed. Sangita Gopal and Sujata Moorti. Minneapolis, MN: University of Minnesota Press, 2008. 85–104. Print.

Shresthova, Sangita. *Is It All About Hips? Around the World with Bollywood Dance*. London: Sage, 2011. Print.

Thomas, Rosie. "Not Quite (Pearl) White: Fearless Nadia, Queen of the Stunts." *Bollyworld: Popular Indian Cinema through a Transnational Lens*. Ed. Raminder Kaur and Ajay J. Sinha. London: Sage, 2005. 35–69. Print.

Vasudevan, Ravi. "Bombay and Its Public." *Journal of Arts and Ideas* 1.29 (1996): 45–66. Print.

Filmography

Salaam-E-Ishq. Dir. Nikkhil Advani. Orion Pictures, 2007. Film.
Love Aaj Kal. Dir. Imtiaz Ali. Eros International, 2009. Film.
Kites. Dir. Anurag Basu. Reliance Entertainment, 2010. Film.
Rang De Basanti [Colour It Yellow]. Dir. Rakeysh Omprakash Mehra. UTV Motion Pictures, 2006. Film.
Gumnaam [The Unknown]. Raja Nawathe, 1965. Film.
Howrah Bridge. Shakti Samanta, 1958. Film.

Kehte Hain Humko Pyar Se Indiawaale: Shaping a contemporary diasporic Indianness in and through the Bollywood Song

Sangeeta Marwah

ABSTRACT

In a contemporary moment rife with cultural reciprocation and symbolized by exaggerated hyper-mobilities, Indianness in general and diasporic Indianness in particular is constantly subject to redefinition and reinvention. Even as the Bollywood song's cinematic fate remains open to speculation, its ability to transcend barriers of space and language, and its near-universal accessibility lend it a unique cultural currency, affording diasporic audiences a space for collective identification. Whether through formal practices, such as dance and fitness classes, or more informal interactions such as wedding performances, appropriation of the song becomes, for the diasporic Indian, a convenient tool for asserting both cultural allegiance and difference even as song themes targeting the diaspora impart a vision of their own that is often grossly exaggerated. Through a combination of primary fieldwork, content analysis and secondary research, this article seeks to understand how the Bollywood song shapes a diasporic Indianness and, in turn, gets shaped by it. My emphasis is on analyzing the diaspora's relationship with the song and the song's potential for diasporic identity negotiation.

> Not burdened by the compulsion to memorialize the nation, this population's consumption of Hindi film songs is radically different from that of their parents. Creatively cutting and mixing elements from Bollywood song and dance clips, they parse their identity as difference within discourses of multiculturalism.
>
> Sangita Gopal & Sujata Moorti (36)

> Looking back, I think it was in watching Hindi film songs and dances that a world of cultural mixing first welcomed me into its midst. In the remorseless blending of movement sources and costume styles, I found a messy, yet appealing, reflection of my own scattered identity.
>
> Sangita Shresthova (xiii–xiv)

Indian Prime Minister Narendra Modi's exuberant Silicon Valley address in 2015 was, perhaps unsurprisingly, preceded by an energetic Bollywood song-and-dance routine performed by the Mona Khan Company, a dance school that offers classes throughout the San Francisco Bay Area. Unsurprising, because the Modi government's rhetoric has consistently advocated the vision of a 'global India' and because Bollywood cinema and its music have, over the past decade alone, come to occupy an undisputed position as globally acknowledged measures of Indianness. Carefully selected songs (a mixture of folk and patriotic music) such as 'Chak De India' (*Chak De! India*, 2007), 'Rang De Basanti' (*Rang De Basanti*, 2006) and 'Indiawaale' (*Happy New Year*, 2014) offered a nationalistic prologue to the Indian leader's entry on stage. For the globalized and digital vision of India that Modi espouses, the Bollywood song-and-dance, in all its modernized glory, emerges as the perfect cultural accompaniment. The song-and-dance's own trajectory of modernization is a direct consequence of the reforms that have transformed the country's economy. Accompanying the widespread economic transformations that neoliberalism introduced to India in the early 1990s was a drastic makeover of the Hindi film industry that, among other changes, significantly updated its production standards. These changes, naturally, extended to Hindi film music as well, transforming it from a mere cinematic construct with debatable narrative functionality to a unique marketing device and an exportable artifact with significant cultural value, especially in the diaspora. What I refer to as the neoliberal song is, thus, essentially a temporally derived construct that started appearing toward the early 2000s that is distinguished from its pre-liberal counterpart through its updated, stylized formal attributes, including both its music as well as its visuality.

The Bollywood song-and-dance today is globally lauded as a cultural icon and as a distinctive marker of contemporary Indianness. Perhaps one of the most tangible transformations in the song's consumption is the unprecedented scale and innovation of its cultural appropriations, especially by diasporic audiences. From dance schools offering intensive choreographic education in a formal, institutionalized setup to collegiate acapella groups competing at the national level, the Bollywood song-and-dance is now a universally acknowledged and celebrated feature of diasporic life in North America and in other nations across the world. In this article, I explore the neoliberal Bollywood song's updated capacities to affect identity negotiation among first- and second-generation diasporic subjects through targeted content and the subsequent emergence of an ancillary cultural industry that promotes an active appropriation of the song as a tool toward the exploration of diasporic Indianness. Employing postcolonial hybridity as a referential framework, I analyze the song's contemporary diasporic appropriations to locate within them traces of identity-construction processes at work and the factors influencing these processes. I argue that the song's contemporary hybridity affords a 'liminal' space of identity construction for diasporic audiences, which is imagined as ethnically ambiguous, even as it raises concerns about authenticity (Bhabha 212). The neoliberal song's text, clearly updated to attract diasporic interest, represents a convenient and easily accessible site for cultural introspection and assertion, while the recent institutionalization of its performative practice in the diaspora attempts to authenticate it as a genuine purveyor of Indian culture. Adopting an ethnographic mode of inquiry, I analyze information such as kinship networks and gender roles in the diaspora to arrive at a better understanding of how the generations of diaspora and the conditions of migration influence diasporic interactions with the Bollywood song (Niyogi 4).

Contemporary hybridities

While hybridity in the Hindi film song and dance is not an entirely new phenomenon, its modernized version, merely by virtue of the collaborations and amalgamations inherent, is a particularly compelling advertisement for cultural fusion. The product of a cinematic form, the nomenclature for which reveals its own hybridized inspirations, the contemporary Bollywood song is a 'dense node of signification' that carries, palimpsest-like, within its layered form the lingering imprints of its eclectic influences (Gopal and Moorti 5). Hybridity, in the song, by lending it a distinct global feel, has radically extended its appropriation in the diaspora. From musical style to visual elements, just about every aspect of the film song now reflects its heightened awareness of the global (and specifically the diasporic), that manifests most often in the form of a fast-paced, club number with high-energy vocals as opposed to the ubiquitous love ballad that was once Hindi cinema's signature offering. 'Hinglish' lyrics, Western-style choreography with a lineup of synchronized background dancers and an MTV-esque esthetic characterize all club numbers which typically tend to gain more popularity, and persevere far longer in the public imagination, than the movies they originate within.[1]

What about the song makes it so amenable to being appropriated as a culturally representative artifact by the diaspora, especially by second-generation migrants, many of who have never even been to India? Its intrinsic hybridity provides a clue. Biswarup Sen writes:

> Bollywood song is the product of a practice that has been characterized by a radical openness to externalities and a consistent engagement with cultural production elsewhere. This strategy has led to the creation of an astonishingly rich and vibrant art whose aesthetic force derives from its radically heterogeneous nature. Incorporating musical styles from the world over, filmigit [film song] possesses a structure of feeling that is emphatically transnational. (Sen 85)

From jazz to rock and from folk to hip-hop, there's something in the Bollywood song to cater to almost every musical taste and the song has continuously evolved to reflect its forever-changing sociocultural context employing, for instance, a more colloquial Hinglish lyrical vocabulary as opposed to conventional Urdu poetry. In its contemporary avatar, the song's characteristic hybridity is a rather distinct incorporation of eclectic, largely Western, musical influences, layered on to colloquially derived lyrics and featuring elements of 'Indian' instrumentation (*sitar*, *tabla*, *harmonium* etc.). The end product is an (often) appealing mélange of the old and the new, the vernacular and the global that attracts an amplified resonance across diverse audience groups. Hybridity is also evident in the song's visuality as depicted through diverse dance forms and thematic inspirations. Choreographed songs, especially, provide abundant opportunities for recreating performances, which open up spaces for audience participation. The decline of the conventional love ballad has further paved the way for choreographed songs with participative potential as a modernizing society relinquishes the cinematically sanctioned space of the song video to enact their conjugations (Gopal *Conjugations*). Thus released from this role, the song is free to either retreat to the soundtrack or to embrace its non-diegetic avatar as a purely choreographed sequence. Finally, technological innovation has made unprecedented instantaneous access to the song's video a reality, thereby inspiring a spate of ancillary offerings in the diaspora which include dance and fitness classes, themed parties and corporate events, concerts and award shows, and wedding choreography. As Bollywood infiltrates diasporic culture like never before, multiple contact zones open up for these audiences to interact with the song both formally and informally thereby affirming the latter's status as an emphatically visible marker of diasporic cultural identification.

Postcolonial scholarship on the concept of hybridity caters to a revisionist paradigm in cultural studies, which involves a move from essentialisms (such as race, gender, class etc.) and polar binaries to a focus on the identity-creation processes that emanate from the 'ruptures in prevailing cultural modes' (Linke and Moller 30). Rooted in the relationship between the colonizer and the colonized, Homi Bhabha's conceptualization of hybridity evokes a 'third space of enunciation' which acts as a potential site of subversive expression even as it provides a safe space for identity negotiation (5, 56). By problematizing essentialist constructions of culture and nationalities, 'hybridity has the potential to allow once subjugated collectivities to reclaim a part of the cultural space in which they move' (Yazdiha 36). Diasporic hybridity, in particular, bridges the divide between the culture of origin and the host culture, affording diasporic subjects the ability to create, and negotiate, consistently evolving identifications (Linke and Moller 30).

My interest lies in finding out how the song, as a hybrid cinematic product, and the diaspora, as a hybridized audience group, interacts with each other to produce transitional identities that are reflective of the latter's highly individualized cultural experiences. Furthermore, I am intrigued by the hybridity evident in the contemporary appropriations of the song in diasporic spaces which reveal the intensity of the diasporic desire to acculturate with the dominant culture as much as to hold on to a relevant interpretation of their originary cultural traditions.

Diasporic appropriation and its discontents

Kinship networks, which at this stage translated to parental authority, and the demographic density of the migrant population in the diaspora determined in large part the relationship that my second-generation respondents shared with the Bollywood song during their formative childhood years. Almost all the second-generation respondents I interviewed between 2014 and 2016 spoke of the 'old' Hindi songs their parents would either watch or listen to, music that most of them steered clear of in an attempt to erase a visible marker of their difference from the dominant culture. Deepali, the daughter of Bengali immigrants from Calcutta, grew up in a small, overwhelmingly white, town in South Dakota with just three other Indian families. Her parents, both ('anti-social', 'conservative') professors, consistently nudged their two daughters toward the classical arts, shunning Hindi cinema and its music as lowbrow cultural forms. Deepali's hybridized identity, further complicated as a result of marriage to a first-generation immigrant and subsequent motherhood, was frequently evoked through the articulation of her interactions with Bollywood songs. Her exposure to contemporary Bollywood music and its social manifestations was strongly imbued with the cultural influences derived from her upbringing:

> When I got married, my sister-in-law really wanted to play Bollywood songs at my wedding but having not grown up around any of that I was almost like borderline offended, like why would she think that I would want to do that… but everyone else wanted to do that…2-3 years later one of our couple friends told me it was like the best wedding they ever attended and it's because of Bollywood [music].

In the absence of any direct familial engagement with the Bollywood song-and-dance during her formative childhood and teenage years, Deepali's associations were solely derived from their formal attributes: she associated 'happy' songs such as 'Paint it Red' (*Zindagi Na Milegi Dobara*, 2011) with an up-tempo track and vocals, and 'haunting' songs such as 'Mere Haath Mein' (*Fanaa*, 2006) with evocative, meaningful lyrics. An examination of the corresponding music videos reveals imagery that conveys a similar essence – the former is a youthful anthem celebrating the joy of life and friendship, while the latter is a romantic ballad that signifies the consummation of the lead couple's relationship.

In sharp contrast to Deepali's narrative of growing up on a self-inscribed cultural periphery was that of Sneha's, a Gujarati woman in her mid-thirties who runs a motel with her husband in Santa Cruz, CA. Sneha's parents emigrated from Africa and the United Kingdom, and her experience of Indian pop culture was as comprehensive as Deepali's was fragmentary, even though both grew up in prominently white towns. Deeply impacted by a childhood (and teenage years) resonant with the presence of the Bollywood song-and-dance, Sneha articulated vivid memories of songs from *Qayamat Se Qayamat Tak* (Mansoor Khan, 1988), *Maine Pyar Kiya* (Sooraj R. Barjatya, 1989) and *Saajan* (Lawrence D'Souza, 1991) which were largely limited to a recollection of their appropriation by her family. Her early interactions with the Bollywood song-and-dance were so entrenched in the cognitive and emotional associations of its appropriations that each time she cited a particular song-and-dance through the course of the interview she expressed in detail the nuances of her own interaction with it:

> It's that song 'Ek Ladki Ko Dekha' – that song in particular always stands out to me as being a very, very sentimental song and so that's also the one I walked down the aisle to at my wedding. And so that song I love – I think it's got a lot of meaning to it.

Significantly, though, Sneha's detailed reminisces did not extend to the neoliberal song-and-dance. She left home for college around the same time that liberalization started making its impact felt in Bollywood' cinema. As a result, her interaction with Bollywood songs changed from a familial appropriation to a peer-influenced consumption that was less emotionally involved and, like Deepali's experience, derived more from the song's formal characteristics.

Importantly, for both Sneha and Deepali, the impact of their kinship networks persevered from childhood to adulthood. Sneha's abundant exposure meant that even as a grown-up, she continued to participate in the occasional dance performance at a family wedding and expressed an earnest desire to introduce her children to Bollywood song-and-dance. Deepali, on the other hand, did not go beyond a casual listen, notably choosing to limit Bollywood song exposure to her own children and, like her parents, steering them toward classical music instead:

> Once they get really sleepy and they're almost sleeping and I put the lights off… I put on my Ipad with the Pandora and with Hindustani classical tracks going so that they're completely immersed in their brain… because music to me is like food, you can eat good food and you can eat bad food… you let them eat some bad food but I also want them to eat healthy.

Deepali's allusion to the neoliberal Bollywood song as 'bad food' was echoed by several other respondents I interviewed, both first and second generation. Concerns regarding the overt sexualization of song elements such as lyrics, choreography and its picturization were consistently attributed as reasons for its ostensibly low-culture status. Yet, the song's diasporic dispersion, and its appropriation, stand at unprecedented levels today.

For all the respondents I interviewed, the neoliberal song's characteristic hybridity greatly facilitates its appropriation in the diaspora by significantly diluting its indigenous distinctiveness while retaining just the right amount of Indianness, thereby extending its acceptance and appeal not just to diasporic audiences but also to non-Indians. Accessibility, and the diaspora's own heightened mobility, have eradicated the need for constant immersion in cultural products and experiences such that objects like the song cease to be artifacts of nostalgic remembrance and, instead, take on the liminality of the interstitial spaces that Bhabha talks about:

> Terms of cultural engagement, whether antagonistic or affiliative, are produced performatively. The representation of difference must not be hastily read as the reflection of pre-given ethnic or cultural traits set in the fixed tablet of tradition. The social articulation of difference, from the minority perspective, is a complex, on-going negotiation that seeks to authorize cultural hybridities that emerge in moments of historical transformation. (Bhabha 3)

Employing hybridity as a mere 'descriptive tool' runs the risk of both oversimplified generalization and theoretical ambiguity (Kraidy 317). More useful, and relevant, is the application of hybridity with a firm contextual and theoretical grounding that demonstrates an awareness of the politics surrounding the same (Kraidy 317). Since classifying any cultural form as 'pure' seems fallacious at best, especially in a globalized context, I refrain from getting into a debate regarding the song's hybridity as a formal construct. Instead, I take as given the musical and cultural amalgam that characterizes the final product and look at it as an accessible and inclusive site of cultural production that allows different generations of diasporic communities an opportunity to variously create and negotiate their unique versions of Indianness.

When describing the song as a facilitator of integrative acculturation, I reference John Berry's model (704), which organizes diasporic response to the dominant culture along a continuum of progressive adaptation. For Berry, a typical acculturative response employs one of the following four strategies: separation, assimilation, integration, and marginalization. These strategies emerge from two basic issues, which Berry defines as 'the distinction between (1) a relative preference for maintaining one's heritage culture and identity, and (2) a relative preference for having contact with and participating in the larger society along with other ethnocultural groups' (704–5). The Bollywood song's modernization can thus be regarded as enabling its diasporic audiences to move toward (2) while still maintaining (1).

While the older first-generation of migrants, in an obvious effort to desperately hold on to the values and memories of their native culture, practiced what may be termed as a 'separation' strategy of acculturation, their children, desperate to fit in the host culture, exhibited a classic assimilation response, the emphasis of which was on absorbing the dominant culture in its entirety. Unable to identify any potential sites of integration into the dominant culture and eager to erase the tags of difference that expressions of Indian culture lent them, they reacted by shunning everything Indian and, often, cultural products like the Hindi film song were the targets of choice. For these second-generation diasporic subjects, the neoliberal song's distinct hybridity and its enhanced accessibility offered, for the first time, an opportunity to openly engage with Indian culture. The newly modernized sound and look of Bollywood songs and their videos, especially those located within films with diasporic themes ('Say Shaava Shaava' and 'Bole Chudiyan' from *Kabhi Khushi Kabhi Gham*, for example) gave second-generation diasporics the opportunity to perform their Indianness in a more democratic manner, as opposed to the often-essentialized, high-culture forms of music and dance that their parents nudged them toward.

For first-generation diasporics, on the other hand, acculturation is not a defined process, split along neat lines of temporality, the way it is for second-generationers. Since most of my first-generation respondents moved out of the country after India's economic liberalization in the 1990s, their experience of the song in diasporic space has solely been with its neoliberal, hybridized version. The song's hybridity, for them, functions as a delineative boundary that defines the outer limits of authenticity where only a genuine, 'pure' Indianness is coded as authentic. The overt hybridities that characterize contemporary Bollywood songs, such as 'Saturday Saturday' (*Humpty Sharma Ki Dulhaniya*, 2013), 'Kala Chashma' (*Baar Baar Dekho*, 2016), 'The Humma Song' (*OK Jaanu*, 2017) etc., are seen as a dilution of an essentialist Indianness, despite their obvious affordance for a performative exploration of cultural identities. Further, my first-generation respondents were able to break down specific components of song production including its lyrics, video, choreography, background dancers etc. as all differently conveying a degenerative Western ethos that is seen as the polar opposite of a purist Indian tradition.

> Some of the songs, like the Honey Singh songs, the tune is very catchy. I want to sing that, [but] the words are so vulgar I don't feel like singing that in front of my kids you know. It's not something I would like to do. (Karishma, mother of twin boys, first generation respondent)

Singer Yo Yo Honey Singh is known for his provocative songs that often contain highly suggestive (and, sometimes, downright misogynist) lyrics yet, despite the social censure his work is subject to, he remains one of the most popular musical artists within and outside Bollywood. While Karishma, a first-generation respondent, originally from Gujarat, did not mention any specific Honey Singh songs by name, it was clear that she generally regarded contemporary, i.e. neoliberal, Bollywood music as a somewhat contaminated form that only showed occasional sparks of creative brilliance. She was especially vocal about her distaste for hybridized song remixes which she argued represented nothing less than an outright theft of original artistry. Another first-generation respondent, Shailja, seemed to share Karishma's views on the cultural bankruptcy of contemporary Hindi songs:

> What's so cultural about it? There's nothing in it—there's nothing Indian in it for me. It's as good as watching an American…[or] Bollywood—sorry… you know… videos. There's nothing cultural about that to me. I think she's wearing some flowing gowns and she has all those dancers in I think black outfits behind her and that's it. There's nothing cultural—Indian, Indian about it for me. (Shailja, describing the song 'Dhoom Macha Le' from the 2013 movie, *Dhoom 3*)

'Dhoom Macha Le' is the title song that features in the soundtrack of each of the three films from the *Dhoom* series (*Dhoom, Dhoom 2 and Dhoom 3*). In the style of most neoliberal Bollywood dance numbers the song, stylistically reinvented with each sequel release, is visually rendered as a glossy music video featuring the lead stars with an entourage of highly skilled background dancers. The song's Aesthetic is overwhelmingly Western as is apparent from the Hinglish lyrics, the costuming and the choreography. Shailja was especially troubled by the song's blatantly Western visuality, something she could not accept as reflective of Indian culture. 'Cultural', for her, is clearly coded as oppositional to Westernization (clothes, choreography, lyrics etc.) while culture, especially authentic culture, is coded as a ritualistic celebration of festivals or as an expression of patriotism. In her later responses, she also mentioned lyricization as yet another element that determines the cultural worthiness of a song for her. She mentioned songs such as 'Gandi Baat' (*R…Rajkumar*, 2013) and 'Ishqiyaun Dishkiyaun' (*Goliyon Ki Raasleela Ram Leela*, 2013) as examples of vulgar lyrics that went against the fabric of what she considered Indian culture.

Choreographic appropriation and cultural experimentation

In a similar vein, choreography also came across as an emphatic parameter of a song's expression or disavowal of Indianness. Songs with more folk-like or classical choreography were deemed as more deserving of the 'cultural' tag. Shalini, one of my first-generation respondents who has lived in the Bay Area for many years, mentioned the song 'Nagade Sang Dhol Baaje' (*Goliyon Ki Raasleela Ramleela*, 2013) as culturally appropriate in this context:

> So I think that's a *garba* style of song. That definitely, you know, appears more cultural than a song like—I don't know—Baby Doll for example that has nothing to do with (laughs)… so that does not… so yeah certain types, I guess you are right, certain types of dance would definitely connect to the culture.

'Nagade Sang Dhol Baaje' from the film *Goliyon Ki Raasleela Ram-Leela* (2013) is a traditionally conceptualized Gujarati song that features the *garba* style of dancing popular in the state. Reportedly, the film's director, Sanjay Leela Bhansali, brought over traditional *garba* dancers from Gujarat to preserve the cultural authenticity of the song's picturization ('Deepika Padukone Learning Garba for 'Ram Leela'', News18.com). 'Baby Doll' (*Ragini MMS 2*, 2014), on the other hand, is a racy, seductive song with highly suggestive, Western-style choreography featuring controversial actress Sunny Leone, a former porn star. It is, thus, clearly antithetical to Shailja and Shalini's views regarding culturally authentic content. As Shalini mentions in her response, choreographic style emerges as a major determinant of whether or not songs are perceived to be cultural or not, where culture is equated with traditional art forms. Importantly, the general impression that my first-generation respondents carried about songs and their cultural equity exhibited a clear divide between pre- and post-liberal India as far as Bollywood content goes. The 'newer' song-and-dances were almost universally perceived as less 'pure' and culturally reflective than the older ones.

Ironically, even as these first-generation migrants consistently decry the loss of legitimate representation in the Bollywood song, they continue to enthusiastically embrace its neoliberal hybridized form especially as an expression of collective identification. The mushrooming of an ancillary culture industry centered around the diasporic consumption of Bollywood including, but not limited to, dance and fitness classes (Mona Khan Company, Bollynaach etc.), Bollywood-themed parties (Jai Ho! Dance Parties, Bay Area Desi Party etc.), concerts and award shows (SLAM 2014, Dream Team Star Show, Rahat Fateh Ali Khan Tour 2015, IIFA awards etc.) is evidence of its hybridization at work. The Bollywood dance and fitness culture has infiltrated diasporic communities across the world but the San Francisco Bay Area, in particular, is inundated with multiple companies offering classes with varying levels of patronage and success. Attending these classes allows students, at a subliminal level, to enact their cinematic fantasies even as it becomes an accessible way to assert their cultural identity. As Ann David writes, the emergence of this enhanced diasporic culture of participation can be located in the diasporic subject's 'need to refresh and recast a sense of Indian identity through cultural (re)production' (217). She ascribes the diasporic desire to participate in cultural endeavors such as Bollywood dance as emanating from the mix of a fantasized longing for the glamor that film culture represents as well as a yearning for an Indianness that might be missing in daily diasporic lives (217–8). The song-and-dance's hybridization enables this desire, especially in diasporic space, by affording a more contemporized and accessible format.

This hybridization of the Bollywood song-and-dance, as it is appropriated by dance classes, is not restricted to an incorporation of Western elements alone. While, historically, classical and folk dance styles routinely made their way into song picturizations, the diasporic appropriation of the song has also now started integrating the classical and the popular as [a] unique new expressions of cultural experimentation. One of my first-generation respondents, a trained *kathak* dancer named Poorva, who had once performed as a background dancer for Madhuri Dixit in the song 'Kahe Chhed Chhed Mohe' from *Devdas* (2002), described the trend to me. Despite her formidable classical training under the legendary Pandit Birju Maharaj, Poorva had no reservations against Bollywood and claimed to have choreographed Hindi film songs for many wedding performances. Even though her own style was firmly in the classical realm, her ability to transcend the high-low cultural barrier between *kathak* and Bollywood dance represents a considerable shift in artistic approaches and the rising trend toward hybrid dance forms that incorporate the classical and the popular. Living 'away' in the diaspora she felt free to experiment with hybridized dance forms, which the Bollywood song allowed her to.

> But here—yes, because I'm free and it's my own world, I'm exploring other songs as well and these [Indian] reality shows, let me tell you, are making a big difference—this 'Dance India Dance' … you see the choreographers and all… you see even my staunch guru, like you know the believer in classical, and classical only—yeah, he's getting involved in movies now. I mean he has a list of so many, 5,6,8 movies that he's choreographing. So, of course I will be and it is definitely moving—shifting the whole way people were thinking of separating the classical from the Bollywood. I think there's this now—you know mix or sort of friendship that they're trying to accommodate both in each other and people of that industry.

Thus, while the hybridized Bollywood song functions as the creative impetus to experiment, the diaspora acts as a facilitator for such experimentation that is characteristic of its neoliberal avatar. The song's hybridity fosters such creative experimentation and facilitates this synergistic collaboration in a way that a pop culture form is granted a heightened respectability while a rigorous classical form becomes more approachable.

Bollywood dance classes in the diaspora, eager to benefit from such inter-mixing, are now, in an imitation of classical forms such as *kathak* and *bharatnatyam,* typically offered as a graded quarter/semester system where promotion to the next level depends on mastery of the previous one as demonstrated through evaluative auditions where students are taught a small choreographed piece and are expected to reproduce it almost instantly. This attempt to 'codify and formalize the way Bollywood dance is marketed and taught' is reflective of an attempt to gain authenticity and respectability for a cultural form that has historically been denigrated as commercial and 'impure' (David 219). Hybridity thus is re-marketed here as both modern and culturally authentic; countering assertions of Bollywood dance as generic and not professionalized is a newly developed system of evaluative examinations, performance showcases and instructor certifications.

As an extension of my ethnographic work, I opted to participate in a local dance class offered by the Mona Khan Company. The Bollywood songs chosen for the class were mostly contemporary numbers ('Kala Chashma', 'Humma Humma', 'Baby Ko Bass Pasand Hai') and typically remixed both to create fast-paced shorter edits more suitable for stage performances as well as to allow for merging together multiple song fragments. The corresponding dance styles ranged from Indian classical (such as *kathak and bharatnatyam*) and folk to mainstream Western styles such as hip-hop, contemporary, afro-jazz etc. Clearly, there is abundant hybridization at play both in the choice of songs and in their appropriation yet, as I observed over a year, the classes were almost overwhelmingly populated by first-generation migrants and it was their children who participated in the kids classes. This is in sharp contrast to responses garnered from my first-generation respondents who, for the most part, expressed no interest whatsoever in participating in a dance class and some of whom, in fact, bore an unmistakable condescension in their tone when questioned about the same.

Diasporic zones and gendered identities

The apparently contradictory attitudes that first-generation respondents exhibit with regard to the Bollywood song-and-dance and its appropriation are symptomatic of a larger debate about diasporic heterogeneity. The contrasting responses and behaviors of a seemingly homogenous audience sample are entirely explicable through a balanced consideration of the diaspora as a variegated demographic. Diasporic identities cannot be retrofitted into structured molds that categorize without contextualizing. Informed by aspects such as gender, class, generation of diaspora and condition of migration, they are more a derivative of the unruly interactions between people, products, and processes rather than of neatly assigned categorizations of cultural conduct.

In evoking theoretical frameworks that highlight the evanescence of cultural identifications, I reference the concept of unsettlement Purnima Mankekar refers to; cognizant of the 'slippages' inherent in the implementation of identificatory processes, she considers as explicative the meanings that emerge from the 'ruptures' that arise as a result of the intermingling of transnational and local public cultures, discursive texts and the audiences that produce and consume them (44). Indianness, she writes, is neither a stable construct nor is it entirely derivative of India as a fixed center; rather it is 'constantly re-produced, reinvented, and unsettled within India and in diasporic communities with varying relationships to India' (Mankekar 8). The contradictions and differentiations revealed through my ethnography point toward the fragmentary nature of diasporic identity creation.

To that end, I consider some of the 'diasporic zones' for identity production, which bear relevance specifically for first-generation diasporic women, as instrumental in the creation of these seeming contradictions. These include their gendered roles as homemakers and perpetuators of tradition, the diasporic space as 'home' and the notion of collective identification with other diasporic subjects. Essentialist notions of Indianness can also be seen as emerging from certain fixated perceptions of gender and sexuality that, despite being the undesirable derivative of a patriarchal society, are critical to constructions of nationhood in diasporic space. Therefore, a reproduction of national culture in the diaspora is contingent upon the representation of a 'heteronormative', controlled 'sexuality', at least for the dominant diasporic population (Mankekar 738). Having spent a substantial part of their lives in India, the first-generation women of my sample all articulated the careful cultivation of a virtuous femininity as intrinsic to a preservation of their Indianness. Expectedly, the most strident criticism of inappropriate cultural influences came from mothers of daughters.

One of my first-generation respondents, Shilpa, is a Sindhi woman married to a Tamilian man; both hail from small towns near the south Indian city of Chennai. Shilpa was extremely vocal about her distaste for certain kinds of contemporary Bollywood songs ('item numbers'), which she equated both with female objectification and cultural degeneration.

> They [item songs] make no sense. Like it is itemizing a woman, objectifying a woman. Why would you do that and the videos are terrible that's why I tell you that I don't let my children watch those movies. A lady dancing in the middle and men trying to grab her, that doesn't give a good picture… 'Chikni Chameli' and what was it? 'My name is Sheila, Sheila ki Jawaani'… maybe as a parent I've stopped liking those songs, maybe I would've liked them when I was

> younger but yeah now it's totally unacceptable. Even the lyrics—like my daughter sings and I'm like shhh…No.

Shilpa's response illustrates her equivocation of Indian culture with its popular forms; her scathing critique of the Bollywood song as sexist and denigrating seemed to reaffirm her larger opinions regarding the unworthiness of practicing Indian culture in its inauthentic contemporary form. Importantly, she admits to viewing cultural products, such as the song, through the lens of parenthood (specifically the responsibility of a young daughter) that, as I mention above, is a critical gendered influencer for cultural interactions.

Shailja, whose responses I included earlier in this paper, also vocalized similar concerns regarding her daughter's upbringing. To highlight the difference between a 'good' (traditional choreography and costumes) and 'bad' (mechanical dance movements and suggestive costumes) songs, she used two item song examples: 'Ghaghra' from *Yeh Jawaani Hai Deewani* (2013) and 'Ram Chahe Leela' from *Goliyon Ki Raasleela Ram Leela* (2013). The former, featuring veteran actress Madhuri Dixit, was coded as graceful and relevant (even though Dixit was the progenitor of risqué, suggestive choreography as epitomized in songs such as 'Dhak Dhak Karne Laga' from *Beta* (1992) and 'Choli Ke Peeche Kya Hai' from *Khalnayak* (1993)) while the latter, with Priyanka Chopra (arguably, Bollywood's most successful transnational actress) was seen as obscene and improper. In her own words, Shailja expressed the contrast between the two performances as follows:

> And she's [Dixit] good at it. It just—it was as if the song is just being made for her you know. And she did it very gracefully. You know as compared to Priyanka's song which was more like you know—there it's all about exercises for me. So definitely songs have come a long way. It's the language, it's the dance… And the clothes—the outfits. So everything has changed over a period of time.

Significantly, there is nothing essentially Indian, per se, about the 'Ghaghra' song other than, perhaps, Dixit's costume. She has a brief cameo as a prostitute wooing a man much younger to her in a red-light district. The song's lyrics are a hybridized Hindi-English and the choreography, while restrained, has definite elements of seduction woven into it. Shailja's assessment of the song then seems to be influenced more by Dixit's persona as a yesteryear's popular actress, belonging to a time when things were widely considered simpler and less 'corrupted aka westernized', as well as an allusion to the folk-like rhythm of the music. The other song, 'Ram Chahe Leela' begins with a shot of Priyanka Chopra, attired in a diaphanous two-piece white outfit, mimicking actions of emerging from a bath. She pretends to dry her hair with a scarf and then proceeds to suggestively tuck the scarf into the waist of her pants. This is the part Shailja took greatest objection to, because of the influence, she claimed, it had on her young daughter:

> Okay… my daughter is still small, she's just 3 years old and she sees that Priyanka song. The other day I actually saw her trying to [*motions the gesture of actress in song tucking a towel into the waist of her dress*] So she's trying to put it here and put this scarf in her pants and I'm sure she didn't know what she was doing. She didn't know what she was doing… so, yes the songs are not for the better you know.

The contradictions and ironies inherent in these responses are not necessarily reflective of opinions, attitudes and beliefs derived from ostensibly stable constructs such as nation, diaspora or even gender; rather they emerge from the chaotic and often incoherent mélange that characterizes identity construction in a globalized, hyper-mobile and postmodern world order. As societies evolve, as cultures assimilate, and as technologies advance, audiences consistently innovate to appropriate cultural products in ever-new formats, both toward a negotiation of their own conflicted identities, as well as for making larger statements regarding collective identifications and mobilizing action toward a social response. The globalization of indigenous cultures, which facilitates their appropriation in this manner, also simultaneously draws criticism for a perceived dilution of a tradition-bound authenticity. For a popular form such as the Bollywood song, which concurrently inhabits multiple discursive sites and increasingly becomes the cultural hook for audiences within the nation and beyond it, in search of an elusive cultural connection or perhaps a mere platform for staging a counter-hegemonic viewpoint, this is a particularly slippery slope to negotiate. Yet, as the increasing subsumption of the indigenous into the popular as well as the institutionalization of Bollywood dance demonstrate, it is not only possible to integrate the traditional with the modern, but also to present the modern in a format that is capable of an authentic cultural dissemination without recourse to 'pure' traditional forms.

Conclusion

From scattered interactions in sequestered spaces to a widespread presence in daily life, the Bollywood song's diasporic engagements today have taken on a radically revamped form. Propelled by the forces of globalization and neoliberalism, the contemporary Hindi film song-and-dance permeates mainstream diasporic culture as a visible and dominant cultural artifact that affords a divergent set of meanings and appropriations to first- and second-generation migrants. Further, as an assertion to its recent popularity that derives, in significant part, from an enhanced choreographic potential, the song is increasingly making its way into a mainstream Western culture, primarily through dance performances. As Bollywood continues to maintain a focus on its primary target audience – the Indian transnational and diasporic youth – and as a globalized world continues to shrink cultural distances between national populations, the song's future travels will likely attract an ever-growing patronage through its varied appropriations and remediations.

Similar to Prime Minister Modi's enduring vision to modernize India and firmly entrench it into the world economy, the Bollywood song-and-dance seems to be on a relentless modernizing mission of its own that most visibly entails its perpetuation as a cultural icon capable of enforcing its own meanings. Audience groups, especially those located in the diaspora, respond by experimenting with reinvented appropriations that facilitate identity negotiations. In a more informal context, whether it is through festival celebrations or weddings, the song's diasporic presence continues to intensify. While both academic scholarship and journalistic writing on the subject have recently questioned the song-and-dance's survival in Hindi cinema, its overwhelming popularity in the diaspora makes a compelling case for its strengthening legacy as a purveyor of contemporary Indianness.

Note

1. Some examples of this are: 'Blame the Night' from the 2014 *Holiday: A Soldier is Never Off Duty*, 'Sau Tarah Ke' from the 2016 *Dishoom* and 'Tamma Tamma Again' from the 2017 *Badrinath Ki Dulhaniya*

Acknowledgments

I would like to thank the editors of this journal for their helpful comments and suggestions regarding this paper. I want to extend a grateful thanks to all the women who graciously participated in my research study. I also want to thank my advisor, Priya Jaikumar, for her constant support and guidance.

Disclosure statement

No potential conflict of interest was reported by the author.

References

Berry, John W. "Acculturation: Living Successfully in Two Cultures." *International Journal of Intercultural Relations*. 29.6 (2005): 697–712. Web. 19 Dec. 2016. <https://doi.org/10.1016/j.ijintrel.2005.07.013>.

Bhabha, Homi. *The Location of Culture*. London: Routledge, 1994.

"Deepika Padukone Learning Garba for 'Ram Leela'". *News18* 24 Sept. 2012. Web. 17 June 2017. <http://www.news18.com/news/india/deepika-padukone-learning-garba-for-ram-leela-511046.html>.

David, Ann R. "Dancing the Diasporic Dream? Embodied Desires and the Changing Audiences for Bollywood Film Dance". *Participations* 7.2 (2010): 215–235. Web. 22 Sept. 2015. <http://www.participations.org/Volume%207/Issue%202/PDF/david.pdf>.

Gopal, Sangita. *Conjugations: Marriage and Form in New Bollywood Cinema*. Ed. Kindle. Chicago: The University of Chicago Press, 2011. 7 Jul. 2012.

Gopal Sangita, and Sujata Moorti. *Global Bollywood: Travels of Hindi Song and Dance*. Minneapolis: University of Minnesota Press, 2008.

Kraidy, Marwan M. "Hybridity in Cultural Globalization." *Communication Theory* 12.3 (2002): 316–339. Web. 16 Dec. 2016. <https://doi.org/10.1111/j.1468-2885.2002.tb00272.x>.

Linke Gabriele, and Hartmut Moller. "Towards a Trans-national Indian Identity? Versions of Hybridity in Bollywood Film and Film Music." *Zeitschrift für Anglistik und Amerikanistik*. 57.1 (2009). 4 Sept. 2016. doi:https://doi.org/10.1515/zaa.2009.57.1.27.

Mankekar Purnima. "Brides Who Travel: Gender, Transnationalism and Nationalism in Hindi Film." *Positions* 7 (1999): 731–761. Web. 16 Dec. 2016. doi:https://doi.org/10.1215/10679847-7-3-731.

Mankekar Purnima. *Unsettling India: Affect, Temporality, Transnationality*. Ed. Kindle. Durham, NC: Duke University Press, 2015. 4 Sept. 2016.

Niyogi, Sanghamitra. *Crafting Identities: Ethnic Incorporation of Two Sub-Groups Among Asian Indians in the San Francisco Bay Area*. Diss., U. California Davis, 2010. ProQuest Dissertations Publishing, 2010. 15 Dec. 2017.

Sen, Biswarup. "The Sounds of Modernity: The Evolution of Bollywood Film Song." *Global Bollywood: Travels of Hindi Song and Dance*. Minneapolis: University of Minnesota Press, 2008. 85–104.

Shresthova Sangita. *Is It All About Hips? Around the World With Bollywood Dance*. Thousand Oaks, CA: Sage, 2011.

Yazdiha, Haj. "Conceptualizing Hybridity: Deconstructing Boundaries through the Hybrid." *Formsssssations: The Graduate Center Journal of Social Research* 1.1 (2010): 31–38. Web. 21 Dec. 2016. <http://academicworks.cuny.edu/cgi/viewcontent.cgi?article=1338&context=gc_pubs>.

Filmography

Baar Baar Dekho. Dir. Nitya Mehra. Dharma Productions, Excel Entertainment/Eros International, Fox Star Studios, 2016. Film.

Beta. Dir. Indra Kumar. 1992. Maruti International, 2007. DVD.

Bunty Aur Babli. Dir. Shaad Ali. Yash Raj Films, 2005. DVD.

Chak De! India. Dir. Shimit Amin. Yash Raj Films, 2007. Film.

Dabangg. Dir. Abhinav Kashyap. 2010. Arbaaz Khan Productions/Shree Ashtavinayak Cine Vision Ltd., 2010. DVD.

Dabangg 2. Dir. Arbaaz Khan. 2012. Arbaaz Khan Productions, 2013. DVD.

Devdas. Dir. Sanjay Leela Bhansali. 2002. Mega Bollywood Pvt. Ltd., SLB Films, 2009. DVD.

Dhoom 3. Dir. Vijay Krishna Acharya. 2013. Yash Raj Films, 2014. DVD.

Goliyon Ki Raasleela Ram-Leela. Dir. Sanjay Leela Bhansali. 2013. Bhansali Productions/Eros International, 2014. DVD.

Happy New Year. Dir. Farah Khan. Mumbai: Red Chillies Entertainment/Yash Raj Films, 2014. Film.

Khalnayak. Dir. Subhash Ghai. 1993. Mukta Arts, 2009. DVD.

Rang De Basanti. Dir. Rakeysh Omprakash Mehra. 2006. Rakeysh Omprakash Mehra Pictures/UTV Motion Pictures, 2007. DVD.

Tees Maar Khan. Dir. Farah Khan. Hari Om Entertainment Company, Three's Company Production & UTV Motion Pictures, 2010. Film.

Yeh Jawaani Hai Deewani. Dir. Ayan Mukerji. Dharma Productions/UTV Motion Pictures, 2013. Film.

The picture is not yet over!: The end credits song sequence in Bollywood

Ajay Gehlawat

ABSTRACT
The end credits song sequence is a recent Bollywood innovation which has emerged in the twenty-first century. Such sequences are increasingly featured in contemporary Bollywood films and can be described as a component of the (preceding) film which also functions independently of it, both internally and externally. Unlike the more conventional, 'Hollywoodesque' outtakes and bloopers that occasionally accompany a film's end credits, the Bollywood end credits song sequences display increasingly choreographed and autonomous song and dance numbers, often featuring additional guest performers. This article explores the make-up of the end credits song sequence and how it specifically relates to the (preceding) film. Through a close examination of a selection of such sequences, starting with those of the original *Dhoom* (2004) and its accompanying sequel (2006), I will examine how the end credits song sequence functions in multiple innovative ways within the film. In the process, this article develops a more nuanced understanding of both the contemporary Bollywood film and the particular role that song sequences now play both within and outside of it.

The end credits song sequence is a recent Bollywood innovation which has emerged in the twenty-first century and which distinguishes this film form from others in a global mediascape. These sequences – one of the first of which appeared in the end credits of *Dhoom* (2004), featuring Thai singer, model, actress, and dancer Tata Young performing an alternative version of the title track in English – are increasingly featured in contemporary Bollywood films and can be described as a component of the (preceding) film which also functions independently of it, both internally, i.e. as a reflexive coda, and externally, as a detachable item which, like the filmic song sequences, circulates among multiple diffuse networks, e.g. YouTube et al. The emergence of these sequences in Bollywood films of the twenty-first century indicates the 'growing trend', in which Hindi film songs 'compete in a globalizing mediascape with diverse genres of popular songs – no longer just music scenes within films, but also music videos that are packaged on websites and television alongside the latest pop videos' (Dutta 235–36). Unlike the more conventional, 'Hollywoodesque' outtakes and bloopers that occasionally accompany a film's end credits, Bollywood end credits song sequences display increasingly choreographed and autonomous song and dance numbers, often featuring additional guest performers.[1] In this article, I would like to explore the make-up of the end credits song sequence and how it specifically relates to the (preceding) film. Through a close examination of a selection of such sequences, starting with the ones from *Dhoom* and its accompanying sequel, as well as those featured in other films, including those of Farah Khan and Maneesh Sharma, I will examine how the end credits song sequence functions in multiple innovative ways, including as remixed reprise, as epilogue, as bonus item, and as a compensatory device for the parallel diminution of song sequences within the film. In the process, this article will develop a more nuanced understanding of both the contemporary Bollywood film and the particular role that song sequences now play both within and outside of it.[2]

If, Tejaswini Ganti notes, 'to those unfamiliar with popular Hindi cinema [aka, Bollywood] song sequences seem to be ruptures in continuity', then they are mistaken, as the song, 'rather than being an extraneous feature … define[s] and propel[s] plot development' (*Bollywood* 91–2). Ganti goes on to claim that the 'skill' of the writer or director is based on 'how well the song situations are integrated into the screenplay' and notes that 'a lack of integration is considered 'sloppy', 'lazy', or simply bad filmmaking' (*Bollywood* 92). Such a sentiment is reaffirmed by other theorists of popular Hindi cinema, including Shoma Chatterji, who even describes the item number – the sequence 'usually introduced as a distinct entity unto itself and unrelated to the story of the film or its characters' – as 'embedded into' the film (233, 248). Kush Varia similarly describes 'the Bollywood song' as being 'embedded within the wider film structure' (41). Such theorization provides an interesting point of entry for the end credits song sequence which is inherently extraneous and yet can, in some cases, still function as a coda to the narrative or as a reprise of key themes. If 'some scholars have described the popular [Hindi] film as operatic', then one might liken the end credits sequence in some ways to an encore (Ganti, *Bollywood* 92). Nevertheless, what is crucial to note is that the end credits song sequence challenges the very premise of the dominant paradigm concerning the song's relation to the larger film, in many ways making such 'integration' a moot point, coming, as it does, *after* the film has concluded. Before exploring the epistemology of such a moment in further detail, however, let us first examine a series of actual end credits song sequences from recent Bollywood films.

Dhoom Dhoom

The series of *Dhoom* films began in 2004 with the first offering, directed by Sanjay Gadhvi, starring Abishek Bachchan, Uday Chopra and John Abraham. The film, which went on to become one of the top-grossing hits of the year, features a series of song and dance sequences, including 'Dhoom Machale', sung by playback singer Sunidhi Chauhan, who went on to win the Zee Cine Award for Best Playback Singer of the year for her rendition, while the song itself garnered the Zee Cine Award for Best Track of the year. At the end of this action film, Bachchan and Chopra, who play police officers Jai Dixit and his sidekick Ali, walk off in a long shot while discussing the bumbling Ali's potential promotion. As they walk away, the film segues to the end credits sequence featuring Tata Young who performs 'Dhoom Dhoom', a remixed version of the earlier 'Dhoom Machale' song, substituting not only Young's voice for Chauhan's but also predominantly English lyrics for what were previously Hindi lyrics. The sequence features Young in a canted rectangular frame within the larger image, in which she dances and cavorts in turn with the film's three male leads even as, outside this canted box, the end credits roll. Along with predominantly English lyrics, this version features more vocoding than the original version and is listed on the DVD song menu as 'Dhoom Dhoom (End Credits)'.[3] This end credits version, along with the added vocoding, different singer and changed lyrics, is shorter than the earlier version featured in the film and also appears in a full-screen version as a special feature on the DVD. Interestingly enough, an additional special feature included on the DVD is an alternate ending to the film, featuring a recurring theme from the film, namely Ali accepting bribes and Jai catching him in the act and then chasing him. After this brief sequence plays on the DVD's special features, a caption appears onscreen, claiming that this original epilogue to the film was subsequently excised. Though not explicitly stated, one can assume that it was removed in favor of the 'Dhoom Dhoom' end credits song sequence which now ends the film.

The follow-up to *Dhoom*, *Dhoom:2* (2006), also directed by Gadhvi, again features Bachchan and Chopra in their earlier roles along with Hrithik Roshan and Aishwarya Rai as the new thieves. Like its predecessor it was an enormous box-office success, in large part due to its numerous song and dance sequences, beginning with the opening credits sequence, 'Dhoom Again (i)', featuring Roshan, an actor known for his dancing prowess, performing an item number with a troupe of background dancers while the opening credits appear onscreen.[4] Interestingly enough, while the original version of the 'Dhoom' song in the first film was primarily in Hindi, the first version here, sung by Vishal Dadlani, features predominantly English lyrics and (thus) no subtitles. As in the first film, there is a segue at the film's conclusion – this time more abrupt – to an end credits sequence, 'Dhoom Again (ii)', featuring Roshan and Rai and a host of background dancers again performing in a split-screen configuration, literally sharing the screen space with the end credits, which continue rolling on the right side of the screen, while Roshan, Rai, and the other dancers continue dancing in a rectangular box on the left (Figure 1). Like the earlier version, this end credits rendition is primarily in English though also features female playback singing and is shorter than the original iteration. A full-frame version, featured on the second disk's

Figure 1. End credits song and dance sequence from *Dhoom: 2* (2006). Source: DVD image grab, copyright of YashRaj Films, India.

special features, is a mash-up of both versions, beginning with the opening credits version and then segueing into the second, end credits version.

What we see in these two *Dhoom* films, then, is the introduction of a particular type of end credits song (and dance) sequence that has continued to gain steam in the twenty-first century. In many ways, one could compare such sequences to music videos (as they themselves are labeled on their respective DVDs) and, in turn, the ensuing process as the 'music video-ization' of the Bollywood song and dance sequence (Gehlawat, *Reframing Bollywood* 145). Yet before considering the further consolidation of such a form, I would like to first examine another iteration of the end credits sequence that emerged at roughly the same time as that of the original *Dhoom*.

Yeh Fizayein

It should come as no surprise that one of the earliest – if not the earliest – manifestations of an end credits song sequence comes from Bollywood choreographer-turned-director Farah Khan. Before embarking on her directorial career, Khan was (and continues to be) one of the predominant choreographers of song and dance sequences in the Bollywood industry, creating a new style that 'practically reinvented the way film songs are staged' (Rangan 380). Along with her own 4 films, Khan has choreographed song and dance sequences in over 90 films and has also choreographed sequences outside of Bollywood, including for Shakira's performance of her song 'Hips Don't Lie' at the 2006 MTV Video Music Awards. It is at the end of Khan's directorial debut, *Main Hoon Na* (2004, hereafter *MHN*), however, that one witnesses the first of what have gone on to become quintessential end credits sequences in all of her films. *MHN* is predominantly an action film, albeit with several spectacle-laden song and dance sequences and humor to boot, in which Bollywood superstar Shah Rukh Khan (hereafter SRK) plays a soldier in the Indian Army who goes undercover as a student at a college in Darjeeling in order to protect an Indian Army general's daughter from the film's ruthless villain (Sunil Shetty). At the story's conclusion, featuring an exchange of prisoners between India and Pakistan after a series of intense fights between SRK and Shetty, the film cuts to an end credits sequence, 'Yeh Fizayein' (This Atmosphere), in which all of the film's stars and also several of its crewmembers, including the director, appear in spoofy sequences in which they cavort and dance with one another at an outdoor fair. Describing this sequence on the DVD commentary track Khan claims:

> I was very clear that my film should end on a happy, musical note, because the last twenty minutes were so dark and full of action and drama … I wanted people to be reminded of the fun they had earlier, and all the characters that they had loved and laughed with … That is why I was very clear I'm gonna have a title sequence in the end, and of course I thought it should be like a curtain call where everyone comes and takes a bow, and me being a technician, earlier, being a choreographer, I thought it would be nice to have onscreen all the people who had worked on our film, not only the actors but all the unit members, because they were as much a part of the film as the people who were onscreen. (*MHN* Commentary Track, 2004)

Thus, Khan, the choreographer turned *auteur*, introduces a distinct type of end credits song sequence, one less like the highly choreographed (read: music video-ized) sequences in *Dhoom* and *Dhoom: 2* which feature guest appearances or reprises by the film's main stars in slick sequences displaying a lot of skin. Khan instead opts for a tongue-in-cheek encore which, in her words, incorporates not only those who appeared before the camera but all the technicians and crew members working behind the camera. Similarly, rather than devising a highly choreographed sequence, as one witnesses at the end of the first two *Dhoom* films, 'Yeh Fizayein' is comprised of what appear to be impromptu moves by performers who, in many cases, have no experience of dancing before a camera, nor display any pretense of doing so. Khan created similar sequences in her subsequent films, including *Om Shanti Om* (2007, hereafter *OSO*) whose end credits sequence features a remixed version of an earlier item song, 'Dard-e-Disco', which is played while numerous members of the film's cast and crew appear on a red carpet for accolades before an assembled crowd who scream and cheer to varying degrees. In keeping with her tongue-in-cheek approach (also on display at the outset of the film), when Khan finally appears at the end of the *OSO* end credits sequence for her 'bow', most if not all of the assembled crowd have already dispersed, thus leaving the director alone on the red carpet, raising her hands in the air with a look of chagrin on her face.

This type of playful approach to the end credits again stands in stark contrast to that taken by the *Dhoom* franchise and illuminates how, from its very inception, the end credits song sequence was far from a stable entity, ranging from a type of 'bonus' item number, to a type of reflexive encore, or curtain call, whose very aim, as expressed by Khan, was celebratory of a different set of performers and realized, in turn, in a different way, i.e. a different type of performance. While both the sequences in the *Dhoom* films and in Khan's are meant to be enjoyable, one set features a high degree of choreography and technical effects, whereas the other almost deliberately eschews such stylization in favor of a campy approach. Before further exploring the implications of such differing esthetics, however, I want to first examine the evolution of the end credits sequence following these initial – and divergent – manifestations and how, in turn, such sequences increasingly reflect the evolving role, more broadly, of song and dance sequences within the Bollywood film.

From bonus items to weddings codas

Following the initial *Dhoom* films, one sees a further consolidation of the end credits song (and dance) sequence as music video-ized form in two films from 2008, *Dostana* and *Singh is Kinng*, both of which include end credits sequences. The end credits of *Singh is Kinng* (hereafter *Singh*), which was released in the summer of 2008, features the film's star, Akshay Kumar, and rapper Snoop Dogg rapping and dancing together before various computer generated backdrops, including the Golden Temple of Amritsar and the Taj Mahal. Despite Snoop's repeated proclamations that 'Singh is the King', the sequence bears little relevance to the film and essentially functions as a bonus item, titillating for its novelty, pairing an African-American rapper with the film's Sikh protagonist, and featuring a similar mix of hip hop and bhangra. As with the *Dhoom* end credits, the sequence at the end of *Singh* shares screen space with the end credits, appearing within a smaller frame within the screen, while the end credits run below it. The sequence also comes subtitled though is not listed on the DVD's song menu, appearing only on the general chapter menu as 'End Credits/ Singh is Kinng'. A full-screen version of the sequence is available as a special feature on the second disk, though this version does not come subtitled. The other major release of the year, *Dostana*, similarly feature an end credits sequence that appears within a smaller frame, sharing the screen space with the credits, and also comes subtitled. The song itself is a remixed version of a song from the film, 'Maa da Ladla', and the end credits version, along with being remixed to a faster, techno beat, features new playback singing by Sunidhi Chauhan. Unlike the original *Dhoom* and *Singh*, however, *Dostana*'s splitscreen end credits sequence is immediately followed by a full-screen version, sans end credits and also sans subtitles. The inclusion of the full-frame version of the end credits sequence on the main disk itself (rather than being relegated to the special features section of the second disk), signals the further consolidation of the end credits sequence as a recognizable form and as an attraction that, through its full-frame repetition, can be seen as 'part' of the larger Bollywood feature.[5]

While both of these sequences – 'Singh is Kinng' and the 'Maa da Ladla Mummy Mix' – can be seen as bonus items, a few distinctions can be made, both regarding their internal composition and their external packaging. To begin with the former, the end credits sequence of *Singh*, compared to that of *Dostana*, is less choreographed, less like a 'pure' music video and more of a mash-up of sequences from the film with scenes featuring Snoop and Akshay dancing and acting silly together. The end credits sequence of *Dostana*, on the other hand, is a tightly orchestrated affair, in which the film's three stars – John Abraham, Abhishek Bachchan, and Priyanka Chopra – engage in carefully choreographed moves, along with numerous background dancers, to the sped up beat of the remixed song. Similarly, and as an indication of its more developed compositional structure, the full-frame version of the 'Maa da Ladla Mummy Mix' appears with the film and not, as with previous end credits song sequences, just as a separate special feature. This inclusion, along with the sequence's longer length (roughly equivalent to the original song featured in *Dostana*) reflects the growing importance being given to this feature 'of' the Bollywood film, which is now presented twice in its theatrical exhibition, once as an end credits sequence (sharing the screen space with the actual end credits) and then as a repeated sonic and visual pleasure – an added bonus, as it were, whose pleasure derives in equal parts from its repetition, its frivolity and its tightly constructed choreography. In the process such a picturization expresses not only 'joy and celebration of the gender and sexual politics that the film has attempted to espouse' but also marks, as Rajinder Dudrah notes, 'a celebration of the feat of the film' itself (*Bollywood Travels* 60), a celebration of new forms of spectacle and sexual politics.

Nevertheless, while the end credits song sequence of *Dostana* could be seen as 'suggest[ing] further queer possibilities' (Dudrah, *Bollywood Travels* 60), it is, as is the case with all of the end credit sequences to have emerged up to this point in Bollywood, not essential to the film's meaning, nor necessary to understanding its plot. Its pleasure derives purely from its excess, something that internal Bollywood song sequences themselves have historically been known for though, in this case, it is inherently an addition to the film, coming, as it does, *after* it. At the same time, to return to Dudrah's claims, one could argue that *Dostana*'s end credits song sequence does constitute 'a reprise of a plot-song earlier in the film' (the original 'Maa da Ladla') through which 'all its former meanings accrue' (Feuer 20). Yet even if one were to borrow Jane Feuer's terms regarding the Hollywood musical and describe such sequences in Bollywood as 'ode[s] to entertainment' (36), in which characters from the film 'comment and reflect on the ensuing action through a mediating communication system' (Pfister 74), more often than not in direct address, these sequences literally extend the parameters of Feuer's analysis concerning earlier manifestations of such strategies, as these end credits songs, rather than appearing, like their Hollywood predecessors, 'at the summit of the show' (Feuer 37), literally come *after* the summit, even as they may still serve what Feuer calls 'the finale function', in which the audience is also invited to take part in 'the celebration of another entertainment triumph' (37). A classic example of the Bollywood end credits song sequence functioning in this fashion follows below.

Maneesh Sharma's 2010 hit film, *Band Baaja Baaraat* (hereafter *BBB*) is about two young Indian wedding planners who grow increasingly attracted to one another even as they organize and celebrate others' unions. The film, which includes several boisterous song and dance sequences featuring the film's leads (Ranveer Singh and Anushka Sharma), culminates with the duo themselves coming together. However, unlike, for instance, the wedding coda at the end of the Hollywood musical *You'll Never Get Rich* (1941) which, contrary to Feuer's claim, exists *within* 'the time and space of the film proper' (82), *BBB*'s wedding coda takes place during the film's end credits, that is, outside of the film proper, even as it 'becom[es] a celebration of the end of the film itself' (Feuer 82). In the film's final scene, we see the wedding planners, Bittoo and Shruti, kissing and finally deciding to be together (after several back and forth struggles and complications) but it is only in the ensuing end credits that we see their wedding, while a remixed version of an earlier song – 'Ainvayi Ainvayi' – plays and the end credits run across the bottom of the screen. The couple sing and dance in this sequence, just as they have throughout the film at others' weddings (and, indeed, to the same theme song, albeit remixed here), while wedding guests include several of their former clients, whose weddings they arranged and in which they also danced. Here, then, one sees a recurring motif from the film – the wedding celebration – reappearing in/as the end credits sequence in which, like the remixed version of the previous song, this earlier element is further augmented, simultaneously fulfilling the 'finale function' and functioning outside of the film proper. *BBB*'s end credits sequence also becomes relevant to the film's plot in a way that previous end credits sequences were not. Thus, the end credits song (and dance) sequence in this instance simultaneously functions as a bonus item and an integral element of the (preceding) film.

Another instance of such a 'wedding coda' can be found in Zoya Aktar's *Zindagi Na Milegi Dobara* (2011, hereafter *Zindagi*), in which key plot elements take place during the film's end credits sequence, itself inspired in part by a 2009 church ceremony in St. Paul, Minnesota (Kamble 11). In this sequence, we see the culmination of one of the film's key themes – individuals choosing to marry for love – even as the sequence itself is, as Jayashree Kamble notes, 'filmed to look like a YouTube video, with the frame reduced to a quarter of the screen to make room for credits' (11). As with the end credits song in *BBB*, the *Zindagi* end credits song, which also does not come subtitled, features the revelation of key plot elements (e.g. who gets married and who does not) while simultaneously functioning as 'a celebration of the film itself' (Feuer 82), i.e. an 'ode to entertainment'. Thus, through films like *BBB* and *Zindagi*, one could argue that the Bollywood realm is extended by broadening the parameters of the film, from story to discourse, beyond the story 'end' to the end credits.

End credits song sequence as compensatory device

While *BBB*, as noted above, includes several song and dance sequences, Sharma's subsequent film, *Ladies vs. Ricky Bahl* (2011, hereafter *Ladies*) contains slightly fewer numbers that can truly be called 'Bollywood song and dance sequences', i.e. those featuring playback and corresponding lip-synching by the actor/actress, as well as intricately choreographed dancing. Not counting its end credits sequence or its opening credit sequence, *BBB* has a total of four song sequences, three of which include all of the elements listed above (playback/ lip-synching plus dancing). While *Ladies* also features three song and dance sequences within the film that adhere to the 'Bollywood' formula, one of these, 'Aadat se majboor', is featured in the opening credits and is a hybrid sequence, featuring singing and dancing by the male lead, Ranveer Singh, but also an introduction to and overview of his character (Ricky Bahl), a consummate con man.[6] Furthermore, all three of *Ladies*' actual song and dance sequences (including 'Aadat') come during the first half of the film, i.e. before the intermission. After the mid-way mark, there is only song sequence in the film, 'Fatal Attraction', which is essentially an instrumental number with minimal vocals and no lip-synching (By comparison, one of *BBB*'s biggest song and dance sequences, 'Dum Dum', comes during the second half of the film). It could be for this reason – the relative dearth of actual 'Bollywood' sequences during the second half – that *Ladies* features an end credits sequence that may very well be described as a 'bonus item'. Yet in some ways this sequence, called 'Thug le', can thus be seen as serving a slightly different function than previous 'bonus item' end credits song sequences.

'Thug le' begins immediately after the final shot of the film – of the two leads (again played by Singh and *BBB* co-star Sharma) kissing in reconciliation – and appears as a full-screen image, without subtitles and with the end credits running horizontally along the bottom of the frame as in *BBB*'s end credits sequence. Unlike the latter sequence, however, which had a more improvised feel, 'Thug le' features a high degree of intricate choreography and a large number of background dancers wearing a series of outlandish outfits while performing various stunts akin to parkour moves. The sequence also features lip-synching and frequent direct address, as the performers reinvoke key themes from the film (cheating, the battle of the sexes, etc.) both in the lyrics and in the choreography (pitting, for example, male and female dancers 'against' one another in large group formations). In such a way the sequence could be labeled a 'reprise' in which 'all the former meanings' of the film accrue (Feuer 20). Similarly, via its excessive direct address (and its more general excessiveness in terms of colors, costumes, numbers of dancers, and movements), the sequence calls to mind the 'ode to entertainment' previously described by Feuer (36). Yet the sequence could also be seen as compensating for the lack of such full-blown item numbers in the film's second half. Given that it literally interrupts a reprisal of the only song in the second half – 'Fatal Attraction' – the end credits song sequence can be read symbolically as a repudiation of the song merely relegated to the soundtrack. In this way, 'Thug le' can be seen as providing precisely what the second half of the film was *lacking*.

An even more vivid instance of the end credits song (and dance) sequence functioning as such a compensatory device is on display in Farhan Akhtar's *Don 2*, released the same year as *Ladies*. This sequel to Akhtar's previous remake of the 1970s Bollywood classic, unlike its predecessor(s), features only one actual 'Bollywood' song and dance sequence (with playback, lip-synching, and choreographed dancing), 'Zaraa Dil ko Thaam lo', which appears early on in this 150-minute film focused more on action sequences and capers. The end credits song, 'Dushman Mera', like 'Thug le', reprises key motifs from the film (intrigue, danger) and pits the male and female leads – SRK, who play the eponymous underworld don, and Priyanka Chopra, the cop dedicated to catching him – as nemeses who dance 'against' one another, echoing the ambivalence both express for each other throughout the film.[7] Thus, even as *Don 2* can be seen as hewing more to a 'Hollywood ecumene' (Bhaumik 202), it also provides a vivid example of an end credits song sequence functioning as compensation for the dearth of song and dance sequences in the film.[8] While the film itself is emblematic of the shift that at least some portion of Bollywood films have recently been making (toward less full-blown songs), the end credits song sequence is, in many ways, the inverse corollary to this trend.

One can see such a trend even more vividly on display in popular Indian films not technically hewing to the Bollywood formula, known as 'hatke', or offbeat, films.[9] Two recent instances of such films that provide song and dance numbers as compensatory devices are *Break Ke Baad* (2010) and *Dum Laga Ke Haisha* (2015). While neither film, in keeping with the general 'hatke' ethos, includes 'Bollywood' song and dance sequences within, both include such numbers as end credit sequences.[10] Perhaps the hatke film *par excellence* in this vein is *Delhi Belly* (2011), which is decidedly not a Bollywood film but rather one that references, quotes and occasionally spoofs this form. The film features a concluding song and dance sequence that, while coming after 'the end of the diegetic story' (Dudrah, "The Retro Noughties" 113), comes *before* the end credits themselves.[11] In thus creating yet another interstitial zone, *Delhi Belly*'s before-the-end-credits ending song sequence illuminates the growing and paradoxical inclusion of the song and dance number as an extradiegetic element in the hatke stratum, a strategy in some part overlapping with that of certain recent Bollywood films.[12]

This general trend leads, in turn, to yet another iteration of the end credits song sequence, namely the title song as end credits song. Such a phenomenon is on display in two recent films, *Shuddh Desi Romance* (2013, hereafter *SDR*) and *Bang Bang!* (2014, hereafter *BB*). In *SDR*, Sharma's third film, following *BBB* and *Ladies*, the end credits song, 'Shuddh Desi Romance' features two of the protagonists involved in the film's love triangle, Raghu (Sushant Singh Rajput) and Gayatri (Parineeti Chopra), dancing together, along with multiple background performers, amidst various Rajasthani settings (As the film is set in Rajasthan, this allows 'former meanings [to] accrue' [Feuer 20]). While one could read such a sequence via Feuer's analysis of comparable situations at the end of Hollywood musicals, in which 'lovers are reunited by being brought onstage together to reprise the title song' (81), a key distinction remains, namely, this is not a reprise but, indeed, the first time we hear the title song, despite its main hook being suggested repeatedly throughout the film, as a teaser of sorts. Thus, the telos of the film is reoriented from the film's conclusion to beyond it – or, put another way, the film's conclusion (or its concluding number, which is also the title number) comes after the film is over.

One witnesses a similar scenario in *BB* which also features its title song only after the film itself has concluded. As the final image of the film fades, the stars of the film, Hrithik Roshan and Katrina Kaif, have the following verbal exchange over a black screen:

Kaif: So, what now?

Roshan: There's just one thing left to do.

Kaif: What?

Roshan: Bang-Bang!

The black screen is then replaced with the opening images of the end credits song sequence, which features the words 'Get ready to Bang Bang on the dance floor' on the screen before cutting to Roshan and Kaif, who engage in a hyper-kinetic song and dance sequence with an infectious beat and half a dozen costume changes over the following three–and-a-half minutes.[13] Whereas, the hook from *SDR*'s title song repeatedly played throughout the film (without ever fully developing into the song until the film was over), *BB*'s title/end credits song was deployed as a teaser in another fashion, having been released a month prior to the film's release (Goswami). In this way, we see how the end credits sequence paradoxically functions as a preview of the film and, pace Kaif and Roshan's brief opening (or closing?) dialog, how such a sequence is simultaneously framed as almost an afterthought ('What now?'), albeit a carefully constructed and deliberately pre-released afterthought.[14] Yet even as these title songs as end credits songs seem to suggest the further distancing of song sequences from the film proper, both *SDR* and *BB* pose challenges to the notion of the end credits song and dance sequence as necessarily being a compensatory device, given that both films include a number of lip-synched, choreographed song and dance numbers within them.[15] So here, again, the end credits song and dance number functions primarily (if not purely) as a bonus item.

Conclusion, or the space of the end credits sequence

To think of the end credits song sequence as a bonus feature is to envision this element literally taking up the last remaining space in the film – at times fully occupying and then sharing the screen with the end credits. In this way, the Bollywood song and dance sequence inhabits a new space, signifying in the process a new causal relationship with the film (cf. earlier paradigms of the song as 'integrated' or 'embedded' in/to the larger film), coming as it does after and thus (re)defining the film *post hoc*, embellishing it, providing a bonus which in many ways is, or becomes, part of the film itself. The end credits song sequence, in other words, embodies both the form of the 'Bollywood film' and this form's most recent mutation into this sleight of hand wherein the defining feature of the film – its 'constitutive limit' (Gopal and Moorti 1) – now only comes after it, accompanies it, signaling through its new space/positioning both its ongoing importance (as a semiotic item) and its relegation to the interstices of the film – its literal and figurative marginalization, the 'constitutive limit' of the form now appearing at or, indeed, after, the limit.[16]

Thus, along with taking place in an indeterminate time – coming as they do after the film yet still, technically, a part of the film – the end credits song sequence more often than not takes place in an indeterminate space, even more nebulous than the 'fantasy spaces' frequently utilized and on display in the films' internal song sequences.[17] The setting of the end credits song and dance sequence, as if corresponding to its temporal amorphousness, could be anywhere and at anytime or, perhaps, to be more precise, at no time, i.e. outside the spacetime of the film, even more so than internal song and dance numbers which, despite their (temporary) departures, *return* – or end with a return – to the film proper (the diegesis). Literally competing with the end credits themselves, the end credits song and dance number begins and ends at unspecified moments, given that it is literally 'out of bounds', outside of the film's realm, no longer 'embedded within the wider film structure' (Varia 41). Conversely, if it can still be seen as part 'of' the film, then the end credits song and dance sequence extra-diegetically extends this filmic structure. Ultimately, one may see the end credits song and dance sequence serving as a reassurance/guarantor of that 'quintessential' Bollywood element – the song and dance number – now located after/outside of the film and thus paradoxically even more tenuously linked to the Bollywood film.[18] If, following a range of recent theorists (e.g. Gopal, *Conjugations*; Ganti, "No Longer"), one were to claim that the song and dance sequence has slowly been disappearing from Bollywood then, even as it 'disappears', to some extent, it increasingly reappears/ is reproduced as an end credits item number.

One could develop this further and see the end credits song and dance number as improving upon the original, amplifying it, doing it one better, an extension not only in space and time but an intensification of a particular mo(ve)ment, one that always outdoes, or 'Bollywoodizes'. In this way, one might compare the end credits song sequence to what Noel Carroll calls 'amplification', in which cinematic innovations are devised by 'synthesizing familiar schemas in fresh ways' (qtd. in Bordwell 152–3). To paraphrase Sangita Gopal in her discussion of what she calls the 'K-Jo effect',[19] if the Bollywood song and dance is isolable (Novak 48), then the end credits song and dance number is always already isolated; if the Bollywood song and dance is rich in spectacle, then the end credits song and dance is even richer, etc. It is precisely in this sense that the end credits song sequence can be considered Bollywood *par excellence* – the pure form of Bollywood marketing itself as such a form. The end credits song sequence allows Bollywood as a media industry and the Bollywood film to both become and unbecome itself with, in some ways, the cart now pulling the horse, that is, Bollywood being defined *post hoc*. But in many cases the aftereffect serves as a stand-in for the actual (absent) signifier, i.e. a metalepsis. David Novak has noted that

> if the standard metaphor for Bollywood films is a *masala*, a blended mix of spices, the song-and-dance sequence is a *masala vada*, a spiced lentil dumpling, which can be eaten alone or added to other dishes at will, but remains a distinct piece. (49)

I would extend this culinary metaphor and say that the end credits song and dance sequence is a carefully packaged *masala vada* that may not even appear on the menu but nevertheless fills in for the larger work in many ways. Ultimately, Farah Khan's quirky end credits sequences remain isolated cases – the only parallel to these stemming from outside of Bollywood, in the films of Gurinder Chadha[20] – while the more frequently utilized end credits song sequence remains the type on display in the *Dhoom* series, the 'Maa da Ladla Mummy mix', 'Thug le', 'Bang Bang', et al, that is, a highly choreographed bonus item. Yet, as this concluding discussion has shown, these 'bonus items' in many ways reflect the larger epistemological instability Bollywood is currently experiencing, where something not even a part of the film now lies at the heart of the film form itself.

Notes

1. The only Hollywood film to feature such an end credits song sequence is *Mirror, Mirror* (2012), directed by Tarsem Singh. The sequence, titled 'I Believe in Love (Mirror Mirror mix)', though sung in English, interestingly has an Indian feel to its music and rhythm, which may explain why Wikipedia describes it as 'a Bollywood-style musical number', even though there is no ostensible Bollywood connection (Director Singh, while born in India, has never made a Bollywood film). My thanks to Jayson Beaster-Jones for bringing this sequence to my attention.
2. In some ways one can compare the end credits song sequence to the earlier phenomenon of the opening credits song sequence. Even as this latter element has also evolved in its composition and relation to the narrative, it still retains a clearer connection to the film/ narrative than the (semi-)detached end credits sequence, often introducing the star(s) and/or key themes as in, e.g. *Muqaddar ka Sikandar* (1978) or, more recently, *Ladies vs. Ricky Bahl* (2011), discussed in more detail below.

3. Technically, the original version of this song is by Canadian guitarist and composer Jesse Cook, whose song 'Mario Takes a Walk', released in 1996, provides the melody for the ensuing versions in *Dhoom*.
4. The repeated use of the 'Dhoom' track throughout the *Dhoom* series (2004–13) also illustrates the use of the end credits song as a promotional device, e.g. for the *Dhoom* franchise, and hook for subsequent films, e.g. *Dhoom:2* and *Dhoom:3* (2013), both of which feature remixed iterations of the original 'Dhoom' song.
5. The full-frame sequence is also available as a special feature on the second disk where, again, it appears without subtitles.
6. Cf. note 2. For more on this opening credits sequence, see Gehlawat, *Twenty-First-Century Bollywood.*
7. In many ways, this end credits sequence calls to mind the opening credits sequences of several contemporary James Bond films.
8. Akhtar's earlier *Don* (2006), interestingly, features several full-blown (Bollywood) song and dance sequences throughout the film and (hence) no credits song sequence. For more on this film and its sequel, see Gehlawat, *Twenty-First Century Bollywood.*
9. For more regarding the 'Hatke' film and its at times agonistic relationship with Bollywood, see both Gopal, "Sentimental Symptoms," *Conjugations* and Gehlawat, *Twenty-First Century Bollywood.*
10. *Break Ke Baad*, whose internal songs merely play on the soundtrack with little to no accompanying dancing, features an end credits song, 'Dooriyan', that starts with a scene continuing the film in a small frame, while the credits roll. After approximately one minute, the sequence transitions into a song, featuring both lip-synching and dancing. The film's director, Danish Aslam, claims that this song was a 'fortunate accident', as they had intended to make it the film's title song but it was then scrapped when they decided not to include an opening title sequence (*Break Ke Baad* DVD, 'Making of Dooriyan' Special Feature). Meanwhile, *Dum Laga Ke Haisha*, whose internal songs also only play on the soundtrack and include no lip-synching and little to no dancing, includes a song sequence, 'Dard Karaara', in its end credits which is formally introduced on the soundtrack (As the film's final image fades, a voiceover proclaims, 'And now let's watch a song composed by Anu Malik …' against the black screen, before cutting to the song's picturization which features choreographed dancing and lip-synching by the film's romantic duo).
11. It is only *after* the 'colorful item number/finale song', as Dudrah notes, that 'the end credits begin to roll' ("The Retro Noughties" 115). In a similar vein, the end credits song sequence of *Dum Laga Ke Haisha* first appears *without* end credits as a full-screen image and then, after approximately one minute, the image is reduced and the end credits appear onscreen, below the image of the song and dance sequence.
12. In another interesting overlap, the end credits song sequences of both hatke and Bollywood films can be seen as promoting not only the stars but, in many cases, the producers of the films, as is the case with *Delhi Belly*'s end credits sequence, featuring the film's producer, Aamir Khan, as the dancing 'Disco Fighter'. Cf. also Farah Khan's frequent inclusion of herself and other crew members in her end credits song sequences, as noted above.
13. The only item that remains consistent throughout the various costume changes is Roshan's open shirts, exposing his sculpted torso.
14. Again, as with the *Dhoom* franchise, we see how the end credits song can effectively function as a marketing device, a form of paratextual media that circulates independently of its 'source' even as it promotes this source.
15. While *BBB* and *Ladies* have more songs overall, all of the (overall fewer) songs of *SDR* and *BB* feature such quintessential elements, i.e. those historically defining the 'Bollywood song and dance number'.
16. One can also note how the end credits song sequence signifies this transition, this intermedial relationship, within its own composition, shifting as it does, gradually (and playfully) at times, from a full-screen image to only occupying a portion of the screen, as the credits return or are re-inscribed.

17. There are, to be sure, exceptions, most notably when the end credits song and dance number functions (more) as a coda to the preceding events, e.g. in *BBB*. Simultaneously, however, in randomly referencing the film (through a selection of filmic moments interspersed throughout the sequence), the end credits song and dance number can be said to both rearrange and truncate the preceding chronology of the film (and thus arguably the film itself), becoming, in a sense, a 'free floating signifier' (Bhaumik 202) that signifies differently – more analogous to the music video's occasional referencing/reordering of scenes from a film 'in' which it appears on the soundtrack.
18. I say 'paradoxically' because it is simultaneously upholding/ guaranteeing the 'constitutive element' of the Bollywood film, now 'produced' as such, i.e. as 'the Bollywood song and dance number', or what Madhava Prasad refers to as 'a self-conscious reproduction of its features' (203).
19. Using the familiar acronym for director Karan Johar ('K-Jo'), Gopal describes such an effect as follows: '[I]f Hindi films are notoriously long, the "K-Jo" film is even longer; if the relation of Hindi cinema to reality is weak, the "K-Jo" film intensifies this artifice; [...] and so on' ("Sentimental Symptoms" 17).
20. See, e.g. the end credits sequence of *Bend It Like Beckham* (2002) or *Bride & Prejudice* (2004).

Disclosure statement

No potential conflict of interest was reported by the author.

References

Bhaumik, Kaushik. "Lost in Translation: A Few Vagaries of the Alphabet Game Played Between Bombay Cinema and Hollywood." *World Cinema's 'Dialogues' with Hollywood*. Ed. Paul Cooke. New York, NY: Palgrave, 2007. 201–217.

Bordwell, David. *On the History of Film Style*. Cambridge: Harvard UP, 1997.

Chatterji, Shoma A. *100 Years of Jump-cuts and Fade-outs: Tracking Change in Indian Cinema*. New Delhi: Rupa, 2014.

Dudrah, Rajinder. *Bollywood Travels: Culture, Diaspora and Border Crossings in Popular Hindi Cinema*. London: Routledge, 2012.

Dudrah, Rajinder. "The Retro Noughties: 1970s Hindi Films in 2000s Bollywood Cinema." *The 1970s and its Legacies in India's Cinemas*. Ed. Priya Joshi and Rajinder Dudrah. New York, NY: Routledge, 2014. 101–119.

Dutta, Aniruddha. "Digitizing the National Imaginary: Technology and Hybridization in Hindi Film Songs of the Post-liberalization Period." *Routledge Handbook of Indian Cinemas*. Ed. K. Moti Gokulsing and Wimal Dissanayake. New York, NY: Routledge, 2013. 231–245.

Feuer, Jane. *The Hollywood Musical*. 2nd ed. Bloomington: Indiana UP, 1993.

Ganti, Tejaswini. "No Longer a Frivolous Singing and Dancing Nation of Movie-Makers: The Hindi Film Industry and Its Quest for Global Distinction." *Visual Anthropology* 25 (2012): 340–65.

Ganti, Tejaswini. *Bollywood: A Guidebook to Popular Hindi Cinema*. 2nd ed. New York, NY: Routledge, 2013.

Gehlawat, Ajay. *Reframing Bollywood: Theories of Popular Hindi Cinema*. New Delhi: Sage, 2010.

Gehlawat, Ajay. *Twenty-first Century Bollywood*. London: Routledge, 2015.

Gopal, Sangita. "Sentimental Symptoms: The Films of Karan Johar and Bombay Cinema." *Bollywood and Globalization: Indian Popular Cinema, Nation, and Diaspora*. Ed. Rini Bhattacharya Mehta and Rajeshwari V. Pandharipande. London: Anthem, 2010. 15–34.

Gopal, Sangita. *Conjugations*. Chicago, IL: U of Chicago P, 2011.

Gopal, Sangita, and Sujata Moorti. "Introduction: Travels of Hindi Song and Dance." *Global Bollywood: Travels of Hindi Song and Dance*. Ed. Sangita Gopal and Sujata Moorti. Minneapolis, MN: U of Minnesota P, 2008. 1–60.

Goswami, Parismita. "'Bang Bang': First Look of Title Track Released." *International Business Times* 16 Sep. 2014.

Kamble, Jayashree. "All Work or All Play? Consumption, Leisure, and Ethics under Globalization in Zindagi Na Milegi Dobara." *South Asian Popular Culture* 13.1 (2015): 1–14.

"Mirror Mirror." *Wikipedia.com* n.d., Web. 1 May 2017.

Novak, David. "Cosmopolitanism, Remediation, and the Ghost World of Bollywood." *Cultural Anthropology* 25.1 (2010): 40–72.

Pfister, Manfred. *The Theory and Analysis of Drama*. New York, NY: Cambridge UP, 1988.

Prasad, Madhava. "Is There a New Subject of Cinema Today?" *Le Cinema Indien* [Indian Cinema]. Ed. Emmanuel Grimaud and Kirstie Gormaley. Lyon: Asiexpo, 2008. 200–207.

Rangan, Baradwaj. *Dispatches from the Wall Corner: A Journey Through Indian Cinema*. New Delhi: Tranquebar, 2014.

Varia, Kush. *Bollywood: Gods, Glamour and Gossip*. New York, NY: Wallflower, 2012.

Filmography

Band Baaja Baaraat. Dir. Maneesh Sharma. YashRaj Films, 2010.
Bang Bang! Dir.Siddarth Anand. Fox Star Studios, 2014.
Bend it Like Beckham. Dir. Gurinder Chadha. 20th Century Fox, 2002.
Break Ke Baad. Dir. Danish Aslam. Reliance, 2010.
Bride & Prejudice. Dir. Gurinder Chadha. Pathe, 2004.
Delhi Belly. Dir. Abhinay Deo. UTV Motion Pictures, 2011.
Dhoom. Dir. Sanjay Gadhvi. YashRaj Films, 2004.
Dhoom: 2. Dir. Sanjay Gadhvi. YashRaj Films, 2006.
Dhoom: 3. Dir. Vijay Krishna Acharya. YashRaj Films, 2013.
Don. Dir. Farhan Akhtar. Excel, 2006.
Don 2. Dir. Farhan Akhtar. Excel, 2011.
Dostana. Dir. Tarun Mansukhani. Dharma Productions, 2008.
Dum Laga Ke Haisha. Dir. Sharat Katariya. YashRaj Films, 2015.
Ladies vs. Ricky Bahl. Dir. Maneesh Sharma. YashRaj Film, 2011.
Main Hoon Na. Dir. Farah Khan. Eros, 2004.
Mirror Mirror. Dir. Tarsem Singh. Relativity Media, 2012.
Muqaddar ka Sikandar. Dir. Prakash Mehra. Eros International, 1978.
Om Shanti Om. Dir. Farah Khan. Red Chillies, 2007.
Shuddh Desi Romance. Dir. Maneesh Sharma. YashRaj Films, 2013.
Singh is Kinng. Dir. Anees Bazmee. Studio 18, 2008.
You'll Never Get Rich. Dir. Sidney Lanfield. Columbia, 1941.
Zindagi Na Milegi Dobara. Dir. Zoya Akhtar. Eros International, 2011.

Index

Note: *Italic* page numbers refer to figures and page numbers followed by "n" denote endnotes.

For Product Safety Concerns and Information please contact our EU representative GPSR@taylorandfrancis.com
Taylor & Francis Verlag GmbH, Kaufingerstraße 24, 80331 München, Germany

www.ingramcontent.com/pod-product-compliance
Lightning Source LLC
Chambersburg PA
CBHW081358090726
47908CB00011B/2714

* 9 7 8 0 3 6 7 7 8 5 6 7 3 *